THE BACKPACKER'S FATHER

By the same author

The Time of Light
Longing

GUNNAR KOPPERUD

THE BACKPACKER'S FATHER

Translated from the Norwegian by Christopher Jamieson

BLOOMSBURY

First published in Great Britain in 2006
This paperback edition published 2007

First published in Norwegian in 2003
by Gyldendal Norsk Forlag AS under the title *Politikapteinens fange*

The author gratefully acknowledges a fellowship at the
Santa Maddalena Foundation, Donnini, Italy,
during which part of this book was written

The publishers gratefully acknowledge a grant from
NORLA towards the translation of this book

Bloomsbury Publishing Plc
36 Soho Square
London W1D 3QY

A CIP catalogue record for this book is available from the British Library

ISBN 9780747586012

10 9 8 7 6 5 4 3 2 1

Typeset by Hewer Text Ltd, Edinburgh
Printed in Great Britain by Clays Ltd, St Ives plc
Bloomsbury Publishing, London, New York and Berlin

All papers used by Bloomsbury Publishing are natural,
recyclable products made from wood grown in well-managed
forests. The manufacturing processes conform to the
environmental regulations of the country of origin.

www.bloomsbury.com

THE BACKPACKER'S FATHER

The ship arrived in the middle of the night. It had approached the island at dusk, anchored two miles offshore and waited. People on the island must have seen it, but taken no notice, probably because only vessels clearly heading for the island interested them; a ship that anchored in the roads was indeterminate, insignificant.

It showed no lights as darkness fell. That should have interested the port authorities at least, and indeed the police, but it didn't seem to attract any attention at all. The ship was just a grey smudge, not far enough away to be on the horizon, but far enough away to be anonymous; it merged almost seamlessly with the encroaching darkness. A police car that was halted at a military roadblock was the closest the island came to discovering what was taking place; the soldier made a friendly request to the two policemen to turn round and go back, because the army was engaged in large-scale man- oeuvres and wanted to complete them undisturbed. The two men exchanged a few words with one another before bidding the soldier goodnight and turning the patrol car round; the roadblock was right in the centre of their area, but they had instructions to give the army their full support. The island had everything to lose from any extension or escalation of the conflict. When their police captain read their report, he gave vent to his feelings in a howl of rage, but by then the ship was long gone.

In the days that followed there was some talk – though not

widespread – of signals from a little fishing village in the north of the island; those who did speak of it tended to ascribe them to the disturbances on the hill behind the village that same night: a house set ablaze, billowing flames, exchanges of fire; not slow, single shots, but intense bursts of gunfire.

Gunfire makes most people stay inside and lie low, well away from doors and windows; gunfire around a burning house reinforces the impulse, and has the additional effect of drawing all attention towards the blaze and roar of the flames.

That was how the ship, showing no lights and with silenced engines, was able to glide right up to the island, probably without being seen by anyone other than those who were meant to see it. It must have started its engines out in the roads and come halfway in before cutting them; the crew on the bridge must have known to the metre how far the vessel would carry on moving and only given a brief reverse thrust as they anchored, which could have been anything: a lorry accelerating, a generator throbbing into life.

Even in the dark the ship looked old, or old-fashioned, high at prow and stern, an antiquated mast with a loading boom amidships. Both hull and superstructure were painted grey, yet without lending it a military appearance; it was and remained a merchant ship that someone wanted to keep as invisible as possible. Name and home port were also painted over, but no military number substituted.

It anchored about thirty metres offshore. The torch that had guided its course stopped flashing as soon as the anchor was lowered. At precisely the same instant the gunfire up on the hill intensified significantly, obscuring the noise of the anchor chain for everyone except those on the beach.

A hatch opened in the side of the ship, which was obviously built for locations without quays or deep harbours. There were no lights in the hold behind the hatch, but from the beach a cluster of figures in white could just be discerned. A voice in the darkness swore under its breath and whispered,

'Can't anyone be religious in this country without wearing white?' Then a grey inflatable was launched, and another, and another; a little further along three more inflatables set off, with two figures in each, two dark shadows dipping black-painted oars into the water and paddling towards the ship and its loading hatch and gleaming white figures. At the rail above the hatch two silhouettes in uniform caps appeared, one shielding a cigarette in his hand that illuminated his eyes with each inhalation. The first rubber dinghy reached the hatch, a rope was thrown and caught, the boat was pulled alongside and the rope held taut while one, two, three, four, five, six white figures half-jumped, half-clambered down into it. The silhouette at the rail flicked the cigarette into the water with a hiss right by the inflatable, and one of the white figures looked up and called out in a low, angry voice. The silhouette at the rail spat.

The rubber dinghies made eighteen trips, plus two with cargo: oblong wooden crates with carrying handles of rope. Each trip took eight minutes, which meant that the ship lay at anchor off the island for two hours and forty minutes: two hours and twenty-four minutes to land 648 men in long white tunics and white skullcaps, and sixteen minutes to bring in the boxes of automatic weapons, fifty-four in each boatload. The grey inflatables were low in the water, but the oarsmen could see the white figures wading out to meet them, to haul the boats in and unload the crates.

They were opened immediately, the weapons unpacked and distributed. Each of the white figures was already wearing an ammunition belt, either over one shoulder or round the waist. The only other thing they carried was a rolled-up prayer mat; some held it in their hand, some had tucked it into their ammunition belt.

Apart from the soldiers paddling the rubber dinghies, there was no military presence on the beach. As soon as the landing was complete, the soldiers carried the boats up the beach and into the woods. None of the white figures watched them go; a few moments later a lorry could be heard starting up, but no heads turned. The exchange of fire up on the hill began again, enough to drown the noise of the anchor chain being raised and the ship's engines coming to life. It was still pitch-black, not a sign of dawn, as the darkness absorbed the grey ship seawards and the men in white inland.

1

ARRIVAL

F rancesco was staring at a pair of boots.

They were welted boots, high and fairly worn. They stood only a centimetre or two from a woman's face: she examined first one, then the other, before closing her eyes and letting her head sink back down on to the white sand. The boots shifted, away from her face, a hand came down and took her by the shoulder, rolled her over, pulling her wet cotton jumper off the shoulder as it did so; the woman grabbed the hand in both of hers and sank her teeth into it. The hand withdrew.

Francesco turned his head. There was a movement behind the woman; a kneeling figure with wet hair plastered to its forehead. The figure seemed to be trying to speak, but couldn't; it fell forward and lay just where the waves were breaking on the shore, one leg bent under and both arms outstretched, the water washing in and out between its fingers. Beyond this figure the sea, a sparkling, uninterrupted expanse in three directions; above the sea the warm blue immensity of the sky.

Francesco's gaze switched back to the woman as she lay staring at the boots. He lowered his eyes, momentarily torn between fear, anger and despair, but something made him look up again almost immediately. The woman had put her arms round the boots and heaved herself towards them, slid her hands upwards till she found the tops and hoisted herself to her knees. Then she took a grip on the olive-green trousers above the boots and raised herself further, past the belt with a pistol in its leather holster, further up the green shirt, past the breast pocket with a cloth name-tag and four decorations in red, green and gold; she went on hauling herself up until she found her hands on a pair of motionless shoulders and her face only millimetres away from the one waiting for her. She drew back a little and spat; the face before her didn't flinch. She spat again.

Francesco waited, listening for something, a sound.

It came. The hand that hit the woman was darker than her cheek, which made the sound seem sharper. The hand struck once, and made him aware of the background noise of the breakers; it struck again, on the other cheek, and he heard a shout, from the figure with wet hair; it struck one last time, and now the beach was full of sounds: wheezing breaths from the figure at the water's edge, squawks from white seabirds, agitated voices from the tropical forest that extended down to the narrow beach, sharp metallic clicks from safety catches.

Then sudden commotion everywhere.

The figure at the water's edge, a man, was first. He lifted his head and surveyed the beach, pressed his hands into the sand to raise his upper body, and drew up his other leg beneath him to kneel on all fours. His activity set off a chain reaction: Francesco rose to his feet and took a few tentative steps; the woman in the cotton jumper backed away, holding her cheeks; three seabirds dived down towards the water, screeching loudly; soldiers with automatic weapons at the ready came swarming out of the forest and on to the beach.

The officer with the bleeding hand pointed at the woman, then at the two men. The soldiers headed towards them, the colour of their uniforms becoming more distinct as they approached. Francesco and the other two looked in surprise at their own wet clothes, as if not comprehending, and when the soldiers seized them by the arms and dragged them into the forest, none of them showed any sign of resistance. The

8

whole beach was spinning, a whirl of images and colours and voices and calls.

There was a low rumble from out at sea. One of the soldiers raised a hand, brought the spinning to a halt, froze image and sound, and turned towards the water. For a moment he was distracted, for a brief moment he stood transfixed, until a brusque command galvanised him into action and reality resumed, but that moment was enough to bring fear to his eyes.

———

The officer from the beach was the chief of police. He had dark bags under his eyes and was writing as he spoke:

'Atlanta, USA. Have you been there?'

Francesco glanced at the woman, who seemed uncertain whether she was the one being addressed. The young man who had been lying in the shallows was fidgeting anxiously at her side. She put a hand on his arm. His hair was still wet. A fan was revolving slowly on the ceiling. Francesco was sitting right behind the other two, breathing heavily, still torn between fear, anger and despair.

'Have you?'

The police captain was giving them his full attention now. The heat from the windows enveloped the woman, waiting for her answer; she seemed to be trying hard to think, but was somehow unable. All that could be heard were the street traders outside, plying their wares.

'I don't know.'

The police captain studied her: wet hair, damp clothes, face with no make-up, eyes without mascara, pallid complexion. Then he turned to his colleague who was tilting his chair back against the wall.

'Ambon, Indonesia. Have you been there?'

His colleague made no reply, just went on scrutinising the woman. Not the other two, only the woman.

'Everyone knows where they've been. But not you. Atlanta, USA? You've no idea.'

'Why do you want to know?'

The police captain returned to the paper on his desk, as if he hadn't heard her.

'In this country women don't ask questions.'

He spoke without raising his head, still writing as he continued, 'Atlanta Hartsfield is the world's busiest airport. 909,840 take-offs and landings in 1999, compared with Chicago O'Hare's 897,290.'

He stood up from his desk and came round to the woman. His uniform shirt was stretched tight across his stomach, his pistol holster slapping against his olive-green trousers. He leant over her, pinched her nose and lips together, nicotine-stained index and middle finger on his right hand, white scar on the left.

'I've done a calculation. If we say the airport is open all 365 days of the year, that's 2,492 take-offs and landings a day. If we assume it opens at five in the morning and shuts down at midnight, it's open nineteen hours a day, which is 1,140 minutes. If we divide 2,492 by 1,140 we get 2.2. If we divide sixty seconds by 2.2 we get twenty-seven. In other words, a plane takes off or lands every twenty-seven seconds, exactly as long as you've been holding your breath now.'

He let go and the woman collapsed with a gasp, tears in her eyes. The young man by her side started to rise, but sat down again when the policeman tilting his chair against the wall slammed its legs to the floor and unclipped his pistol holster. The nicotine-stained and scarred hands blocked the woman's nose and mouth again.

'Twenty-seven seconds to the next one, twenty-seven seconds till the next plane takes off or lands at the world's busiest airport and you can breathe again. If we reckon that each flight carries 150 passengers, that's more than 135 million people, more than 135 million people a year taking off or landing at the world's busiest airport, and you don't know whether you've been there or not. Atlanta, USA; don't know.'

He let go of her again and went back to his desk; she gulped desperately for air. Francesco looked at the man by her side, wondering what to do, and the policeman by the wall put his hand to his pistol.

'Atlanta, USA, you don't know; the world's busiest woman, we don't know. We've never seen you before, we don't know who you are. All we know is that you suddenly turn up on a beach here with this other pair – three Europeans with no visas, no passports – and you start yelling as soon as we take you in for questioning. You haven't stopped yelling for the Danish Embassy for two hours. Do all European women yell like that, for God's sake?'

He tapped a cigarette out of a crumpled packet and lit it.

'We'll let you phone the Danish Embassy, one, when it suits us, and, two, when we get a connection. Remember, you're on an island.'

He marked off the two points on his fingers.

'And remember, the capital is a long way off, six hours by the quickest flight. In the meantime, find yourselves a hotel and stay there, in your rooms; don't stand at the window; don't sit on the balcony if there is one; order your meals and have them sent up. We'll be keeping an eye on you. The first ship or plane to leave the island after the Embassy has sent your passports, you'll be on it.'

Francesco held up a hand. The police captain looked at him in surprise as if unable to accept that there might be anything more to say, or that any of the three Europeans had a right to speak. Francesco pointed at his chest.

'May I show you something?'

The police captain frowned.

'What, for instance?'

Francesco undid a button on his shirt and drew out a beige

canvas pouch hanging on a cord round his neck. He opened the zip, took out a bundle of wet banknotes and laid them on his lap, then eased out something that only just fitted in. It was a small pack of photos, sealed in plastic. He flicked through to one of them and proffered it to the police captain. Over by the wall the policeman dropped the front legs of the chair to the floor and stretched himself.

The police captain gave a curt dismissive laugh.

'What, are we going to show one another our photographs now? Sorry, I left my album at home.'

'This might be of interest.'

Francesco handed him the picture. The police captain accepted it with some reluctance and gave it a cursory glance. Then as the other policeman stood up and took a few silent paces forward the police captain studied the photograph more closely, looked up at the still-damp European with the canvas wallet, compared the two. The policeman turned aside with his hand to his mouth, but not fast enough: everyone in the room could see his smile. The police captain read what was written on the back and then perused it more carefully. The picture was of the damp European with an Asian officer. The latter had an arm round the European's shoulder. His epaulettes suggested the rank of general.

'So you've met our President?'

The police captain's tone was entirely neutral. Francesco nodded, straightened his back and allowed himself a new feeling: superiority. The police captain glanced over at the policeman against the wall, who had sat down on his chair again and was leaning back, his expression suggestive of laughter – laughter that took wing and flew out of the room and along the corridor, in through door after door, and as it flew on it carried a trail of laughter in its wake, from every single room, laughter that crossed the courtyard and was borne on fluttering wings up the street, to the market; people looked up and grinned, called to one another and grinned, and the skies darkened, from the blue of honour to the grey of shame.

Francesco said: 'I thought it might be of interest.'

He waited expectantly.

'What do you want?' the police captain said, handing back the photograph.

Francesco took it and glanced enquiringly at the other two Europeans.

'A little more appropriate treatment while we wait for the Embassy? For instance.'

The police captain sat for some time with his gaze fixed on him. There was complete silence in the room. Dark circles of sweat were forming under his arms. Then he stubbed out his cigarette in the ashtray and said, 'You can go out into town to eat and shop, but straight back to the hotel afterwards. Within reason.'

'And if there's a balcony in the hotel?'

The police captain did not deign to reply, just jerked his head towards the door. Francesco and the others rose to their feet. Francesco had a faint smile on his lips. He didn't seem to be aware that he had caused the police captain to lose face, that in some cultures that can be a dangerous thing to do. He came from a part of the world that knew all about guilt and little about shame. Now he was in a part of the world that knew all about shame and little about guilt.

A policeman escorted them out, first along a narrow corridor with closed, dark-brown doors on both sides. There were fans on the ceiling, at ten-metre intervals, none of them working. Two elderly women stood weeping in front of one door, and screams could be heard from behind it. The policeman gave the three Europeans a look, and they averted their eyes from the door and followed him, down some stairs and out through a heavy steel door. The policeman touched his cap and left them; the three Europeans stared about them.

Asia stared back at them: an enormous mask with dark holes for eyes and a black pit for a mouth, a contorted angry mask in luminous green with streaks of blue; in the eye sockets they could see rickshaws and scurrying coolies and crouching women, images they had seen before, images they had brought with them, and now suddenly there were images of themselves there as well, three overgrown white apes in the crowd, that too an image they had brought with them, but it seemed to surprise them all the same.

The young man spoke in an undertone: 'Thanks. Whether the photograph was genuine or forged. We'd rather not know.'

Francesco smiled in acknowledgement. They surveyed the street. It was predominantly yellow and brown, with low buildings on each side, some with balconies, some without, but all with shutters at the windows, oblique slats that let in light but not sun.

Francesco inclined his head towards the houses. 'Dutch? Colonial style?'

The woman responded, 'Shall we get ourselves something to drink? Something cold, with green leaves and a taste of mint? Something that's good for hysteria?'

Both men could hear the quaver in her voice. She put a hand to her chest and continued rapidly, 'I'm Helen. Danish. This is Kurt. He sounds Danish, but he's actually Dutch. We make TV programmes together, documentaries. What about you?'

Kurt interrupted sharply, 'I thought we had an agreement.'

Helen covered her mouth.

'Sorry. Forget the bit about Dutch. What about you?'

'Francesco. Italian-Portuguese. Tourist.'

He indicated that they should follow him and they all three crossed the street. There were traders filling every available space, some roasting nuts and bananas on metal grills, others selling fruit and vegetables, bolts of bright-coloured cotton, Coca-Cola, drinking-water, beer, brandy. Some of them sat on low stools; most sat directly on the pavement beside their wares. Their eyes followed the three Europeans, but they left them alone, didn't attempt to invite their custom.

'Thank God we came ashore on the right island, so at least the money's not a problem.'

Kurt stopped at a crate of cans and bottles. He took out a bundle of soggy notes and read the cans to find a beer. Then he held up three fingers and looked enquiringly at the vendor. The latter shook his head. Kurt held out the money, the trader shook his head again, motioned them further along the street. Kurt raised his eyebrows in perplexity at the others and they all walked on without comment. He tried the next drinks stall, whose owner also shook his head and motioned them on.

'What's the matter? Aren't these people poor? Is there something wrong with my money?'

He was angry. Francesco said under his breath, 'Perhaps we're being followed. Maybe the locals don't like doing business with foreigners who are being followed by plain-clothes police.'

It was the middle of the day and the street was full of people. Some of the stalls were playing music over raucous loudspeakers. The music blended with the smoke from the grills and the scent of spices being sold in little cotton bags. The street opened out into a large square sloping down towards the harbour. Two jetties were built out from the quayside, two narrow strips of concrete projecting into the vast, empty ocean. The three Europeans stood for some time, staring out to sea, and between them guessed at the number of all those who had gone down with the ferry. Then they turned to take a good look at the island, at the town extending a kilometre each side of the harbour, at the densely wooded hill beyond, five-hundred metres high, and the similarly wooded hill behind that, which must have been about a thousand metres high. A woman at a grill called to them and pointed at three roasted sweetcorn. They exchanged glances and sighed with relief; evidently they were alone, at least for the time being.

'How much money have we got?'

Francesco put the question between a sip of beer and a bite of sweetcorn. They were sitting on wooden crates, surrounded by interested spectators.

Helen leant forward and whispered, 'It'd be a bit stupid to get our money out and start counting it here. I've got about a thousand dollars and a hundred dollars' worth of local currency in a money belt round my waist. It's sopping wet at the moment, but it'll dry out. How much have you got, Kurt?'

'Roughly the same.'

Francesco stuck two fingers under his leather belt, pulled it out a little and let it go again.

'Hidden pocket on the inside with a zip. Two thousand dollars. And two hundred dollars in local currency in the wallet round my neck. I guess you've both got credit cards too, but that you've heard the same as me, that they can only be used in the big hotels and with the airlines, and then only to pay, not to get cash?'

The other two nodded. Francesco sighed. 'We could have been just normal well-heeled tourists if that idiot of a ferry captain hadn't made us leave our passports and visas with him during the crossing.'

He stood up and the other two followed suit. He picked up the crates and carried them over to the woman with the grill and thanked her. Then he gestured down the street and looked questioningly at the others: 'Shall we go and find a hotel?'

They walked in silence while the street life swirled around them. Francesco seemed to have taken on a kind of leadership role. He didn't like the first two hotels they tried, having seen the lobby and attempted Portuguese with the staff at the desk. In the third he grinned when he saw the lobby; he grinned even more when the young girl at the reception desk answered him in slightly faltering Portuguese.

The rooms were small but clean and opened on to a communal sitting-room and shared a toilet and bathroom. So they could have their privacy and one another's company as well.

They were given three registration cards to fill in and one ball-point pen between them. They all left the spaces for passport and visa numbers blank. The girl frowned when she saw that, and turned to call through the open door to the street. A man stuck his head in, she said something to him, he disappeared, they could hear him shout, a voice on the other side of the street replied, and he came back and said something. The girl nodded, looked at the three Europeans again and nodded.

They took less than a minute to move into their rooms, leaving their doors open. Without cases or bags to unpack they had to content themselves with trying out the beds and chairs to make the rooms their own. The shared sitting-room was spartan, to say the least: one sofa, a table and three chairs.

Footsteps on the stairs and the girl came in with three sarongs. She indicated their damp clothes and rubbed her clenched fists together, miming washing actions.

———————

Francesco woke with a start. More footsteps on the stairs outside the window. He sat up to see. It was the girl again. She didn't turn her head.

They had all seemed to agree that they needed some sleep. They had stood in the doorway in their sarongs, a little embarrassed, and given their clothes to the girl. And then, without further words, they had withdrawn to their rooms and closed their doors.

Francesco looked at his watch: it was almost four o'clock. Hearing a knock, he tied his sarong around him and opened the door. The girl stood there, holding out his clothes. He fetched his wallet of local currency from the bedside table, extracted two notes and proffered them. She shook her head. Then she bent down and took his shoes out of a plastic bag, light canvas shoes, also dry.

He dressed quickly, slipped the waterproof envelope of photographs out of his wallet and followed her down the stairs. He caught up with her as she went behind the reception desk. She could have been in her late teens, with dark, serious eyes and high, slender shoulders under a white T-shirt. He smiled and held up the photos. She looked at him in surprise. He took out the top picture and laid it on the counter, swivelled it the right way round for her, and she picked it up.

The next one was identical: a smiling young woman with cropped brown hair, leaning against a rock face. She was wearing shorts, a sun-top and heavy boots, and had a coil of red rope over her left shoulder. It was a proud smile, as if gratified at an achievement.

He turned over a publicity leaflet lying on the counter, laid the photograph in the centre of the blank side and said in Portuguese, 'Could you write something for me in Malay?'

The girl stared at him in bewilderment. He asked again, but more slowly and clearly this time, pronouncing each word carefully as he pointed at the paper and the picture.

'Please could you write for me in Malay?'

He pointed at the picture of his daughter again, then pursed his lips and blew, waving both hands out in front of him, *disappeared*, pointed at the picture once more, made a question mark with his finger in the air. Has anyone seen her, here here here . . . ?

The girl nodded, she understood. She took a pen from under the counter and leant over the paper, wrote a word in large letters directly beneath the picture and underlined it. Then looked up to ask, 'Daughter?'

Francesco nodded and dropped his eyes. A voice whispered inside him. Dead, or in danger. He shook his head, tried to silence the voice.

'Anya.'

He said it quickly, almost harshly, faced the girl and repeated it, 'Anya. A-n-y-a.'

The girl wrote some brief sentences. Then straightened up and read aloud, translating into Portuguese, 'Anya. Have you seen? Her father looking for her. Ring hotel 38 44, local call.'

Francesco thanked her, indicated that he needed more sheets of paper, was given a pad and went and stood at the end of the counter to begin laboriously copying out what she had written, first one sheet, then the next; when he started on the third, the girl held out her hand for some. Francesco gratefully gave her four, keeping three for himself. She finished her four in less time than it took him to do two. She waited patiently until he had finished the last, and then she brought out a glue stick from under the counter.

'Thanks.'

He spread out the photos from the plastic envelope, all copies of the same original, and carefully pasted them one by one on to the ten sheets of paper. Then he held a sheet up against the wall, as if to hang it.

'Where's best?'

The girl thought for a moment and answered hesitantly, 'Hostels, lodgings. Backpackers before. Not now.'

'But proprietors? Who might remember?'

He put words into her mouth, nervously. She nodded. Then she said *hostels* and went on to list a series of names, counting them off on her fingers. Francesco listened eagerly, repeated the names after her, closing his eyes and saying them aloud. The girl smiled. Francesco pointed to the street: 'Go to the hostels and hang up the photos?' The girl called something to the open door and a man answered, shouted across to the other side of the street, received a reply. Francesco noted the pattern, the same as earlier in the day. The girl behind the desk had permanent contact with a man just outside, presumably a doorman, and he had permanent contact with someone on the other side of the street, someone with the authority to give the go-ahead or not; he had given the go-ahead for their incomplete registration cards – would he do the same for a circuit of hostels?

The plastic bead curtain in the doorway parted, a man in a tracksuit came in, pulled down the zip on his jacket and showed a police badge fastened inside with a safety pin. A leather belt was strapped diagonally from his right shoulder and under his left arm. The girl spoke to him rapidly and gestured towards the European. The policeman listened, reflected for a moment, took a mobile phone out of his pocket and keyed a number. A voice answered, the policeman spoke, paused, listened. Francesco took the picture of himself with the President from the bottom of the pile and put it on the counter. The policeman picked it up and looked at it, gave it back with a hasty glance at the girl, said another few words into the phone, which he then abruptly handed over. Francesco looked at it uncertainly; the policeman said something to the girl, and she translated.

'Speak. He wants.'

Francesco took the phone. It was the police captain.

'What is it now?'

His voice sounded threatening.

'My daughter, backpacking. As I told you, she said she was coming to this island in her last postcard. I must get started on my search; it is a matter of life and death to me. Missing-person posters in the most popular backpacker hostels would be the obvious thing to do first. Please, I beg you.'

Francesco was clutching the sheets of paper bearing his daughter's photo, his knuckles white.

'There aren't any hostels for backpackers in this town. There's reasonable accommodation for our own people, which is sometimes occupied by young Westerners with dollars. We haven't got any of them now, thank goodness; they all fled when the troubles started. You are the only Westerners here.'

Francesco said nothing, just let his request hang in the air and waited. The police captain at the other end of the line was also silent.

'Well, Mr Portuguese-Italian stew.' The police captain was obviously breaking his silence unwillingly, very unwillingly. 'Listen to me. It's true that we can't touch you when you've got a photograph of yourself with the President. But don't push your luck. Don't push your luck too far.'

A long pause followed.

'Let me talk to the police officer on surveillance duty.'

Francesco gave the phone back to the policeman in the tracksuit and felt a huge sense of relief. The policeman listened, responded with a single brief word three or four times, then put his mobile phone away and said something to the girl behind the desk.

'He says go with him.'

Francesco thanked her and followed the policeman, who held the bead curtain aside for him as they went out. He felt his shoulders relax with another surge of relief.

The policeman's vehicle was a yellow pick-up, Malaysian or South Korean. It was parked on the pavement across the street. The policeman got in, leant across and opened the passenger door, and Francesco climbed in.

The policeman drove down a side-street, using his horn and the truck itself to scatter a flock of goats, crossed a small square and jolted down a bumpy alley. Francesco wanted to wind down the window, but the policeman stopped him. None of the people outside even glanced at the truck, oddly enough. As the narrow alley opened out into a dried-up river bed, the policeman slowed down and negotiated it carefully, continued up a hill and out on to a main road. A little further on he stopped outside a low brick apartment building at a crossroads. An elderly woman came out, he said something to her, she asked something, he replied, she shook her head. Francesco held out one of the posters with his daughter's photo on, *please, please*. She took it, studied the photo, shook her head again. Francesco felt his heart sink. The woman looked at him, nodded her head towards the door and indicated with a gesture that she would pin it up. They thanked her, went back to the truck and set off for the next lodging house. Francesco observed the signs of life along the main road. There was an air of resignation about everything, of indifference almost. Broken-down vehicles were parked along the side of the road, here and there a ripped-off car door or a seat. In front of most of the houses clothes were hanging out to dry on bushes. He tried to get a glimpse of a market as they passed, but the shade under the woven straw canopies was too dark for him, and all he could see were silhouettes moving, some turning away, some watching them. He leant back and closed his eyes.

'Have you got children?'

He spoke to the policeman without opening them.

'If so, you'll know that's the real purpose of life, perpetuating the species. Everything else is just frills.'

He opened his eyes and continued his inspection of the street life.

'When you've perpetuated the species you've done your bit. Like an actor who's been on stage and spoken his part. There's no more, it's over, and life in its deepest sense becomes meaningless. In its deepest sense. All you've got to look forward to is your next obligation, dying, so that the species doesn't get too prolific. Perpetuate the species and die, not much of a life.'

They parked outside another hostel, had another poster displayed, went on to the next. 'Relationships can relieve the meaninglessness. Human relationships. With a partner, with children.'

He continued his monologue, gazing out of the window. 'But it all falls apart if your partner vanishes. Or your children. Who can bear growing old alone?'

They drove on in silence; Francesco stopped talking. They visited hostel after hostel, he showed the picture of his daughter, one after another the proprietors shook their heads. Anticipation, disappointment; anticipation, disappointment. In the end he just leant against the car window with his eyes closed.

'Why have you stopped?' Francesco said. 'We haven't got any more posters.'

Francesco put the question without even opening his eyes. Then he heard the policeman step out, opened them reluctantly, and saw the woman from the first hostel standing with his poster in her hand, talking to the policeman. He felt hope welling up within him and leapt out of the car; the policeman held up a hand to restrain him.

'Has she seen her?' Francesco was shouting now. 'Has she heard anything about her?'

He was at their side, grabbed the poster. The text had been written with a blue pen, and now something had been added underneath in red.

'What does it say?' he gasped.

The policeman pointed at the woman. She pointed at the paper, said something, thought for a moment, said something else. The policeman was staring at the paper in silence.

'What does it say?'

He shouted at the woman when she tried to give him back

the paper, *pin it up again, leave it there longer!* But when she ceased trying to explain and registered sympathy in her expression he lowered his voice. All the way back to the hotel in the car he was whispering, *what does it say, what does it say?* The girl behind the reception desk looked up in fright when he came racing in.

'Someone has written on the poster!'

He gestured at the policeman behind him, the policeman spoke to the girl. She asked a question, as if unsure of something. The policeman repeated himself and added a little more.

'He say someone wrote when owner out.'

'What have they written?'

'Hard to translate.'

The girl was making a huge effort to find words. Francesco held his breath.

'Does it say they've seen her?'

She shook her head.

'No, not seen. Hard to translate, no word Portuguese.'

She continued struggling. Francesco was still holding his breath.

'Big danger big death.'

'Is Anya dead?'

'No, not dead. Big danger big death.'

She shook her head helplessly. The policeman said something in her ear, which she translated, 'Written in red. Blood. Warning.'

She hunted for a new word and finally found it: 'Serious warning.'

2

WITNESS

The fire started when they were sitting on the balcony with a can of beer each.

While Francesco had been making his tour of hostels the others had been out shopping, for themselves and for him: shaving gear, toothbrushes, toothpaste, bottled water, brandy – they felt they needed a drink after all they'd been through. Later on the three of them had found a café right by the hotel for a meal, fried fish with rice. Now they sat contemplating the harbour and the evening sky.

It was a warm night, not a breath of air to make the candle flame flicker. A faint smell of seaweed drifted up from the harbour. They drank their beers and chatted, exchanging their impressions of the day in a desultory fashion: *I wonder what happened to the rest of them, did you see the mother with the two children, there was a second life-raft, wasn't there?* Sipped their beers and lapsed into longer and longer silences. Kurt went down for three more cans and they sat with this second round and exchanged further thoughts; *my daughter said she was coming here, how long can they hold us here, how can we get in touch with the Embassy, how long can they hold us here? My daughter said she was coming here.* But the tropical darkness enveloped the words and muffled them; muffled the anxiety, muffled the despair; the gaps between the words became longer and longer, the conversation softer and softer, as if they were no longer talking to each other, but only to themselves, or to the candle flame. The street below was empty, the buildings opposite in darkness.

The fire broke out over to their left, on a hill behind the buildings a little way up the street, and within seconds the house was completely engulfed in flames. The wood must have been tinder-dry or doused from floor to ceiling in petrol. The flames appeared almost instantaneously, soon rendering the whole framework starkly visible, and they could hear the noise of exploding glass. Two young men and a middle-aged woman came out on to the balcony next to theirs, staring at the burning house, the woman holding her hand up to her mouth. The two young men turned to greet the three Europeans, with a smile and a nod towards the conflagration. The Europeans smiled back cautiously, not sure how to react. One of the young men drew his finger across his throat and made a whistling sound, then they both laughed and switched their attention back to the inferno. The flames were still raging and leaping high into the blue-black tropical sky, when they heard the clatter of a helicopter. The young men shouted out and rushed into their room. The woman was about to follow, when she suddenly seemed to remember the Europeans, paused in her flight and pointed agitatedly at their door and at the noise of the rotors, shouted bang-bang-bang, making the stuttering motions of an imaginary machine-gun in her hands.

Helen needed no more persuasion. She flung herself in just as the first salvo of shots came from the helicopter, dropped to the ground and rolled to the door, opened it and crawled through and down the stairs a little way, with her head against the wall and her face in her hands. Kurt was right behind her, crept down a few steps beyond her and huddled into a foetal position.

'Isn't the Italian coming?'

'Portuguese.'

'Kurt, for Christ's sake!' Helen screamed in exasperation.

From behind the counter at the foot of the stairs two pairs of eyes stared up at her: the receptionist and the young boy who had gone out for their beers. Francesco came stumbling out on to the landing and pulled the door shut behind him, running semi-upright, as if he couldn't manage a crouch, sat down on the top step, turned round to make sure he had cleared the door and drew a deep breath, obviously terrified. The noise of the helicopter was directly above them now, the judder of machine-gun fire hammering across the roof, the thud of bullets striking buildings. Helen ran her hand through her hair and it came away covered in plaster and she screamed again, but this time in fear, looked up at the flaking ceiling and closed her eyes tight. The din of the helicopter was subsiding, sounding more normal, the noise of the bullets receding, becoming less threatening. She opened her eyes, looked at the two men above and below her on the stairs. They were pale and panting heavily. Francesco had beads of sweat on his brow. A voice called in English from the balcony outside, probably one of the two young men.

'Hey! *Tuan!*'

'Do you think he means us?' Kurt asked the others in disbelief.

'*Tuan?*'

The voice from the balcony was tinged with laughter. Kurt glanced down at the reception desk, the girl nodded to him and pointed to all three of them. He climbed the stairs past the other two, opened the door, crossed the sitting-room and went outside on to the balcony. The two young men and the woman were back on the adjacent balcony. They all turned when they heard him coming out, indicating by gestures that the danger was over, pointing at the helicopter that had suddenly veered off and was fast disappearing. One of the young men said slowly, searching for the right English words, 'When a house is set on fire, an army helicopter often comes, shooting at everything that moves in the area round the house.' The young man paused, then added, 'Perhaps they hope to kill the arsonists. Or perhaps they just want to scare the shit out of the neighbours. Difficult to say.' The house was nothing but glowing embers now. The two young men made a sign of leave-taking and went; the woman remained, standing with her hand on the door to the room, and said something to the three Europeans, now together on the balcony again: *goodnight*, in English. They thanked her and said goodnight in return. She smiled and shook her head sadly, saying in halting English, 'I rent room, move here, escape, now it follows me.'

She sighed and went in. The three Europeans watched her go, unsure of her meaning.

An hour or so later Francesco was still sitting on the balcony with a glass in his hand. Helen stood in the doorway, watching him, before advancing somewhat hesitantly to sit beside him. They gazed out together at the lights of the town.

'Do you have any special reason to fear for your daughter?'

'I haven't heard a thing from her for more than a month. No letter, no card, no e-mail. It's not like her. It's not like her at all. She must have run into trouble.'

The thought went through Helen's head, *more likely she's run into the Tropics, or someone special*, but she refrained from saying anything.

'And this is a country going through enormous changes right now, and change brings violence in its wake. Something might have happened to her. Or might be about to.'

'Our Foreign Office hasn't issued any advice about not coming here. Has yours?'

'No, but a government department can allow itself greater equanimity than a father.'

Helen turned and looked at him. She perceived a man who wanted something more than to protect his daughter from danger, someone who wanted to preserve a story in order to cling on to it. She was right. No one can step into the same river twice, however much he wants to.

Francesco took a swig from his glass and leant towards her. 'Do you dance?'

She stared at him in astonishment.

'On an Asian balcony? After being shipwrecked, nearly drowned, arrested and now shot at from a helicopter?'

Francesco nodded to each of the questions. He got up and danced a few steps by the railing.

'Foxtrot: fast ballroom dance with four beats to the bar. Quickstep: equally fast ballroom dance, but only two beats to the bar. Try to hear four beats inside you as you dance to two beats. That affects the way you move.'

He was dancing up and down the balcony with his eyes half-closed. Helen stood up and found the rhythm, danced forwards as he danced backwards, backwards when he came forwards. Neither of them hummed a tune, neither beat time; the sound of the two beats of the dance against the four beats inside them was quite clear. Helen thought *the desperate dancer* and smiled inwardly – an exciting title, it would make a good documentary – and the two figures could be seen from darkened windows around the town, two dancing Europeans, on a balcony, in the middle of the night. A quickstep with two beats to the bar against an inner pulse of four is also the basic rhythm of the samba, the South American expression of the same feeling. Two beats to the bar against a pulse of four: could that be mankind's joy wrenching itself loose from despair?

———

Francesco shut the door, took the chair over to the window and picked up the plastic bag of items the others had bought earlier that evening. He lined them up on the window-sill: a night-light, a packet of cigarettes and a box of matches, an empty film canister with an airtight lid that would serve as an ashtray, and a hip-flask. He opened the window a chink, lit the tiny candle, switched off the ceiling lamp, took the lid off the film canister, lit a cigarette, unscrewed the cap of the hip-flask and filled it. Then he sat down with a deep sigh, leant his elbows on the window-sill and looked out. He could just discern the glow of a charcoal grill, tables and benches throwing long, almost grotesque shadows in the moonlight. There were three dark windows in the building directly opposite; he closed his eyes and took a sip from the cap. Was he listening to a faint melody, or was he lost in thought? Was he longing for something?

He sat for nearly two hours with the candle at the window; five cigarettes, the whole contents of the hip-flask. From time to time he rubbed his eyes with the thumb and index finger of his right hand, as if he were tired, or wiping away tears. Eventually he blew out the candle and became invisible. There was a sound of two heavy expulsions of breath in the room, almost like the sound of someone dying, then all was quiet and still.

'What would you like for breakfast? Did you stay up long?'

Helen's head appeared round the door. Her questions seemed to imply more than the actual meaning of her words, as if there were a silence in the room that frightened her.

Francesco raised his head from the pillow, 'Till dawn.'

'Egg?'

'Please.'

'I'll be downstairs.'

She started to say something else as she closed the door, but changed her mind. She walked down the stairs a little stiffly, took a paper from the reception desk and went on into the breakfast room. It was quite small; four tables with white cloths, a white ceiling, brown varnished walls and floors, a stocky woman in a yellow apron standing against one wall. She came over and spoke in English.

'Tea?'

'Coffee.'

'No have.'

'I know.'

Helen smiled and showed her the jar of instant coffee she had bought the previous evening.

'Can you bring me a jug of hot water? And two slices of toast with butter and marmalade? And a full breakfast with eggs for my friend.'

Helen gestured towards the chair by her side. The woman nodded and disappeared. Helen opened the paper, scanning first one picture and then another, turned the pages, scanning more pictures. When Francesco came down, she folded it neatly and pulled out the chair beside her. Francesco pushed it back in and sat down opposite her instead. She looked offended. Francesco nodded at her jar of coffee. 'You've been in this part of the world before.'

'A bit.'

They sat in silence for a while. Helen played with the fob on her room key, let it dangle from the key and tap against the salt cellar. The waitress arrived with a tray. Helen waited until she had laid the table and departed.

'It's odd. I've been shipwrecked with you, shared a life-raft with you, been washed ashore with you, arrested with you, put under house arrest with you, been shot at from a helicopter with you, yet I don't even know what you do for a living.'

'I'm a book restorer.'

'What sort of books?'

'Medieval manuscripts mostly.'

'Oh. Preserving the past.'

The sounds of Asian life came suddenly pouring into the

room, as if a door or window had been opened somewhere, opened on to another reality. Then they ceased just as abruptly, as if someone had deliberately locked them out.

Helen said, 'If God let you relive one day, or one week, or one month of your life, do you know which you'd choose? Have you ever played that game? It makes you think. What you choose tells you a lot about yourself.'

Francesco's face tightened, but she didn't notice.

'The most significant thing of course is whether you choose the past or the present. That tells you most. And then the question is what aspect of yourself you've chosen.'

She looked up and paused.

'Sorry. I've touched a nerve.'

She laid her hand on his.

'Someone who's ill?'

He nodded.

She watched in silence as he ate his breakfast, then gathered up her cigarettes, lighter, newspaper and room key.

'Shall we go?'

They left the breakfast room, hesitated in the reception lobby as they saw the sunlight shining in at the main door, took a few tentative steps towards it. Across the street a man in a tracksuit was sitting sideways on his car seat with the door open.

'Shall we see what's permitted?' said Francesco in an undertone. Helen agreed and put her hand on his arm. They went out of the hotel, paused on the pavement, looked up and down the street. The man was watching them. Francesco made the motion of drinking from a glass and raised his eyebrows in a question. The man touched his watch and held up his thumb and forefinger, slightly parted. Francesco nodded, not long, understood. They set off down the street, examining the wares on the stalls, peering into the windows of the shops in the buildings behind, enjoying their feeling of freedom. After just a few blocks they found a little pavement café with white-painted tables and chairs. Helen ordered a glass of tea. Francesco pondered a moment then ordered a beer. Helen cast a glance at him before pointing towards the hill beyond the town.

'There's a dam in a high valley up in the middle of the island. That's our reason for being here. What about you?'

Francesco's eyes followed the direction of her finger. The café proprietor brought their drinks. Francesco took a long swig.

'Tell me.'

Helen grinned and sipped her tea.

'If you tell me your story afterwards. Is it a deal?'

Francesco smiled and nodded. Helen gazed at the hill pensively.

'There's a valley the other side of that hill, a valley that drops quite steeply towards the east. Originally there was a lake in the lowest part of the valley with a village on its shore. The lake was formed by a spring at the head of the valley, a spring that never ran dry, however late the rainy season came. The people of the village had built an altar at the spring, which they worshipped as a gift from God. They always had water for their terraces along the sides of the valley, they always had water for their animals, they always had water for themselves. They always knew in some way that their security was dependent on there not being too many of them. Anthropologists who've studied the tribe think it's stayed the same size for centuries, without anyone being able to explain how or why. It might seem natural enough, but not in a society and culture that worships fertility. Population growth in neighbouring tribes has apparently never been less than two per cent, but in this tribe it was a constant zero.'

She became more animated.

'One day civilisation reached the valley. The authorities wanted to dam the valley to build a power station. A bigger valley basin would collect more precipitation in the rainy season in addition to the spring water. An even bigger basin would collect even more, so two reservoirs were planned.'

'And the tribe opposed them?'

'The tribe opposed them.'

'But the authorities were stronger?'

'But the authorities were stronger. It's the usual story. And as usual the authorities had capital behind them. Chinese capital in this case.'

'So the tribe moved? Or was moved?'

'Both. Some took the offer they were made, and it wasn't bad by local standards. Some tried to stay put. But even the ones who stayed put seemed to realise their days in the valley were numbered. It became increasingly obvious with every piece of construction machinery that arrived. So when the final offer came, they packed up their belongings and left.'

'Leave or die?'

'On the contrary. Leave and come back. The tribal elders were offered a special deal which they accepted: once a year the power station turbines had to be switched off for maintenance, a job that normally takes a month. The authorities offered to close the upper dam and open the lower one to empty the reservoir before the maintenance period, so that the tribe could return to its village. The level in the upper reservoir would stay the same, so the turbines could be started up immediately once the maintenance period was over.'

Helen paused and drank some more tea. Francesco finished the rest of his beer and swung round on his chair towards the café.

'So this was going to be one of the best documentaries ever.'

The café proprietor brought another beer.

'Imagine the sight: the village houses gradually coming into view, the inhabitants standing on the banks of the reservoir watching their homes rise from the water; imagine them walking into the streets and alleyways, touching the walls to make sure they're not dreaming; they've returned to the past, for one month they're back in a bygone age.'

A pained expression crossed Helen's face and she paused again. They sat silently observing the life on the street. A young couple arrived at the next table, an elderly man sat himself down at another and opened a newspaper. From time to time a street-vendor would come past and hold out his tray of goods over the green hedge: watches, sunglasses, hairclips. The couple at the next table simply said no, the two Europeans shook their heads, the man with the newspaper didn't even raise his eyes.

'I can understand them.'

Francesco was slowly rotating his beer glass as he spoke and he left his words suspended for a moment as he thought about how to continue.

'When I was a child, I used to regard myself as young. When I was a youth, I used to imagine myself as an adult, and when I became an adult, I saw myself simply as more grown up. Now I am grown up, and I won't get any more grown up than I am. Always before I had a clear image of what was coming: as a child I always had a clear image of the young boy, and as a young boy I always had a clear image of the grown man, but now I can't see anything ahead of me clearly at all. I know that what comes next is old age and eventually death, but I can't see how it will happen. It would be different if we lived according to the classic Buddhist tradition, of couples leaving one another in the last phase of life to seek insight and quench their thirst for life. But we're not Buddhists, and we're not Asian. Above all we're not Asian. I think there's a natural desire in Europeans to stick to what is known. For me as a child there was something familiar in the image I had of myself as a youth; and as a youth there was something familiar in the image I had of myself as an adult. Now I suddenly have no images, I cannot envisage myself as an old man; there's nothing familiar about it at all, and it frightens me. So I think it's natural for us to want to retain the dream of what is familiar, to try to hold on to it.'

Helen interrupted, 'If you could be young again for one month a year, wouldn't you choose to be?'

'You mean get older and older for eleven months, and then revert, say, to the age of eighteen for one month every year?'

Francesco sat thinking about this for a long time. On the pavement passers-by slowed down, even stopped, as if waiting for his answer, though for most of them it would be in a language they didn't understand.

'Would I spend the eleven months waiting for the one? Eleven months not aware of what I was doing? And what about that one month? Would it be so precious to me that every minute gone would leave a sense of loss?'

Helen didn't reply. Francesco went on with a little smile. 'I heard of a boy once who paid a final visit to his father in a condemned cell. One hour, and the boy knew it was to be the last hour he would ever have with his father. Sixty minutes, with sixty seconds in each: 3,600 seconds; the last time he would be with his father, the last time he would see him, hear him, smell him, touch him. The boy decided to divide the seconds equally between sight, hearing, smell and touch, 900 seconds each, since these would be the last memories he would have to live with for the rest of his life.'

'What happened?'

'The boy became so engrossed in counting the seconds that he didn't take in anything of what his father said. He eventually fell asleep. When he woke up, his father had gone.'

The café proprietor had come out and was wiping the table behind them. He put his cloth down and called out to a street-vendor on the opposite pavement, *he fell asleep and was executed while he slept*. The street-vendor shook his head dolefully and called to a boy shining shoes further along the street, *his father didn't wake up till after his son was executed*. The shoe-shine boy put his hand to his head and called out to the owner of a tea-stall, *after the father was executed he woke his son*, adding, *Europeans are weird.*

The café proprietor and the street-vendor and the tea-stall owner all nodded in agreement.

———————

Kurt closed his door quietly with a glance at the doors of the other two. Then he went outside, stood on the hotel steps for a moment and gazed about him. The hotel was in a side-street with few vehicles and low buildings. Every roof sprouted aerials and lines of washing. He cast an eye at the man in the tracksuit across the street, who the others had said was a policeman, and walked off to the left, expecting a shout, which didn't come, so he continued making his way in the opposite direction from the main road and found a street-market which he slipped into before slowing down to look over his shoulder. He was a tall man, even by European standards, and here he towered above everyone.

He surveyed the street in both directions. People bustled round him as he stood like an island in the human stream. He inspected the walls of the buildings on both sides of the street till he found the sign he was looking for, then headed for it at a brisk pace.

The bar was cramped and dark, with a counter along one wall and tables along the other. There was a cigarette advertisement and a clock above the bar, and five cans of Dutch beer and a bottle of Chinese brandy on a shelf. A young woman appeared from the back room, with her hair hanging loose and too much make-up.

Kurt said, 'Beer,' slowly and clearly in English and pointed to the cans behind her. 'Please.' She opened a metal container full of cans in water, dried one and set it in front of him.

Kurt broached it and drank the first mouthful straight from the can, then took the glass she gave him, filled it to the brim and emptied it in one swig. The young woman watched his actions.

'Same again, please.'

He wiped the foam from his lips as he spoke. The woman nodded but went into the back room. When she returned she was carrying a bowl of roasted nuts that she put on the counter before getting out another beer. Then she leant against the wall, just watching him. He smiled at her, and she reciprocated. He drank this one in a more leisurely fashion, taking small sips as he examined the room. The lower half of the walls was covered in dark wood-panelling, the upper half in a cream floral wallpaper.

'When does the next boat leave the island?'

The woman looked at him as if trying to read his lips. Then she shook her head.

'Boat? No − no boat.'

Kurt tried again, spoke even more slowly and clearly; 'When does the next boat leave the island?'

'No, not when.'

Kurt heaved a sigh, glanced towards the door with no real hope, tried another tack. 'What about aeroplanes? How often do planes go from here?'

The woman held up a hand, *wait*, and pulled out a telephone from under the counter, held her hand up again, *wait*, picked up a worn, handwritten book of phone numbers, searched for a number and dialled it. She listened to something being said at the other end in a staccato voice, then shouted back, laughing, looking at the man with the glass of beer as she laughed, shouted again, listened, laughed. Then she put the receiver down and turned to him with a beaming smile. She lowered the palm of her hand to the bar, *wait here*. Then she pointed towards the street and said, 'English. Here.'

She lifted his empty beer can, shook it and gave him a questioning look. He nodded. She took another can from the metal container and opened it. Once more he took a swig straight from the can before filling his glass. She watched his movements and mimicked him; first a swig from the can, then pour it into the glass, right? Kurt grinned in acknowledgement. She giggled. They stood in silence for a while, the only sound coming from the clock on the wall behind the bar next to the cigarette advertisement. Kurt looked up at it, the woman's eyes following his. The silence continued unbroken.

She put on a music tape; drums, strings and a slightly melancholy song brushed the silence between them to one side, brought them closer. Then suddenly Kurt was aware that someone had come in the door. He turned. A voice said in soft, fluent English, 'That was the first test. Whether you have time. You've passed. Now comes the next. Don't stare. And don't gape.'

Kurt kept his attention on the voice from the moment it came in till it was right by his side. The voice spoke quickly in Malay to the woman behind the bar and she went out to the back room. Kurt tried to look away from the voice, but couldn't. He kept taking sidelong glances at the long black hair and chiselled profile, the slim neck, the brown skin in the vee of her blouse, the long legs in blue track-suit trousers and the dark-brown bare feet with red toenails in plastic sandals.

'Don't stare. And don't gape.'

The woman now at his side tapped on the bar as she spoke, two light but firm taps. Kurt averted his eyes. The woman from the back room reappeared with a bottle of lemonade which she opened and put on the bar with a glass in front of the woman in the blouse and track-suit trousers. He tried to reply, but had to clear his throat and start again.

'You speak English?'

'That's right. Now you can look a bit. Not much. What's your name?'

'Kurt. Danish. What's yours?'

'Rosalind.'

He scrutinised the woman as she drank her lemonade,

39

noticed her fingers holding the glass, an engraved silver ring on every finger, even her thumb. He looked at her black hair that was swept back and held in place with a plastic slide; her parting was rust-coloured, probably dyed with henna. He let his gaze move from her eyes and nose and mouth, down her neck and blouse to her legs and blue trousers.

'That will do. Turn away now.'

Kurt did as he was told, put his elbows on the bar, his hands together, his thumbs under his chin and his index fingers against the tip of his nose. Rosalind studied him from the side; his hair, his hands, his armpits; leant behind him to see his back. Kurt blushed. Rosalind moved closer and put a hand on his stomach.

Kurt looked at her, looked away, braced his muscles.

'In good shape. Excellent. Try this.'

She took his hand and pressed it to her thigh as she flexed it under the blue cotton cloth of her trousers. He withdrew his hand and nodded.

'Good shape. Excellent.'

He motioned towards the young woman behind the bar.

'This woman thought you could tell me when the next plane leaves.'

'*This woman?*'

Kurt blushed again. He looked at the woman behind the bar and pointed at himself.

'Kurt.'

The woman behind the bar smiled and replied, 'Fidelis. Like Semper Fidelis. Sousa.'

'Fidelis thought you could tell me when the next plane leaves.'

'Good. You learn fast. But you ought to dye your parting with henna. Fidelis can do it for you.'

Rosalind reached out and ran three fingers along his parting as she said something in Malay. Fidelis nodded and responded. Kurt looked embarrassed.

'Do you know when the next plane leaves?'

Rosalind withdrew her hand.

'Fidelis rang me because I can speak English; my mother's a teacher. No one knows when the next plane will be. The last ship went two weeks ago, with seven hundred refugees on board. The sides of the ship were completely covered with people trying to climb aboard. The ones already on board tied ropes and threw them over the side, to their children, to their relatives, to their friends.'

'What a sight.'

Kurt tried to imagine the scene, the ship covered in a swarming mass of bodies clambering up. Rosalind's eyes narrowed.

'What a sight? What drama! What do you think happened next?'

Kurt shook his head. 'No idea.'

'The crew went along the rail slashing the ropes, all of them. Weeping, screaming refugees tried to prevent them, but the crew were armed. The refugees clinging to the sides fell into the water; some managed to swim ashore, some didn't. That was the last ship to dock. News spreads. Every captain knows that if he comes here he'll get a ship full of refugees that he'll never be able to get rid of, because no one will take them.'

'But can't they just be put off at the next island? They're citizens of the country, aren't they?'

Rosalind gave him a long look before replying.

'There are a few things you don't know. But you learn fast, and you've got plenty of time.'

'What about air connections?'

'The same. All civil flights have been cancelled indefinitely. Military planes are flying, but they won't take civilians. And now comes the sixty-four thousand dollar question. What is the sixty-four thousand dollar question?'

Rosalind waited expectantly. Kurt emptied his glass and glanced enquiringly at hers. She shook her head.

'Kurt? What is the sixty-four thousand dollar question?'

He turned to face her.

'Why are people fleeing this island?'

Rosalind gave him a swift hug, felt in his breast pocket and found a black leather wallet, asked something in Malay over his shoulder, received a reply, extracted a note and laid it on the bar, replaced the wallet, took him by the hand and led him to the door.

'Come with me and I'll show you something.'

———————

She had a man's bicycle parked outside. Kurt watched her as she bent forward to unlock it: her movements were delicate yet firm, the muscles of her back taut against her white blouse. She straightened up and smiled at him, handing him the bike.

'You're the man. In our country it's the man's job to wheel the bicycle.'

'And if they each have their own?'

'He wheels both.'

'And when they have children?'

'Then there are lots of bikes to wheel.'

Kurt laughed. He'd never been ordered around like this by anyone; he felt like hitting her and calling her a bossy bitch, but at the same time he was fascinated by her and her authoritative manner.

They walked down the street with the bike between them, he with one hand on the centre of the handlebars. She was pointing things out and commenting on them, occasionally touching his hand to draw his attention to them. 'A Greek merchant lives there, he's been here for years; that hotel is owned by Lebanese; Greeks and Lebanese will travel to the ends of the earth to trade.'

'Yes, they've always been like that.'

They had the same lightness of step, the same physical demeanour.

'Do you think it's all right for me to be walking around with you? We've been told not to be gone for too long.'

'Did anyone try to speak to you as you went out?'

'There was a policeman sitting in a car opposite. He didn't attempt to stop me.'

'No one on this island would dream of making problems for someone from your culture. Anyway we're not going far. We'll just put them to the test. We can walk for an hour today, and then a little more each day. In the end we'll have the whole day.'

Kurt turned to look at her, and she seemed aware of it, though she didn't reciprocate.

'And provided we stick to the areas that are under the control of the police, we're safe. They're on our side.'

'Our?'

'Christians. The army is on the Muslim side. We have to keep out of their way.'

'The army or the Muslims?'

Now it was her turn to look at him.

They had left the market behind them, the smell of barbecues and spices and smoke. They were strolling beneath street lamps, in a cool breeze off the sea. Kurt stopped and took a breath of the fresh air. The girl smiled and waited for him.

'If this were a film,' Kurt said, 'we'd be kissing by now. But it isn't. I've heard that you don't show your feelings in public. And that everything you do in this country is seen; however alone you think you are, there are always eyes out there in the darkness, watching you.'

Rosalind put an arm round him and drew him slightly closer.

'Where on earth did you get that from? Lonely Planet?'

He was about to reply when out of the darkness a voice

suddenly whispered her name. She whirled round abruptly and answered. Kurt lost his balance, tripped over the bike, caught her on the back of the knees and pulled her down with him. As she fell she laughed, 'Some film!'

Kurt murmured, 'All he could see was her white smile in the velvety tropical night.'

The anonymous voice repeated her name, more imperatively this time. Rosalind responded from her semi-prone position. Kurt lay where he was while the voice continued an insistent stream of words in a stage whisper.

Rosalind gasped and said, 'Come on. Quick.'

She stood up, grabbed his hand, retrieved the bike, patted the saddle.

'Get on. Can you manage to ride it with me on too?'

She didn't wait for an answer. As soon as he was on, she sat sideways on the crossbar, supporting herself with both hands over his and indicating with her head, 'Down that street there. As fast as you can.'

'What's happened?'

After a shaky start, Kurt found his equilibrium and pedalled faster. Rosalind balanced gracefully in front of him, leaning into the bends with him, straightening up when he did.

'What's happened?'

'Someone's been attacked. That's all I know.'

They swung into a side-street, across a square and were immediately at the harbour. There was a brick church in a park by the beach-front promenade, separated from the street by a white fence. Next to it, within the park, was a low house, also of brick. The lights were on, and furious voices could be heard from the door and windows. There was a group of people gathered at the gate. Rosalind said something to them. They turned and looked at her, and at the European with the bicycle, and stepped to one side. Kurt pushed the bike through the gate, she shut it behind them and went on towards the house.

'Why did they stand aside for us?'

'Because you are *tuan*.'

'Don't lie to me.'

She stopped abruptly and turned to face him.

'I'm not lying. To them you're *tuan*.'

She narrowed her eyes at him for several seconds before walking up to the house. Kurt stood and watched her for a moment, then wheeled the bike after her. The voices from the door and windows were louder and the light brighter now they were up close. Rosalind indicated the wall to the right of the door, 'You can put the bike there.'

He put it on the left. Once again they exchanged glances, then she indicated to him that he should follow her in. A man accosted them in the doorway, an elderly man in dark trousers and white singlet with a deeply furrowed brow. Rosalind asked him something; he replied in Malay, short, angry phrases. Then he drew his finger across his throat.

Rosalind addressed herself to Kurt, 'You're a cameraman, you must have seen blood before?'

'How do you know I'm a cameraman? Lonely Planet?'

'I have a friend who's in the police. Come on.'

The man drew back to let them in. They found themselves first in a sort of lobby, full of people, some weeping, some praying, but all stood aside for them and they came into a larger room with long brown benches, a meeting hall or a school. In the middle of the room a crowd of people were standing in a circle around something, the women with handkerchiefs held to their eyes, the men tight-lipped. Rosalind eased her way forward until they were at the front by two benches that had been placed together to form a make-shift stretcher. On it lay a woman dressed in a full-length white dress, with a man kneeling beside her pressing a blood-soaked white towel to her neck. Her lips were moving, and there were beads of sweat on her brow. Rosalind dropped to her knees beside her, taking the bloody towel from the man and raising it carefully. The woman's throat was slit from ear to ear. Bubbles of air rose from the centre of the wound. Rosalind laid the cloth gently back in place.

Kurt whispered to her, 'Is there a doctor on the way?'

She replied without looking up, 'Of course. But he'll be too late. The priest too. Have you got a camera with you? They say photographers never go out without one.'

Kurt nodded. She looked up, and he nodded again.

'The one I had went to the bottom with the ferry. But I've bought myself a new one.'

'Don't take it out for a minute.'

She bent forward and spoke in the woman's ear. A slight change in her expression seemed to indicate that she heard.

Rosalind said, 'I told her she won't die in vain; she'll die without a priest, she'll die without the sacraments, but she won't die without a witness.'

Kurt took the witness from his trouser pocket, a metallic digital camera, and slid the cover to one side. He pressed a button, held the camera away from him and looked in the screen. There was a rattling sound from the woman, and more blood seeped into the white towel. Rosalind gave him a rapid glance.

'Too dark. Too many people crowding round. They're blocking the light.'

The woman was trying to raise her head.

'Can't you use a flash?'

'I never use flash. It flattens the features.'

He moved the camera back and forth, held it down near the floor and up at head height.

'Can you get them to kneel?'

'And pray?'

The dying woman coughed, blood spurted out from under the towel and on to the white shoulder of her dress. Rosalind said something to those nearest, and they stared at her and at the camera. Then the first of them knelt, an old woman, and clasped her hands in front of her forehead; another woman knelt and put her hands together; a young boy followed suit, and then it seemed that the whole room was kneeling, the whole room had clasped hands up at their foreheads, filling the universe with prayer. The sound of the people in the lobby faded, and of the people by the door, and in the street. The prayers flowed over the dying woman; she turned her head the little she could, as if attempting to see the murmuring lips and clasped hands.

Kurt watched them in the camera screen, the woman twisting round against the background of closed eyes and sombre faces moving up and down, up and down, then he pressed the shutter button and the picture froze. For a second or two it was fixed on the screen while the camera stored it, then motion resumed. The woman was trying to sit up, trying to push the towel away; the noise of prayer intensified, sounding more fearful. Kurt pressed the button again and froze the picture: the woman's action was suspended on the screen, half-leaning on her left elbow with one hand on the towel; the people praying froze for another second before the picture was back in motion. Then Rosalind took the towel away from the woman's neck, blood pumped out of the wound, the woman tried to hold her throat and fell back; the camera froze her movement and the faces behind her, crying out now, for another second, quite still, until the picture on the screen began to move again, and the people opened their eyes and lowered their hands and silenced their prayers and gazed at the woman on the stretcher, the only one now on the screen who was no longer moving.

———————

' "You won't die in vain; you'll die without a priest, you'll die without the sacraments, but you won't die without a witness." That was rather melodramatic.'

Rosalind's eyes were lowered as she spoke. Kurt didn't respond. She looked up at him, seeking an answer, in his eyes, in his face, but didn't find any. They had taken the bike and joined the onlookers outside the gate. An ambulance had arrived to collect the dead woman, a doctor had come, a priest too. Kurt had fastened the camera to his belt and hung it inside his trousers. Rosalind touched it discreetly.

'The witness is here, is it?'

Kurt blushed.

'It would be best if you go back to the hotel now. If there's still a policeman outside, make some contact with him, at least exchange a few words. We've been away less time than you might think. Everyone knows that *tuan* have lengthy drinking sessions and think water makes their stomachs rust.'

She reached up and put a hand round his neck and kissed him. 'I'll come when the streets have quietened down a bit.'

Kurt lay down on his bed in the hotel room and waited. He lay with his hands behind his head, looked at the light from the naked bulb hanging on its wire from the ceiling, and waited. An oscillating electric fan on the bedside table sent a breeze of warm air from side to side across the room. Having studied the ceiling, he rolled over and lay on his stomach. There was something he didn't understand and maybe didn't want to understand. Were they using him? He buried his face in the pillow. What did they want the photographs for? Couldn't they have taken photos themselves? They must surely have cameras of their own?

He rolled over again, put his hands back behind his head and whispered to himself, *this is where they have them, this is the part of the world where they have cameras*. After a while he got up and turned out the light. The window to the stairway glowed pale yellow with dark shadows.

48

How long does it take to die when your throat has been cut?

Kurt whispered it into the semi-darkness. The shadows whispered in response, *no time at all, no time at all.* It must have been an attack they had forewarning of, an attempted kidnap, maybe. The slitting of her throat must have happened less than a minute before the girl and I arrived. Some of the people there must have seen it, and that many people can't assemble in one minute. Does that bother me?

He put one arm over his eyes. The shadows continued to whisper, *there's something that should bother you more.*

What?

He opened his eyes with a start.

They stood aside for her, not for me. It's more than fifty years since this country got its independence; all that about *tuan* is rubbish.

The shadows were interrupted by a sound from the door. Rosalind entered the room and locked the door behind her. Kurt heard them no longer. He swung his feet off the bed and stood up as she came towards him. She began to undress, without a word: first blouse and bra, then sandals, trousers and pants, and finally the plastic slide holding her hair in place. She shook her hair loose. Kurt reached out and touched her cheek, ran his fingers down her neck towards her breast. She undid his belt buckle, pulled out his shirt, began unbuttoning it from the bottom.

———————

Later Kurt said, 'Have you ever had the feeling of living behind high walls?'

He was lying with one hand beneath her neck and whispering in her ear while running the index finger of his other hand along her profile, first over her forehead and down her straight nose, then over her dark lips, round and under her chin and along her throat.

Kurt went on: 'A wall of expectations? Achieve, better yourself, achieve, better yourself, until one day you're sitting behind a wall of suits and ties in a room full of men?'

He let his hand lie on her breast; she looked down at it. He took his hand away, extracted the other hand from under her neck, rolled over on his back and linked his hands behind his head. Rosalind stretched herself and laid her head on his shoulder.

'Are we out in the exercise yard? Is this when the dream of jumping over the wall is born? And the thought of what's on the other side?'

Kurt fell silent. She looked at him, put her fingers to his lips, drummed them lightly and whispered with a smile, 'Perhaps a big jar of honey? That you land right in? And then I'd have to come and lick you clean?'

He smiled, leant over her and ran his fingers through her hair. Then he lay back down again and stared up at the ceiling.

'Kurt. Fancy calling me that. King Kurt the Great. Or Pope John Kurt. Anyone can hear it's wrong. I sometimes wonder whether there was a reason my father gave me that name, or whether it was just chance.'

'It suits you.'

Kurt turned and kissed her, drew her towards him. She slid her arms round him with a smile and sniffed at his neck. He put his hands behind her head and brought her ear close to his lips.

'When I was a boy I used to keep a list of jokes about Danish country bumpkins on the wall of my room and mark them off every day when I came home from school. Not a day went by without one and there can't be a single joke about country bumpkins that I haven't heard. There was a joke competition every week, and the winning joke was the one that had been told the most times. I eventually became a dab hand at predicting which it would be.'

'What was the prize?'

Kurt smiled and drew her ear even closer, whispered

something almost inaudible. Rosalind grinned at him: 'Danish girls don't do that.'

He rolled her over on her back and lay on top of her, took her face in his hands and looked into her eyes.

'When I was sixteen I moved to my mother's. She was Flemish. Also from the country. That was when it occurred to me that country bumpkin and Flemish were two different expressions for the same thing.'

Rosalind said nothing. The word *Flemish* hung in the air between them for a moment, then divided in two: Belgian Flemish and Dutch Flemish, an unavoidable distinction in a part of the world where one side has almost four hundred years of colonial history on its hands and the other hasn't.

After a while she rose and sat with her legs astride his back and massaged his shoulders. She was bathed in the light from the stairwell, which made her skin glow.

Later, when they lay in one another's arms, drifting off to sleep, he said in a low voice, 'Do you think a country bumpkin could jump over a wall?'

Rosalind waited until his breathing was regular, then took one of his hands, pressed her thumb into his palm and whispered, 'Do you remember the name of the girl in the bar?'

He mumbled something.

'No. Fidelis.'

She turned on her side and snuggled up to him, wrapped his arms around herself, one hand on her breast, the other on her stomach.

'Do you know who I am?'

She moved her head to hear better whether any answer was forthcoming. He just carried on breathing gently. She smiled, closed her eyes, and said, 'Now you have your wall.'

A gentle breeze of whispering voices came in through the open window from the sea. The whispers were like waves; rising, falling, rising, falling. Rosalind wrinkled her brow in her sleep.

3

BARTER

The men in white from the ship had gathered together in
the grey light of dawn in an Islamic compound of
mosque, hospital and school. High walls hid it from view on
all sides. They had unrolled their prayer-mats and were
kneeling with their faces to the ground, straightening up to
utter a few words and then bending forward again. A mullah
stood watching them from the entrance to the mosque before
shaking his head and going inside.

After their prayers they withdrew singly or in groups to the
area they had been allocated by the centre's leaders, a wooded
grove between the hospital and the school. Several of them
checked the padlock on the store where they had been
required to leave their weapons, giving it a tug to test it.
Soon all were sitting or reclining on the ground, and the sun
rose above the roof of the mosque, forcing those who could
find space into the shade under the trees. They were obviously
waiting for something, their presence here only temporary.
Baskets of white bread were produced and distributed, two
jugs of tea followed with ten plastic cups hanging round the
rim of each. The men in white queued up, some still eating
the bread they had been given. They stood in silence in
groups of ten and drank the tea, before rinsing the cups in a
bucket of water and handing them on in the queue.

The first lorry arrived four hours after prayers. It reversed
into the grove and came to a halt. Two men stepped down
from the cab, dropped the tailgate and called for thirty men to

work on a clove farm, board and lodging included, counted off the hands that went up, you, you, you and you, pointing to the lorry, closed the back when it was full and drove off. There were already four more lorries waiting to enter the compound, and two more arriving further down the road. The first truckload of thirty men swung out into the street and rumbled off in low gear, passing a military machine-gun post where the soldiers didn't even look up, and a military checkpoint without being stopped.

It drove on, out of the town and uphill. One of the men in the cab stuck his head out of the window and shouted two words, 'Christian village', repeating them as he pointed ahead. The men in the back looked at one another and crouched down, holding and supporting each other, so that they could no longer see or be seen over the sides. The lorry accelerated, bouncing at breakneck speed over potholed roads; some house roofs appeared, some more, then an unbroken sequence, the men alert and watchful. A gap, slightly longer to the next, and it was over. The lorry reduced speed, the man in the cab put his arm out of the window and banged with the palm of his hand three times on the door. The men all stood up. Now the road wound between open fields, with a house here and there, a booth, a little market. They came to a halt in a quiet village, the two men in the cab jumped out and dropped the tailgate, pointed to a tea-stall. The owner must have been expecting them: he had tea and fifteen glasses ready. The men drank in two relays while being addressed by one of the men from the cab.

'About half an hour to go. We'll be passing an isolated Christian church on the way. We'll make a brief stop there.'

The men in white nodded, exchanging glances. Some of them wandered a few metres away from the tea-stall, others were having a stretch, rotating their shoulders, trying to exercise the stiffness out of their joints after a night without sleep and being buffeted about on the back of a truck. The two men from the cab took the tea-stall owner aside, paid him and held a hushed conversation with him. Then they clapped their hands and walked over to the lorry. The men in white climbed aboard, the tailgate was raised into position, the driver started the engine and they moved off.

It was an attractive scene: the lorry was painted gold, the load-space dark blue, and even the men's white clothes had a warm glow, as if there was a lot of yellow in the white. The tea-stall owner stared pensively after it as it receded into the distance. There were two men sitting on a wall, each with prayer beads, also pensively watching it go. When it finally disappeared round a bend in the road, the countryside was totally quiet, totally peaceful, not a movement anywhere, a green island in an endless sea with the sun directly overhead.

The police captain tightened the belt of his uniform, took down a cap with a shiny peak from a shelf, stood in front of a washbasin with a small mirror above it and put the cap on. Then he left his office, walked down the corridor, across the courtyard and out into the street. The police guard on the door presented arms. The police captain raised his hand to his cap in salute and gestured to the blue and grey open-topped car parked outside. A young, armed policeman sprang out and held the door for him.

'Army Headquarters.'

He didn't look at the policeman as he spoke, and the young man merely nodded. The police captain put on his sunglasses, big black ones with gold frames, keeping his eyes on the pavement as they drove along, as if inspecting his people. From time to time they passed policemen who saluted and received an acknowledgement in return.

Army Headquarters were down by the harbour, near the mosque. The entrance was surrounded by sandbags, taciturn soldiers lying flat with their machine-guns at the ready in front of the building. The police captain appeared not to notice them; he went straight up to the guards behind the sandbags and said, 'The colonel. I have an appointment with the colonel.'

The two guards admitted him. He went up the stairs, along a corridor with a worn red carpet and stopped at a solid, dark-brown door. He knocked and gazed out of the window as he waited, perusing the crowd of figures in white inside the mosque compound, and glancing over towards the cranes in the harbour, two of which were at work.

'Come in.'

He opened the door and went in. The colonel was sitting at a desk in the window, only his silhouette visible against the light. It was a large, high-ceilinged room, at the other end of which was a set of leather chairs around a small glass table, with a picture of the President hanging on the wall above. The colonel stood up and waved his hand towards the chairs. The police captain thanked him and sat down.

'How are you, Captain?'

'Fine, thanks. And you, Colonel?'

'Fine, thanks. And your family?'

'Fine thanks. And yours?'

'Fine, as far as I'm aware.'

The colonel pressed a bell-push and a few seconds later there was a tap on the door and a soldier came in. The colonel ordered tea without looking at the police captain. The soldier saluted and went out.

'Have your men had a quiet night?'

'Not bad. Two houses burnt down in the early hours, one yesterday evening, exchange of fire outside the Christian rehabilitation centre just after midnight, two small bombs in the Muslim business district. How about yours?'

'The same.'

The colonel and the police captain sized one another up.

The soldier entered with a pot of tea and two glasses and left again immediately. The two men sipped their tea.

'It looks as if there are increasing numbers of refugees in the mosque compound?'

The police captain gave the impression of putting a question, but only just.

'Possibly. Are new refugees still arriving at the church?'

'Probably. Will you be having a talk with the leaders of the mosque at Friday prayers?'

'Not out of the question. And you're still talking to the church fathers even though you don't go to Mass?'

The two men took another sip of their tea, the hint of a smile playing around their lips. The colonel could have been in his fifties and looked as if he had spent his whole adult life on active service. He had a line of colourful decorations above his left breast pocket. He was watching the police captain and waiting. The police captain was gazing out of the window, as if seeking inspiration from outside, seeking inspiration from the light and the sea and the harbour before getting down to business.

'We've arrested three Europeans. One woman and two men. They must have been on the ferry that sank, and come ashore on a life-raft. We found them semi-conscious on a beach after a tip-off from fishermen and brought them in for questioning.'

'Interesting. Where are they from?'

The colonel took another sip of tea.

'The woman and one of the men are Danish, the other man Italian, with a veneer of Portuguese. They abandoned ship in what they stood up in, no visas, no passports. We've put them under loose house arrest.'

'Interesting. Why loose?'

The colonel kept his eyes on the police captain while he waited for an answer. The police captain stared at the window and the sea and the harbour again, drawing a finger ruminatively along under his collar. The colonel leant back and crossed his legs and added, 'You're the police on this island. We've only been sent here to calm a – what shall we call it? – a collective outburst of emotion. If you think loose house arrest is appropriate, that's up to you. But we like to be kept informed. Loose house arrest means they've got some limited freedom of movement?'

The police captain nodded.

'Limited. For eating and shopping.'

'I'll make sure my men know. They're the only whites on the island now? In this sea of yellow faces?'

The police captain gave him a quick glance to see whether he was being ironic, but the colonel was inscrutable.

'We're only aware of one other. Our three are staying in the hotel near the Christian rehabilitation centre.'

The colonel nodded. The police captain picked up his cap, as if getting ready to leave, shuffling it from one hand to the other.

'The Italian is a book restorer. What God's intention was with him is anybody's guess.'

'Maybe using him to restore books?'

'Maybe. The Danish man and woman work for Danish TV. They're making a documentary about the submerged village in the mountains. You know about that?'

The colonel nodded again. The police captain stood up, put on his cap, straightened it and said, 'That was all I came to see you about. Thanks for the tea.'

He went to the door, the colonel's eyes still on him with a smile hovering round his lips as he noticed the police captain hesitating. The latter turned too slowly to catch a glimpse of the smile before adding, 'Oh, there was one other thing that occurred to me.'

'I'm all ears.'

'Could we make use of the Europeans in some way? What do you think?'

'Not a bad idea. But how?'

'Difficult to say. But if there was something in which we had a common interest . . .'

The police captain didn't finish his sentence.

'We?'

'The army and the police.'

There was silence in the room. From the window came the sound of the cranes in the harbour and the men in the mosque compound. The colonel smiled again, with a twinkle in his eyes.

'You're a man of perspicacity. Not many would have thought of that. Not many at all.'

The police captain returned the smile fleetingly, as if gratified. Then took his leave again. 'Let's think about it. The first to have an idea can get in touch.'

The colonel watched him go, smiling tentatively, when the police captain paused once more with his hand on the doorknob. The smile had vanished by the time he turned.

'Are you really convinced it's necessary to send in an army helicopter every time a house is set on fire?'

'Absolutely. It emphasises the severity of the situation.'

'And to shoot from the helicopter?'

'Ditto.'

'But shooting at everything in the vicinity? Up to a radius of three blocks?'

'Well, obviously there wouldn't be a lot of point in shooting into the burning house itself. Not many arsonists would stay in a building they'd set fire to. We're here to restrain. One way is through fear. We want it to be known that setting fire to other people's houses can be dangerous.'

The police captain finally took his leave and withdrew.

———

The colonel sat at his desk and waited. He knew the police captain would come back in person if his plan required active participation by the army. If not, there would just be a phone call. He took out his mobile from his briefcase, checked that it was on and laid it down beside him on the desk. Then he slowly swivelled his chair and looked out of the window. On the grass by the mosque a group of young men in white headbands was training. His experienced eye told him it was battle training. He stared across at the harbour and the cranes and the horizon beyond, then brought his gaze in over the town and the church. He knew that the same battle training was in progress on the square in front of the church; he had passed by it enough times in his car. He folded his hands in his lap and looked at the horizon. Reflected in his eyes was the grove by the mosque, full of youths now, all with white headbands, shouting excitedly, many with spears, other with bows and arrows. He turned his attention to the church, from where a second group of youths was streaming down the street, those too reflected in his eyes, all wearing red head-bands, shouting slogans and brandishing their spears, or flailing wooden clubs. He sighed. That's what happened when people sacrificed their intelligence to their religion. The young men at the mosque had no concept of the inevitable relationship between cause and effect; they believed reality to be a mirror image of God's will. The youths at the church believed the same thing – not a sparrow falls to the ground without God's will. The most significant difference between them was the colour of their headbands. And when both groups were motivated by blood vengeance, there might be no end to the violence.

He sighed again.

No end to the violence and no end to our ignorance, he thought. If the philosophers are right that knowledge is the knowledge of causes, then we know no more in this society today than we knew a hundred years ago, or two hundred, or five hundred.

He watched the two groups for a while. The demonstrators

from the church had been halted by the armed police. His own soldiers had blocked off the area round the mosque. He thought about his country that had once been a disparate weave of Hindu kingdoms and Islamic sultanates. So it should have remained. But the Dutch had wanted it otherwise and forced them to live together as one people. Yet they weren't.

He heaved another deep sigh. The Dutch had gone. The blood spilt then should have been washed away. But that wasn't what people wanted. At least not the Malays in the capital.

He closed his eyes and could hear the shouting of angry demonstrators, decade after decade, separatist movements and ethnic revolutionary groups: he heard the cries of the peoples who were forced to flee, from one island to another, two million at least; he heard the cries of those who lived on the islands to which the displaced were transported; he heard the shots, the spears and arrows, the burning houses; he heard the torture and the screams of pain, the executions and the sobs of the bereaved. Then he opened his eyes and looked at his mobile phone. It was ringing.

'Violence is nothing new in any society, least of all in ours,' he said out loud. 'But on this island they have a different attitude to violence.'

He picked up the phone, pressed the connect button and listened for a while. Then he interrupted the voice on the other end: 'You don't mean, Captain, that the *tuan* make better films than we do? Just because they're *tuan*?'

The voice at the other end was silent for a moment before replying. 'Of course not. But there are other doors open for them. Where they come from. If we could get them to film this collective outburst of emotion, as you yourself called it, Colonel, the doors would be open to European TV companies in an entirely different way than if it came from us. The *tuan* would rather have reports from their own people.'

The police captain paused slightly before using the nickname for Europeans, as if it cost him an effort.

The colonel took up the idea, a wry smile crossing his face. 'And if European TV programmes show pictures of this collective outburst of emotion, that will have quite a different effect on our leadership in the capital? And our reports with appeals for reinforcements will be taken out and reread?'

The police captain replied, 'Something like that.'

The colonel rose to his feet, turned towards the window, stood with the phone in one hand and the other behind his back, gazing out.

'You're right, of course. It's good to see that the army and the police can sometimes have common interests. But what if the two TV people suddenly leave the island? It won't take the Embassy many days to send them replacement passports, will it?'

'They think we have scarcely any telephone contact with the outside world. Only intermittently.'

The colonel turned back to his desk. '*Tuan* have strange ideas.'

He was on the point of terminating the conversation and hanging up when something suddenly occurred to him. With his eyes on the portrait of the President hanging above the coffee table, he said, 'What about the book restorer?'

'It's harder to think of any common ground there,' was the police captain's terse reply.

'Maybe you have your own plans for him?'

There was silence at the other end. The colonel waited. Then he said, 'Rumours travel fast. Especially among people who have too little to talk about. I wish you and your men a good day, Captain.'

A police car called for the three Europeans directly after breakfast. An officer came into the breakfast room and beckoned them, and they got up uncertainly and followed him out to the waiting car. The driver didn't turn his head. The trip to the police station took only a few, completely silent, minutes. The officer who had fetched them got out and opened the door for them. Francesco set one foot on the pavement but was restrained. The policeman put a hand on his shoulder, indicating that the other two should leave the car, which they did, looking confused and annoyed. Francesco watched through the window as they were led through the steel door. He tried to open the car door, but the policeman at the wheel prevented him; he tried to wind down the window, but the same policeman stopped him again. He peered at the façade of the police station. It was yellowy-brown, a rather heavy, central European twenties' style, two low blocks joined by a long, single-storey wing.

'Why are you keeping me here in the car?'

The policeman stepped out, lit a cigarette and leant against the bonnet without so much as a glance in his direction. Two chickens were clucking behind the car and he turned to try to see them; the policeman came and stood in front of the window, effectively blocking it. Francesco swung round irritably and looked out of the other window, where he could see the street, but street life didn't interest him at that moment – he wanted to know why they were keeping him in the car, and even found himself asking the question aloud, realising the pointlessness of it as he did so. *What will the President in the capital say when he hears you've been holding me prisoner in a car? An insignificant police captain in a windswept outpost holding me prisoner in a car.* And he could hear the police captain give a curt laugh; 'Holding prisoner, what are you talking about? We asked you to wait in the car while we had a talk with the other two; even Europeans wait in cars – we asked you to wait in the car because the sun was high in the sky, and we didn't want to expose you to the heat.' Francesco put his hand to his throat and cleared it. There was sweat on his brow, he was thirsty, he banged on the window where the policeman's back was still blocking his view. 'Water, something to drink!' The back didn't move. He leant over to the free window and wound it down, and the policeman with the cigarette shouted something and three armed policemen came out of the guardroom towards the car. Francesco stared at them, stared at the automatic weapons hanging from straps over their shoulders, all three barrels pointing at him; the guards were looking at him, straight at him, and he tried to interpret their expressions; disinterested, neutral, indifferent, yes, indifferent, he said the word to himself, they would kill me with the same indifference with which they would let me live. The guards were at the car now and took up position with their backs to each of the three uncovered side windows. Francesco gasped, locked in; he stared out of the front windscreen, the only free window, facing straight into a wall, a flaking yellowy-brown wall. He leant back and touched his throat again, the sweat running off him now, water, water, the temperature in the car rising by the minute, his pulse getting faster; he was wheezing for breath, wiping the sweat from his face, leant forward with his arms over the seat in front of him and his head hanging down. Something glinted at him, not on the floor beneath his face, but something in front, something he had spotted as he leant forward. He raised his head and was looking straight at a shiny key in the ignition; he ran his eyes along the instrument panel till he saw a switch marked 'air-conditioning', smiled in relief and reached out to turn on the ignition for a cold stream of air, sighing in anticipation as if he could feel it already, a cool refreshing stream of air, half out of his seat reaching for the key in the ignition. One of the policemen cocked his weapon, then the second, then the third. Francesco froze, leaning over the front seat with his hand only a few centimetres from the key, and then sank back down with tears in his eyes.

He was still sitting like that when the others returned. He didn't know whether he had passed out, he didn't know whether he had noticed the guards at the windows leave; he only knew that he had a sensation of coming round when the door was opened and he felt a hand on his shoulder.

'Aren't you feeling well?'

It was Helen. She looked worried. Kurt was right behind her, trying to see in.

'I'm fine. Must have dozed off in the heat. Have you got any water?'

With a searching glance she handed him a plastic bottle of water. He took some long swigs and turned his face to catch the air coming in through the open door. Then he moved over to make room for the other two, the policemen climbed into the front seats and the car started up.

'What did the police want you for?'

Francesco had to clear his throat twice before he could get the question out. Helen was still scrutinising him.

'We asked why you were having to wait in the car. He said you weren't coming to any harm there.'

She laid her hand on his arm. Francesco smiled.

'I was OK. Was it the police captain? What did he want?'

Helen seemed reluctant to change the subject. Kurt answered for her.

'He wanted to know if we'd been woken by the noise on the first night. If anyone had tried to explain to us what it was. We said no. He asked what we had seen and heard. We said a fire, a helicopter, shots. Then he opened a drawer in his desk and took out a video camera and a MiniDisc player with a microphone and long lead and asked us to test it.'

Helen took over: 'It sounded more like a command. We tried the equipment and it worked OK. Then he explained that what we had seen and heard that first evening was regrettably not an isolated incident. This island is not what it used to be; neighbour has turned against neighbour, group against group. The army has been sent in to keep the peace, but it hasn't succeeded in doing so. Then he asked whether our accreditation was in order, even if it was at the bottom of the sea. We said it was, and he only needed to ring the press department in the capital.'

'But the Embassy first.'

Francesco's tone had an element of bravura in it. Helen laughed.

'Then he started being ironical – he said we had come here to make a documentary about their culture, and that was fine, they were always interested in European documentaries about their culture . . .'

Kurt interrupted, 'Forget the irony. He wanted to know whether we would also consider making a documentary about their anti-culture.'

'Anti-culture?'

Francesco was puzzled.

'He said that what we saw and heard the first night was anti-culture, and that things shouldn't be like that. The police and the army could put a stop to it, but not without reinforcements. So far their requests have fallen on deaf ears in the capital.'

Francesco saw at once what the police captain had in mind.

'And that's what they need you for?'

Kurt nodded.

'For him – and them – we are the way into European TV. Dutch, British, French, there's no limit to the demand for good quality programmes with plenty of drama; German, Italian, Spanish; Danish TV could handle the sales.'

'So his proposal was . . . ?'

'That we should make one or more reports about the disturbances here, with commentary in English, so that they can understand what's being said, and then we could use their same equipment to make the documentary we actually came here for.'

Francesco closed his eyes and saw before him a pair of scales: we let you work on your documentary if you work for us, that's a nice balance. He looked further into the darkness at another pair of scales; we let you search for your daughter if you . . . But he couldn't see what was on the other side of the scales. If you, if you . . . All he knew was that they had told him something now, they had locked him in a dark, over-heated car and told him something.

'What's the problem?' Francesco looked from one to the other. 'He lends you their equipment so that you can make the documentary you came for, in exchange for you filming something for them. I don't see the problem.'

Francesco looked at them uncomprehendingly. Kurt was drawing lines in the condensation on his beer glass. Helen lit a cigarette. Neither of them responded. They'd gone out for a drink after the police car had set them down at the hotel. Francesco was still on edge; the other two were indignant and frustrated.

'Isn't the equipment good enough? Or is it who's commissioned it?'

Kurt removed his finger from the patterns on the glass and replied, 'The latter. We work for Danish TV. Not for the police in an Asian dictatorship.'

Helen added, 'Also, it's a matter for our editor. That kind of decision is what we have editors for.'

Francesco almost felt sorry for her.

'But your editor isn't here, and you can't contact him.'

'Her.'

'Her. Your equipment is lying at thirty thousand fathoms, and you've got a concrete offer, a quid pro quo. What do you think your editor will say when she finds out you could have filmed but chose to come back empty-handed?'

'Don't bully us, please,' said Kurt quietly. 'The point is, neither of us is used to working on news. But we do know a bit about sources and checking them out. We've got no way of checking our sources here. We've got no other sources at all except our friend the police captain. He can wind us round his little finger – select what we should cover, choose where we film. We could end up being partisan without even realising it and be a laughing stock among our colleagues all over the world.'

Francesco stared at him in disbelief.

'Are you telling me that TV reporters aren't partisan?'

Kurt grinned for the first time since the meeting with the police captain. 'Manipulating and being used are like eroticism and pornography: two sides of the same coin, but at the same time as different as they could possibly be.'

'Kurt's always very good with words,' said Helen matter-of-factly, taking a drag on her cigarette before continuing, 'but he also happens to know what he's talking about.'

A long pause ensued. They were sitting in a pavement café down by the harbour. There was a constant stream of passers-by in both directions, and the whine of cranes in operation along one quay where there was a rusting cargo ship. Francesco tried to see what was going on, but there was no sign of any loading or unloading.

'And there's another thing,' said Helen, still in a dispassionate voice. 'How dangerous is it?'

The other two waited for her to continue.

'Who wants to end up between screaming, unpredictable Muslims and Christians on an Asian island six hours' flying time from the nearest embassy?'

She looked at the two men. Neither of them said anything. She leant forward and wrote a word on the table with her finger: *afraid*. Then pointed at herself, got up and wandered off. Kurt's eyes followed her.

'Poor Helen.'

Francesco was taken aback. It was the first time either of them had shown concern for the other.

'She's afraid of covering the riots, and afraid of saying no.'

'And of what the police captain might come up with next?'

'Exactly.'

Francesco wondered for a moment whether the young cameraman realised that a refusal from them could also have a negative impact on his own search for his daughter, but he refrained from saying anything. Instead he asked, 'What about you? Are you afraid?'

Kurt nodded. 'Yes, very. But I've heard from colleagues who've filmed in conflict areas that the camera seems to give you some kind of protection, a sort of immunity. We'll have to hope that's the case.'

He too got up and left. Francesco emptied his glass and followed. Helen was waiting for them outside the café, standing with her hand on a lamppost, watching the street life. They walked back to the hotel in silence. There was one question none of them put into words: how did the police captain intend to get the TV recordings transferred without a telephone link? They all had their own reasons for not coming to grips with the question. Francisco needed all the time he could get for his search, Helen could see the chance of getting what she called the documentary of all documentaries. And Kurt was beginning to find that the exotic mix of sensuality and brutality had a certain appeal.

4

AN EXECUTION

The priest could have been in his mid-fifties; he had big rough hands and deep lines in his face.

'Ye have heard that it hath been said,' he intoned, 'an eye for an eye and a tooth for a tooth. But I say unto you: that ye resist not evil; but whosoever shall smite thee on thy right cheek, turn to him the other also.'

He raised one hand and stroked his right cheek with his finger, as if to verify that nobody had smitten him. He kept his eyes on his notes and gave his congregation only occasional glances.

'And whosoever shall compel thee to go a mile, go with him twain,' he said, looking up. 'And whosoever shall compel thee to go a mile, go with him twain,' he repeated, and two women in the back row turned their eyes towards the half-open door and the sunlight streaming in.

'Ye have heard that it hath been said,' the priest continued, bending his head to his notes again, 'thou shalt love thy neighbour and hate thine enemy. But I say unto you, love your enemies, and pray for them that despitefully use you and persecute you, that ye may be the children of your Father which is in heaven.'

Now there were more than just the two women in the back row who were watching the door. Unease seemed to have spread throughout the congregation, carried from one row to the next; one after another they swung round in their best Sunday clothes to look towards the door.

'For he maketh his sun to rise on the evil and on the good, and sendeth rain on the just and the unjust,' declaimed the priest, raising his eyes again, raising his eyes and falling suddenly mute, for the whole congregation had turned their backs to him: a hundred people, young and old, adults and children, the men in dark suits, the women in bright frocks; a hundred people sitting with their backs to the priest and looking towards the door and the sunshine and the sound of a lorry; a hundred people exchanging glances, whispering, staring at the door again, and the noise of the lorry was growing stronger than the sunlight, and the noise came in through the door and up the nave to the altar. Row after row of eyes followed the noise as it went by. 'If ye love them which love you, what reward have ye?' the priest was asking, running his finger under his collar. The noise of a lorry was on its way up the steps to the pulpit now and the priest looked at it uncertainly, shook his head in confusion, caught his breath. The noise went on growing till it filled the whole church, then the lorry swerved into the square outside and came to a halt.

'Costa da Silva climbed on to the pillion of her boyfriend's motorcycle at 7.35 yesterday evening.'

The priest stirred his coffee as he spoke – a different priest, a different part of the island. His black cloak was shabby, the crucifix on the white wall behind him thick with dust. Kurt had set up his camera on a tripod and was following him in the viewfinder, zooming in, pulling back a little. Helen was sitting on a chair at one side of the priest and supporting her microphone hand with her elbow on her knees.

'God was generous when he created her: every time she sat on the motorbike her boyfriend had to lean forward to stop the front wheel lifting off the ground. Has either of you ever ridden a big bike?'

Helen shook her head. Kurt didn't reply.

'A shame. You ought to. Anyway, the point is that speed compensates for weight. And a passenger on a motorbike naturally leans forward as the speed increases.'

The priest took a sip of his coffee and went on speaking, almost as if to himself, 'It's one of nature's many remarkable concepts. Man reacts to speed by leaning forward, not backwards. As if taking a dive. Could that be a metaphor for how we react to life?'

Helen cleared her throat.

'Sorry, I'm getting off the subject. Costa da Silva, 7.35, on her boyfriend's motorcycle. She had been to evensong here in the church. I stood on the steps and watched her go, saw her lean forward and put her arms round her boyfriend, on the straight stretch past the palm trees over there.'

He paused again.

'Just as they disappeared behind the palms, I saw him turn his head and grin at her. Big bikes often have that effect. I think it must be something to do with the combination of speed and balance, of position in space, as ballet dancers say.'

'I'm not entirely sure I understand.' Helen made a show of resting the microphone on her lap and switching off the tape recorder.

'Forgive me.'

The priest fetched more coffee for the three of them. Kurt declined, preoccupied with adjusting his camera. The priest sat still for a moment, eyes lowered as if concentrating on an inner vision. Helen, watching him, put her hand to her mouth in alarm when he suddenly jumped up and mimed riding a motorcycle, holding both hands out as if gripping the handlebars, his right hand twisting the throttle, his legs slightly apart, his knees bent. He leant forward and wriggled against something behind him; he reached back with his left hand to something on the pillion and touched it with a smile. Helen turned and whispered, 'Kurt, do you see what I see?'

Kurt looked at her in some surprise and replied under his breath, 'An old man sitting drinking coffee?'

'He's not old, and he's not sitting.'

'Helen, are you OK? He's sitting there, right in front of us,' said Kurt in a tone of concern.

———————

'Kurt, I need some air. Do you think we can ask to come back another day?'

'Well, I like that! It was you who thought we ought to get the story while it was still fresh.'

Helen looked at the priest. He was sitting astride a motorbike with someone behind him. She tried to rid herself of the image by covering her eyes with her hands, but the room was filled with noise: a motorbike coughing and spluttering and the sound of voices approaching in the distance. She took her hands away from her eyes and the noises ceased. She murmured, *let me see it but don't make me hear it*. She saw the priest peering anxiously at the handlebars, pulling on the clutch, putting it in a lower gear and trying to jump-start it. The engine gave a few coughs and died. Then it seemed that someone on the seat behind him called out; the priest turned his head and looked back beyond the bike, first to one side of the road and then the other. He was clearly afraid now, his breath quickening. Helen covered her eyes again; the noise of someone trying to start a motorbike filled the room ever louder, first the self-starter, then the kick-start. She took her hands away, and the priest had dismounted. Another person was standing there with him, someone he had put his arm round.

'Kurt, are you seeing what I'm seeing?'

'An old man telling us a story?'

Helen bit her lip.

'Why didn't they attempt to flee? Why did they just stand by the bike and let them come?'

'That's what he's telling us now. Aren't you listening? They were coming at them from every direction. There was nowhere to flee to.'

Helen's eyes were filled with tears as she looked at the priest again. He was staring about him, left and right, ahead and behind, his mouth open, pushing the person he had his arm round behind him, presumably in an attempt at protection.

The first blow hit the priest in the face, tearing one side of his nose, splitting both his nostrils. He tried to shield his face, but he was evidently surrounded now and his hands and arms were pinioned behind his back. Helen closed her eyes. The room was full of noise again, of screams, from many voices, wild, agitated screams, out of control, and between the screams the sound of blows, dull thuds, punctuated by breaking bone.

She opened her eyes; the priest had disappeared. She looked around fearfully and saw him lying by a wall, lifeless, his face pressed sideways into the ground. She looked for the motorbike – it had gone or fallen over, but at the spot where it had been there was someone moving. The room was revolving round the place where it had stood, slowly at first, then spinning faster and faster, as if to a rhythm, before suddenly coming to a halt. It looked as if someone were being lifted up. Helen put out her hands and clasped them in prayer, *Dear God, don't make me see this*.

A thin streak of blood was trickling down what was lifted up, the streak opening up slowly, so slowly that the blood only seeped out; *I can't cope with this, I can't cope with this*.

She sobbed, and a jet of blood suddenly spurted right out into the room, as if from a slash. She cried out in fear for her life, *Dear God, don't make me see this*! Now there was blood flowing everywhere in the room, pouring from cuts and gashes. Helen put her hand to her head, rubbed her temples. Kurt leant over and said, 'Helen, aren't you feeling well?'

'Kurt, close your eyes.'

'Why?'

'Do as I say.'

Kurt closed his eyes.

'Can you hear anything?'

'No.'

'The sound of weeping?'

'No. Just the traffic outside and the birds and the priest taking a sip of his coffee.'

Helen looked at the priest. He was still sitting there in his shabby cloak with the dusty crucifix on the wall behind him. He was holding up a coffee pot and looking enquiringly towards her.

When Costa's girlfriends told one another the next morning about the execution, a rape had been added to the tale.

'The leader of the mob, the smith, the one with the callused hands. First of all he tore the clothes off the upper part of her body and displayed her to the others. They clapped. Clapped and laughed.'

'Were there women there?'

'Women and men. Mostly men.'

Her friends had assembled at the gate in the low wall bordering the graveyard; they were formally dressed in white blouses and lace, with black mourning bands, as if they had prepared themselves for the news of the dreadful events by dressing up for a solemn occasion. They had their hair up or tied back and only very little lipstick or eye make-up on; teenagers, adolescents, young women, jolted out of their everyday lives.

'Then he stripped the rest of her clothes off her, bit by bit.'

The friends glanced over their shoulders at their parents on the steps of the church.

'When Costa was completely naked, the smith laid his huge hand on her, right here.'

One of the friends was lowering her gaze and pointing. The others gave little shrieks.

'Then the smith's wife stepped forward. She bent over and spat into her. Like this.'

The others blocked their parents' view while one of them demonstrated.

'To think that a woman could do something like that.'

'That's what Muslims are like. They don't have feelings, only hatred. Then the smith's wife undid her husband's trousers and took it out.'

'Wasn't he already standing proud?'

'Yes, but he hadn't come yet.'

Their faces twitched with barely suppressed sniggers, and then they burst out laughing, surprised at themselves. They huddled closer together and continued in a whisper. Their white clothes shone out clean and untouched against the thick green foliage of the trees above them and the scorched brown grass beneath their feet and the silent gravestones behind them.

When a group of men were talking about the execution a couple of hours later, a gang rape had been added. The table was full of bottles and each man had a glass in his hand or within reach on the table. As the story unfolded, more and more of them added their own contributions.

'There were eighteen in all. The cobbler counted them.'

'Who was the leader?'

'The male nurse from the hospital. He's just back from pilgrimage. They tore the clothes off the boy and took him first, every single one of them.'

'The boy?'

'That's what Muslims do. Then they slit his throat. Costa screamed when they turned him towards her and let the blood spurt all over her. Muslims get off on seeing blood.'

The men around the table agreed and drank deep. At the other end of the room a young woman emerged from behind a curtain, went to the bar and switched on a stereo. The sound of Whitney Houston filled the room.

'They tied her hands to a tree and her feet to two stakes they'd driven into the ground.'

You-uu-uu. I will always love you-uu-uu.

The young woman had picked up a microphone and was singing along. A man came out from behind the curtain, crossed over to the table of drinkers, greeted them and sat down. The other men paused in their conversation, one lifted his head enquiringly and the man nodded.

And I'll always be true-uu.

'Then they cut her clothes off her.'

'No, no, no, that's all wrong.'

It was a newcomer, uncorking a bottle as he spoke.

'Muslims aren't clever enough to tie knots, nor to drive stakes into the ground.'

The others fell silent.

'And they would never dare cut her clothes off her. Their wives would beat them if they came home with clothes that were cut to ribbons.'

The men at the table agreed.

'Lots of repair work before they could be sold. Lots of unnecessary work.'

'No, they put a gun to her head and forced her to strip.'

'A home-made pistol made of iron pipes and bamboo, and saltpetre gunpowder.'

'And a knife to her throat, a curved sickle.'

'And then someone fetched a flautist so she could strip to music.'

'They didn't need to fetch anyone: all Muslims play the flute.'

'She took her blouse off first. Slowly, in time to the music.'

And I'll always love you-uu-uu.

Whitney Houston and the young woman had company now, the tones of a flute weaving in and out of their melody.

'Then she took off her bra, danced a few dainty steps.'

'Her breasts didn't move at all, not when she freed them from her bra, nor when she danced. They stuck straight out, as big and firm as melons.'

The man who was talking made the shape of two huge breasts in the air as he spoke; the men at the table groaned.

'Not floppy and droopy like the ones at home, but firm, and high.'

The men's eyes lit up, and in them shone the image of a naked body with large breasts slowly gyrating, and a smile played on their lips.

'Then she was passed from man to man, so that everyone could lick her nipples, bite them, feel them.'

A sigh went round the table, many of the men taking a swig from their glasses.

'No, no, no, a Muslim would never take a woman's nipple in his mouth with onlookers present, or he'd risk being called a baby, and that would be shameful, and he would have to kill the nephew of the man that said it, to free himself from the shame, and then the brother of the nephew would kill the cousin of the one who had killed the nephew, and so it would go on.'

The men at the table muttered and wiped the froth from their lips, *absolutely right, absolutely right.*

'And then some fool of a Hindu, probably a snake-charmer, would say the cupola of the mosque resembled a woman's breast with a nipple, and then holy war would be declared, *jihad, jihad*, and all because of the fact that an adult Muslim had taken a woman's nipple in his mouth and been seen by others.'

'They don't show much tolerance.'

Rosalind appeared at the door of the bar. She looked at the men seated at the table, most of them with one hand at their crotch. She was wearing a red headband. She stood watching them for a while, then went over to the young woman with the microphone. She took it from her, turned to the men, pulled her cloak aside and placed a hand on her hip.

'Are you coming?'

You-uu-uu. Will always love you-uu-uu.

'We'll avenge it now.'

And I'll always be true-uu-uu.

The men at the table exchanged glances. Rosalind took out a short, black, rubber truncheon and drew it across her belly.

'Are you ready?'

One of the men emptied his bottle and stood up; the others looked at him and at one another, emptied their bottles and got to their feet. Rosalind handed back the microphone and headed for the door, grinning at the men as she went by. A couple of them reached out and touched her cloak and she turned and gave them a smile, opened the door and beckoned them.

———

Helen adjusted her blouse, held the microphone slightly away from her and spoke to camera:

'A long, low, drawn-out moan echoes through the room behind me as a coffin lid is passed over outstretched arms and a priest reads a quiet prayer. The lid is placed on the open coffin, a weeping mother has to be restrained, an uncle is given a hammer and nails. In the square outside a hundred people stand like pillars of salt and listen to the hammer blows: three nails on each side.'

Helen paused and let the hammer blows resound in the silence.

She was standing in the doorway, positioned so that she could see both those gathered outside and the mourners round the coffin inside. Kurt had set up the camera by an open window, and alternated between filming Helen, the coffin, and the people in the square. Helen looked at the coffin, relieved that it was closed now. She had had trouble concentrating while it was open; it had felt as though the swollen face were watching her.

'Costa da Silva, thirty-four years old, is gone for ever. A Christian, engine failure in a Muslim area, hanged. This is everyday reality. No one can explain why Christians and Muslims have suddenly started attacking one another on this peaceful spice island. It is the very island which used to be held up as an example of tolerance in this island state, *pela gandung*, an alliance of Christian and Muslim villages. There are as many Christians as Muslims on the island, fifty-fifty, as against ninety per cent Muslims in the rest of the country. That is why this idyllic island was so important, as a symbol.'

Helen shut her eyes and saw again the swollen face in the coffin, heavy eyelids and a brown line down from one ear, across her throat and up to the other. She heard herself ask why is her face so swollen, why is her face so swollen, and heard a man whisper that they hung her upside down before they slit her throat, hung her upside down for slaughter, *halal*.

'Today that symbol is crushed, today the island is a society at boiling point. Christians and Muslims no longer dare cross each other's territories without an armed guard, and thousands have sought refuge in churches and mosques. The thump of bombs can be heard every day, brutal nail bombs designed to maim rather than kill. Many shops are shuttered up, the island is running out of food and consumer goods, most normal activity has ceased. Each side blames the other: the Christians maintain the Muslims started it; the Muslims say it was the Christians. There is no one in a position to determine who is lying and who is telling the truth.'

Inside the room six men stood round the coffin, bent down and lifted it, adjusted their hold and hoisted it on to their shoulders. A priest walked in front of them to the door.

Helen dropped her voice. 'The particular history of the island may provide an explanation for the tension. Five hundred years ago this island and its immediate neighbours were the world's sole suppliers of nutmeg and cloves, two spices which at the time were worth more than gold on the European market. The Dutch, Portuguese and British fought bitterly and ruthlessly for control of the islands, and at the same time each introduced their own brand of Christianity. On this island Catholicism counts as one religion, Protestantism as another.'

The cortège of the priest and the six coffin-bearers passed her, went down the steps and through the courtyard. The crowd divided and let the procession through; a chorister sang *Nearer, my God, to Thee*, the congregation responded with *Nearer to Thee*. The family of the deceased followed, many of them in tears. Kurt followed the last relative, walking along with his camera on his shoulder and filming, holding the focus on the coffin, sweeping over the congregation. Helen stayed where she was, saying nothing. Kurt turned and beckoned her, pointed at the coffin. She shook her head, couldn't do it, we can add the commentary later, or let the pictures speak for themselves. Kurt shrugged his shoulders and went on filming. Helen stood in silence and watched the procession turn into the little graveyard by the side of the building, a lush green graveyard with a few headstones and rusty metal crosses, waiting till the last of the congregation had followed. Then she counted the heavily armed police positioned all along the stone perimeter wall at ten-metre intervals. She walked slowly round to the back of the house, until she could no longer hear the singing and weeping. A telephone was ringing inside. With a sorrowful smile, she sat down on a bench by a table and switched on the tape recorder.

'In the final phase it was the Dutch who emerged as victors and were able to tap the resources of the island state, undisturbed, for nearly 350 years. The island developed during the colonial period as an important source of recruitment for the army. The Dutch colonists trusted Christian soldiers more than Muslims, and gave privileges to the former which were withheld from the Muslim majority. After independence the tables were turned and now the Muslims have the upper hand. The dictator has been careful to keep a substantial proportion of Christian ministers and officials around him over the years, but the dictatorship is on the verge of collapse and Islamic confidence is growing. The dictator's successor will probably be equally careful to surround himself with a substantial proportion of Muslim ministers and officials.'

She paused for a break and listened to the birds singing, took out a notepad and flicked through it, then continued:

'It is only this island that is different; only here are the Christians so strong that they can risk challenging the Muslims. The last thing we saw as we left the capital this morning was a Muslim being dragged out of a car and beaten up by angry Christian demonstrators, right in the centre of town. The demonstrators had gathered in protest at what they see as giving in to Muslim demands, screaming their rage at the police who were trying to restrain them.'

Helen stopped and lit a cigarette, inhaling deeply before going on:

'The island is now being held in an iron grip by the military. Heavily armed soldiers are on guard everywhere, in doorways, at roadblocks and in concealed positions. Three thousand elite troops have arrived on the island to try to put down the unrest. They are managing to keep the two sides apart, but they can't prevent the house-burnings, bombings and executions. And everyone is aware that the soldiers will not be here permanently. Firstly because it costs money to keep them here, and secondly because they are needed elsewhere. On this island there are many dry haystacks and many people with matches, as the local expression has it. This island constitutes a warning for the whole country. A tight lid has been kept on all ethnic and religious opposition throughout the thirty-year regime of the present dictator. No discussion of it has even been permitted – quite a feat in a country with three hundred ethnic groups, five religions and three hundred and sixty-five languages. With the dictatorship on the brink of collapse, a transitional figure is needed, and there will be a free-for-all. Hundreds of political parties are sure to demand to be registered as soon as there is any talk of free elections. Sparks are beginning to fly in many parts of this huge nation of thirteen thousand islands.'

A car started up in front of the building and moved off slowly across the courtyard and into the street. As it left Helen could just make out the police captain's head in the rear window. She opened her notebook, took out the fact sheet he had given her, unfolded it and slowly tore it into shreds.

———

'If we live by the principle of an eye for an eye and a tooth for a tooth, we'll finally end up with a world which is blind.'

Francesco was more or less talking to himself. They were sitting on the veranda outside the hotel lounge, a natural meeting place at dusk. Kurt was studying the day's filming in a little screen on the camera, making occasional notes. Helen had the tape recorder on her lap and was listening to her commentaries through headphones. Her eyes were closed. Francesco looked out over the town and the harbour and said it again, almost under his breath: 'An eye for an eye, a tooth for a tooth, a blind world that can't see, can't relate to anything beyond itself, doesn't feel empathy.'

'And is also toothless?'

Kurt uttered these words without looking up from the camera. Francesco made no comment.

'If you as a Christian on this island had been accustomed to centuries of equality in relation to the Muslims and then after independence had experienced nothing but repression, for more than fifty years, how long would you go on putting up with it?'

Francesco still didn't answer, still said nothing to the younger man.

Kurt raised his head now and his tone became angrier. 'If you as a Christian saw your father hounded and humiliated by Muslim soldiers, officials, employers, how long would you put up with it? How long would you go on accepting it?'

Helen took off her headphones with a jerk. 'Where do you get this from? You're always out now, where do you go? I hear your door in the mornings, and it's not you going to the bathrooom. Who are you seeing?'

'That's none of your business,' Kurt replied, going red in the face.

'Not even if it prejudices your work?'

'I can handle it.'

Francesco waved them apart. 'You've had a hard day. Take it easy.'

Helen gave him a withering glance. 'It's not a question of taking it easy. It's a question of neutrality. We are reporters. We report. We don't get involved.'

In the silence that followed the darkness seemed to envelop them, three Europeans on an Asian veranda, surrounded by darkness, like an immobile sculpture against a backdrop of sounds and smells. Then the sculptural unity dissolved. Kurt went inside; Helen sat down and picked up her headphones again, fiddling with them in her hands.

'We have a source problem,' she said. 'Kurt says the Christians on this island are accustomed to centuries of equality. Who is his source? Do you think a Muslim would have used the word equality about the centuries up to independence? On an island with a Christian elite who cooperated closely with the colonial powers?'

She put on her headphones without waiting for a response. Francesco closed his eyes and leant against the wall behind him.

'Kurt ought to find himself a Muslim source to check. And he daren't. Because he knows he would soon have her father and all her brothers after him.'

She said this aloud, too loud for the soft darkness, as if to drown out the voice in her headphones or to be sure of it carrying into the sitting-room. Then she sat in silence to the end of the tape.

'What are you thinking about?'

'Anya,' said Francesco, opening his eyes.

'Still no news?'

'Still no news. The same circuit every single day, the same lack of response. Since the words in red on the first day, nothing. Absolutely nothing.'

Helen wound the headphone lead round the tape recorder and stood up. In the doorway to the sitting-room she turned and said, 'You'll tell us if there's any way we can help?'

Francesco nodded.

'Remember the old expression, "No news is good news".'

He nodded again. Helen looked at him with a mixture of concern and resignation. Then she shook her head and went in.

Francesco was about to lean back against the wall again when he suddenly sat up with a start. The moon had risen and was casting a broad path of light over the dark sea. In the centre was a pair of eyes, staring at him, biding their time.

5

A CRUISE SHIP DOCKS

The congregation sat in silence, all eyes on the priest. No one drives a lorry around here on a Sunday, a voice whispered, and the congregation nodded, looked enquiringly at the priest, as if expecting an answer: who could be driving a lorry on a Sunday around here? You have a Father in heaven who knows your every desire because He hears your prayers, said the priest, joining his hands. The congregation put their hands together in prayer and bowed their heads, *Our Father, which art in heaven*, and now came the noise of a tailgate being lowered, *Hallowèd be Thy name, Thy kingdom come*, and feet thudded on the ground, many feet, *Thy will be done, in earth as it is in heaven*, steps, a woman sobbed, more marching steps, *Give us this day our daily bread*, and a woman shouted, 'Bread, who the hell can think about bread!' and the congregation gasped and stared at her, the priest gasped and stared at her, and for a split second time stood still, for a split second the steps outside were silenced as the priest and the congregation stared in shock at the woman who had shouted; she blushed and lowered her eyes and sunlight streamed up the nave as the door was opened wide, first one half and then the other; *And forgive us our trespasses, As we forgive those that trespass against us*, and shadows appeared in the sunlight, first a couple, then a few more, then more and even more, and the next line of the prayer was drowned by the commotion of people turning towards the door and the group of white-clothed men standing there, *And lead us not into temptation*, thirty silent, white-clothed men standing in the doorway looking at the congregation, not with arms folded, not with their hands on their hips, but with their arms at their sides, in absolute, indifferent power; two men in one of the rows at the back clenched their fists and repeated *Lead us not into tempation, Lead us not into temptation*, the women next to them laid their hands on their clenched fists, trying to calm them, the men threw them off and glanced round at other men, seeking out other men, *Lead us not into temptation*, and suddenly a force surged out from the men in the doorway, as if they had become aware of the clenched fists and were responding to them, a force that seemed to be generated by the resistance it met; the force pushed against the resistance, drove it before it, wordlessly, the resistance retreated, in between the rows of pews of motionless praying figures, up the stairs to the gallery, a scream was heard from above, but no one looked up, no one moved; the congregation sat like pillars of stone gazing at the silent white figures in the doorway, *For thine is the kingdom, the power and the glory, for ever and ever*, and another scream came from the gallery, and still no one looked up, the force from the white-clothed men came back down alone, made a sweep across the church and prostrated itself before the men in white.

Amen.

It was the priest who said it, as if he had almost forgotten it and had remembered at the last moment, *Amen*; the word rolled out over the congregation, in an almost inaudible whisper. The men in white paid no heed to the word; they stared at the congregation with the same indifference, until there came a call from behind them; they stared at the congregation for a few more seconds, then turned and left. The tailgate slammed as they climbed aboard, and the lorry started up and drove off. The congregation sat where it was while the noise of the engine gradually grew fainter and fainter, the priest cleared his throat and turned the pages of his notes, Ye have heard it said, an eye for an eye and a tooth for a tooth, and in the front row a man took the hand of the woman at his side and brushed his groin; the woman bit her lip and lowered her head, turned to another woman, the other woman nodded; in the row behind a man put his hand on the thigh of the woman by his side and squeezed it, the woman closed her eyes, the hand squeezed till the knuckles showed white, the woman's shoulders drooped as if she knew that something awaited them, and knew what it was, But I say unto you, Forgive them that trespass against us, said the priest, Forgive them that trespass against us, and sunshine poured in through the church door with the sounds of a peaceful landscape, completely still, completely tranquil, not a movement, a green island in an endless sea with the sun directly overhead and men and women in a church in their Sunday best.

Francesco peered at the ship on the horizon. He shaded his eyes and squinted. The people round about laughed, shaded their eyes too and squinted at each other, giggling. A man took him firmly by the hand and led him over to a hut on one of the two harbour jetties. A small crowd of onlookers followed. Painted on the wall of the hut in white letters, first in Malay, then in English, were the words, 'Sunda Steamers and Barges. Arrival Wednesday mornings, departure same day. Allah willing.' Someone had crossed out Allah and written God, and then God was struck out and replaced by Allah and a note in red: 'The next person to cross out Allah will get his throat cut.' That seemed to have brought the argument to a conclusion.

Francesco read it aloud, the people round him nodding. The man who had taken him by the hand put his finger on the word 'Wednesday'. Then he let go of his hand, placed his own hands together like a spire over his head and sang an imitation of church bells. Francesco understood: Sunday, today was Sunday. The onlookers were becoming uneasy; the man brought his hands down, kicked off his sandals and knelt down to pray. Francesco got it: Friday, so today was either Sunday or Friday, not Wednesday. He pointed at the word 'Wednesday' on the wall and shook his head, not Wednesday, then pointed at the ship on the horizon, not ship. The man clapped his hands approvingly, and the spectators heaved a sigh of relief.

Francesco thanked the man, waved to everyone else and walked away. Some of the other people followed, but at a distance now. It was calm, with clear skies, the sea as smooth as glass, and quite obviously a holiday. There was no sound from the rusty freighter moored at the second jetty, the cranes outside the warehouses were motionless, and the middle classes were promenading along the quayside in white or yellow dresses and blue or black suits. On the inside of the pavement, nearest the wall, sat men and women with fruit piled high for sale, crates of mineral water and brandy, sweetcorn on little tripod grills and trays of sweets. There was an aroma of cooked food and spices, mingled with the smell of seaweed from the harbour.

Francesco took a seat at a stall and asked for a beer. The can was moist with condensation and he downed it in three long gulps and asked for another. Then he put the empty can on a box in front of him, leant over and peered through the ring on the lid, moving the can until the ship completely filled the ring. A man in a blue suit stopped and bowed to him, turning to present the woman on his arm. Francesco bowed his head in return.

'You're a machine-gunner, I see,' the man said, indicating the can. 'My father was one too. In the Dutch army. First Fusiliers.'

Francesco gave an interested smile.

'That's how he spent his final years.' The man gestured again towards the beer can. 'Like you. With his chin resting on the table and his eye to a sight. Then one day he didn't lift his head again.'

The man shrugged his shoulders.

'That's life. Machine-gunners come and go, machine-guns go on for ever.'

He bowed once more, made a sign to the woman on his arm, and walked on.

Francesco sipped at his beer, more slowly now. After a while he leant over and took another sighting through the ring: the ship was bigger, so it must be on its way to the island. He got up and paid, tucked his shirt more neatly into his trousers and strolled off. It was hot, the sun was nearing its zenith, and he joined the flow of promenaders, trying to fall into their rhythm, but not quite having the patience. He paused at a kiosk, glanced at the newspapers and shook his head apologetically to the vendor, walked on to a café with brown wooden tables inside and two white plastic tables outside. The waitress came out to him as he sat down, smiled and said in halting Portuguese, 'Back. You back. Welcome.'

Francesco stared at her in amazement, 'You speak Portuguese?'

She smiled again and mumbled, 'Little. Learn now.'

She returned his gaze. She might have been thirty, with short hair and high cheekbones, her body slender, almost too thin beneath her loose-fitting waitress uniform. She proffered the menu. He threw out his arms and shook his head.

'I don't understand what it says.'

She smiled, produced a little notebook from her pocket, opened it and showed it to him. On the first page, written in pencil in unjoined script, was chicken cooked with pepper sauce, chicken wings, octopus. She pointed at the menu, here, here, here. With rice.

Francesco said, 'Have you translated this for me?'

She looked at him uncertainly.

'You.'

He pointed at the book and wrote in the air. Then pointed at himself.

'For me?'

She nodded and smiled, pointed at him, pointed into the street, mimed with her fingers someone coming into the café and sitting down at a white plastic table, held up five fingers, five times. Francesco smiled back and mimed her coming out of the café five times to take his order, her expression of despair when she couldn't manage to explain to him what the dishes were; he reminded her how she had mimicked chickens cackling and fish swimming, fish being caught; she smiled, blushing a little. Then she stood just looking at him. Francesco also fell silent, seemed embarrassed. Something had passed between them that they were both a little fearful of.

He pulled himself together and held up the menu. 'Octopus?'

She took his hand and moved it until his finger pointed to a word. His eyes followed her hand. She said a word in Malay, repeated it with her eyes still on him. He repeated it back slowly, she corrected him, he repeated it again, she nodded. Taking the menu, she went back into the café, her hand brushing his shoulder as she passed.

He closed his eyes, sat quietly and let his face relax. Then he opened them again and turned towards the harbour. The waitress reappeared and set a brown bottle of beer and a glass down in front of him with a friendly gesture. He smiled in gratitude; he hadn't needed to ask for it. She pointed at the ship far out at sea, giving him an enquiring look.

'Ship? It's called ship.'

She repeated the word, saying it several times to herself, wanted to know more. She pointed at him, pointed at the ship, made a motion to indicate someone leaving. Francesco shook his head. 'I'm searching for my daughter.' She didn't understand. He took her by the arm and showed her. 'I,' he pointed at himself, 'have daughter.' He moved her arm backwards and forwards. 'Like you.' She gazed at him wide-eyed.

He held out his hand for the notebook, picked up a pen and drew the figure of a man. By the side of it he drew a child figure in full-length dress. Then he turned and made a broad gesture towards the town and the hills beyond. 'Gone.' She followed attentively, took the notebook and pen from him and wrote above the child figure, 'Years old?'

He replied by writing twenty-five on the table with his finger. She leant over him to see the number as he wrote, her forearm touching his. She straightened up and put her hand to her chest, me, and wrote thirty-five on the tabletop.

He nodded. She gave him another look and went back into the café.

Francesco poured himself a drink and his eyes filled with tears. He picked up a paper napkin from the table and dried them.

She came out with a plate of octopus and salad and a bowl of rice, noticed the crumpled napkin, removed it and brought a fresh one over from a neighbouring table. Then she stepped back and said, 'Enjoy hope?'

She was clutching the screwed-up napkin in her fingers.

Francesco helped himself to rice and tasted the octopus before answering, 'Hope you enjoy it. But you're right, we enjoy hope, just as we hate despair; hope is the taste of something new, despair is the smell of something old, something that once was.'

She looked at him in confusion, trying to keep up with the stream of words in Portuguese. Then she stood behind him and placed her hands on his shoulders.

'Eat.'

She wanted to say more, but had to consult the word list in her notebook.

'Drinks water.'

She squeezed his shoulders and went inside. Francesco ate reflectively, his thoughts isolating him from the cacophony of Asian noises. The cries of street-vendors and the hooting of car horns hovered around his white plastic table without encroaching, as if his silence frightened them off. Only one sound seemed to penetrate, that of the bead curtain in the doorway of the café every time it was parted and the waitress peeked out at him. When he had finished eating she cleared away his plate and cutlery and rice bowl and then came back and asked if he would like coffee, making as if to drink from a cup. He nodded.

She went in and re-emerged a few minutes later with the coffee. As he drank it, she gestured towards the harbour and to herself and him, together down to the harbour? A ship hooted and he jumped, having completely forgotten the vessel that was on its way to the island. She took his coffee cup and glass and disappeared, and when she returned she had changed into blue jeans and a red shirt hanging loose; she was wearing plastic sandals and her toenails were painted red, and she was carrying a rolled-up shawl. He looked her up and down, taken aback, and there must have been something in his expression that pleased her, because she smiled at him and laughed as they went out on to the street. They walked in the direction of the harbour, and after a few metres she linked her arm in his and he felt the urge to say something to her, started a word, as if to ask her what her name was, or whether she had family, to get to know her as a person, but he didn't.

The ship was in the process of docking at one of the harbour jetties, the one belonging to the steamer company. It was white with a yellow funnel and classic shape of high bow and stern and low midship. A rope of multicoloured pennants ran from the bow up to the mast and along the full length of the ship to the aft mast and down to the flag at the stern. The pennants over the funnel were blackened with soot. Passengers were crowded at the rail on the shore side, and the blink of camera lenses could be seen; an orchestra was playing on the aft deck, a waltz for piano and strings, and a voice was making an announcement over the loudspeaker system.

The jetty was already full of people, and still more were pouring on: beggars, street-vendors, men and women in their best clothes; in the water below, canoes bearing fruit and vegetables were jostling alongside, and strong brown arms were holding their wares up towards the rail high above. A man in white uniform was leaning over the rail with a megaphone and ordering the canoes out of the waters between the ship and the jetty, where it was already so congested that there was scarcely room for the canoes to manoeuvre. The ship went into reverse and moved further away from the quayside, and the officer continued bellowing at the canoes, until eventually he could dock.

The young woman tugged gently at his sleeve and nodded towards the gangplank. The white tourists were descending it now, in a somewhat hesitant throng, as if unsure whether it would take their weight or whether the natives were friendly. Most of them were middle-aged or older. As the onlookers made way for them they headed for the promenade and the town, walking awkwardly as if unused to such activity. Several of them muttered to one another after passing the white man and his young, dark-skinned companion. Francesco spoke into her ear under his breath, 'At this very moment we are being christened, you and I. In this instant we have acquired a name.'

She touched his arm. The flood of tourists was thinning out, had almost dried up, when suddenly there came a final flurry: six men of almost equal age, around fifty, in good shape, four of them with grey ponytails. They were waving their arms in the air, and the onlookers clapped. They were all wearing black jeans and black T-shirts, two of them had colourful waistcoats, one a red leather cap. It was obvious they were used to being the centre of attention. Francesco whispered *rock* into the young woman's ear. She looked puzzled, so he rocked her from side to side, like a dance, *rock*, and she put her hand to her mouth and stared at the six men in disbelief.

They walked in silence until they came to a park down by the beach promenade, where they sat on a bench and gazed out to sea. They broke their silence with names, Maheeba, Francesco, then withdrew into silence again. There were tall palm trees in the park, beneath which families sat picnicking, and some children were playing on the grass with a little dog. Men lay asleep here and there, a young lad and a girl sat chatting by a fountain, two teenage boys carrying schoolbooks were walking together past the fountain and out of the park, one wearing a white skullcap and robe, the other in Western clothes.

Maheeba looked up a new word, 'Tell.'

Francesco remained immersed in contemplation. Maheeba put her hand lightly on his shoulder, as if to reassure him of something, laid her rolled-up shawl on the bench, stood up and left him for a moment. Francesco seemed to be sinking further and further into his own thoughts. When she came back with a can of beer and one of mineral water, he accepted the beer absent-mindedly. He thanked her and watched her slim fingers taking a pack of tissues out of her pocket, pulling one out and wiping the rim of the cans, though his gaze appeared unfocused. He took his first swallow with closed eyes, then he turned to face the sea and stretched his arm towards the horizon.

'Europe.'

He painted it on the horizon, a continent in cheery colours, light, bright lines, big white spaces. Europe: source of music,

94

strings, wind instruments, a whole symphony orchestra. Maheeba put her head on one side, listening, entranced, with a smile on her face, shut her eyes, then swayed her head and body in time to the music.

'Italy.'

Francesco went on painting his picture. Maheeba followed, still smiling. He painted rolling hills with their dense foliage reaching skywards, he painted people gathering in the squares every evening in the hour before darkness, just to talk, to be together, he painted Saturday mornings and men with guns and baying dogs in the woods.

'Tuscany.'

He painted houses of pale brown stone and towers with bells, he painted green cypresses planted in straight lines along roads crossing the landscape, golden fields and mansions with arched windows. Then he stroked his brush over the distant horizon.

'Portugal.'

And now he used stronger colours, thicker lines, denser areas; the music was faster, harder; he painted a woman, and a man, and a house, he painted curtains at windows and smiled to himself; he opened windows so she could hear children crying; she laughed and clapped her hands, leant forward to listen to something in the background: typewriters, a cash register opening and closing, the children's tears changing into words, song, laughter, youthful voices. Then he stopped painting, held his brush poised. Maheeba looked at him, and at the horizon. He painted a little dark spot, sat and contemplated it, painted it bigger. The spot was stationary, silent itself, and seemed to be absorbing the sounds in the picture, silencing them, absorbing the colours in the picture, darkening them.

Francesco turned towards her, tears in his eyes. Then he reached out a hand to the horizon and pulled a curtain across. They sat for a while saying nothing. He sipped a little of his beer, she of her mineral water. He touched her softly on the shoulder, made the sign of a question mark, spoke the word she had found, 'Tell.' She blushed, shut her eyes, as if to find peace to think, came to a decision, opened them again. She swivelled on the bench to exhibit the island, encompassed it with outspread arms, showed the ocean all around. Then she bent down and planted something in the soil, a seed, or a seedling; it grew, centimetre by centimetre, divided, grew branches, the branches grew blossoms, golden flowers; the plant went on growing until it became a shrub, a little tree; the tree went on growing, stretching up its branches to the sky and its roots down into the earth; the tree grew before their eyes until they could hardly see the ocean, and there were children playing in the tree now, climbing and laughing, and someone had made them a swing. Birds built nests high up and the sun filtered through the leaves; the tree had now become so big that they could no longer see the horizon at all; they rose from the bench and sat down with their backs against its trunk, with their backs to the ocean, and above them the children continued to play.

6

AMONG MUSLIMS

'Maheeba wonders if you'd like to go with her to visit her family.'

Francesco gave the café owner a searching look and whistled.

'Don't be so European about it. She wants to know whether you'd like to go with her to visit her family. Full stop.'

Maheeba was following the exchange with rapt attention.

'Where do they live?'

'A bit outside the town. You'd have to rent a scooter.'

The café owner mimed the action of steering a scooter and gave him a quizzical look.

Francesco tossed his head back and replied, 'And me an Italian? No problem.'

The café owner laughed, 'Now you are being European, all right.'

Maheeba had her hand up to her mouth, but with a smile in her eyes. The café owner turned to her and they exchanged a few words.

'She wants to know if you can afford it. The scooter will cost ten dollars, the bodyguard twenty.'

'Bodyguard?'

'You have to drive through two Christian zones.'

Francesco merely nodded. The café owner seemed about to say something else, but stopped himself. He gave a casual wave of his hand and said, 'Have a good trip. Let her arrange everything.'

The proprietor of the scooter-hire shop was Indian, with thick, shiny hair and a broad gold ring on the little finger of his left hand. Maheeba spoke to him in Malay; the Indian replied in English, 'Number one quality. We have scooters of what we call number one quality. Thirty dollars.'

He held up three fingers. Maheeba said something angrily to him and he responded unperturbed. She retorted in rapid tempo, he replied as unruffled as before, then continued in English, 'We also have scooters of what we call number two quality. The same as number one quality, but we call them number two quality. Twenty dollars.'

Maheeba's eyes were fixed on him, attempting to understand. Francesco held up two fingers to her, twenty dollars. She took him by the arm and led him out, without another word. They had barely gone a few metres down the street when the Indian called after them, 'We also have scooters of what we call number three quality. The same as number one quality and number two quality, but we call them number three quality. Ten dollars. Didn't think we had any left, but we have.'

They went back in with him and through to the rear of the shop. There were two mopeds and a light motorcycle in the yard. The Indian took them over to the motorcycle.

Francesco pursed his lips, 'That's not a scooter, is it? That's a motorbike.'

The Indian nodded. 'Yes, but it's also a scooter. Same thing.'

He sat himself on the motorcycle. He was a big man, his shirt was straining over his stomach; the motorcycle sank beneath him.

'Good quality. As good quality as number one quality and number two quality. Better, in fact.'

Francesco squatted down and inspected the brake lever, the brake fluid, the level in the little round window marked SAE30 and min and max, ran his fingers over the tyres, peered along the length of the frame. Then he stood up, kicked the starter four times before the engine spluttered into life, revved the engine and listened for odd noises. Then he switched off the ignition. Maheeba gave him an expectant look. OK? Francesco pointed towards the other side of the island, 'Inshallah.'

Maheeba laughed. The Indian laughed too.

'Allah or Christ or Ariel Sharon, it's all the same.'

———

The three of them on the motorcycle made a pretty sight – Maheeba, Francesco and the bodyguard they had hired, along with the live piglet he had tied on the back, a gift. The light flickering through the fronds of the palm trees made it look as if they were moving faster than they actually were. The town was thinning out around them, the gaps between houses increasing. The bodyguard with his rifle had closed his eyes and seemed to be asleep, his head dropping on to his chest, his body sagging. The woman in front turned to look at him, saw he was asleep, checked both sides of the road – no people to be seen – rested her head on the shoulder of the man steering, reached up a hand and drew his face down to hers. He took his hand off the clutch lever and put his arm round her briefly. She smiled and straightened up. He could hear Helen's voice whispering in his ear, *what do you think she wants from you, are you a bridge to the outside world, is she promised to a man who'll never finish paying the dowry instalments?*

They approached a small lagoon, went over a bridge with a fast-flowing stream beneath it and on beside the shore. There was a breeze from the sea, and they both turned their faces towards it; their bodyguard was still asleep, and the pig looked as if it were paralysed with shock. She put her hands on his, he raised one hand a little and they entwined fingers. Helen's

99

voice whispered again, *what do you want with her, do you want to get involved in yet another story, risk regaining your own separate identity and thus lose something of your daughter?* He squared his shoulders, tightened his grip on the throttle. She took her hands away, leant back against his chest, put her hands on his arms. He smiled, started humming, and she smiled.

'Hey, boss.'

It was the bodyguard.

'Boss, how many wives you got?'

Francesco smiled again. Maheeba seemed to understand the question, turning her head slightly to hear the answer.

'None.'

'None?'

The bodyguard looked as if he couldn't believe his ears.

'A man your age and your clothes, and you got no wife?'

Francesco smiled again.

'I had a wife, but haven't any longer. How many wives have you got?'

'You only had one wife? Didn't it get boring?'

Maheeba was watching the road ahead now without displaying any particular interest. Francesco changed down and twisted the throttle as they started an incline.

'Two. I've got two. When I get promoted, I'll have the money for another one. Three. A man needs three wives. The two I have now menstruate at the same time. That means for one week a month I don't have a wife. Another wife will solve that problem.'

'Do they sleep outside?'

'What the devil business is it of yours?'

'All primates that sleep outside adopt the same cycle. It's the moon.'

'Are you calling my wives primates?'

The bodyguard put his rifle in his lap and grabbed Francesco in the groin with both hands. Francesco's eyes and mouth opened wide.

'I'll give you primates.'

He squeezed hard. Francesco jerked and let out a howl. Maheeba shrieked and kept her eyes on the road. The bike swerved off the road and down a slope; the pig squealed in terror, the bodyguard laughed. The bike hit a mound and careered on downwards into a bush. Maheeba shot over the handlebars and disappeared from view. Francesco pushed the emergency stop button and the engine cut out. In the sudden silence that followed they could hear birdsong, a distant vehicle, and a piglet frightened out of its wits. Francesco and the bodyguard were still sitting astride the motorbike, surrounded by green foliage.

'Hey, boss, wasn't that taking it a bit far?'

The bodyguard heaved himself clumsily off the bike. Francesco pointed to the other side of the bush, where he could hear Maheeba moaning softly.

'She must be OK. How can anyone hurt themselves on a bush?' said the bodyguard, pushing his way through.

Then he looked over his shoulder and said, 'Hey, boss, can you bring the gun here?'

Francesco picked up the rifle that was still lying across the motorbike, lifting it carefully, first by the barrel, then the stock, as if he were afraid of it or knew nothing about guns. He carried it in front of him like something sacred as he waded through the bush to the other side and looked down. Maheeba was lying on her stomach with her head hanging over a dip in the ground, motionless; her hands stretched out in front of her, her fingers clenched in the earth. Just a centimetre or two from her face was another face, with staring eyes and a grossly swollen mouth, a swarm of flies crawling and buzzing around the severed neck. Francesco cried out and dropped the rifle. It fell to the ground butt first and a shot exploded into the trees above them. Maheeba yelled, made an effort to rise, first on all fours, then to her feet. The bodyguard took charge of the gun.

'Not your day, is it, boss?'

Maheeba started screaming, in fear and horror, expelling her breath in sharp sobs. Francesco put an arm round her shoulders and pulled her close, turned her head away from the grisly sight. The bodyguard nodded.

'She thinks it's a relative. Try and get her back to the road. I'll get the bike.'

Francesco clambered up the slope, dragging the distressed woman with him; she was resisting, as if she didn't want to leave the severed head behind. The bodyguard had overtaken them and was struggling with the bike to turn it round.

'And boss, it's better if she doesn't see the head any more. There's something stuffed inside its mouth.'

'What?'

Francesco came to a standstill while he waited for the answer, confused and bewildered.

'Something that tells us there's another person been murdered too. A father, a brother, a husband.'

The bodyguard got the motorbike back up on to the road.

Maheeba's father had strong, slim hands and spoke fluent English. He held the syringe up to the light, expelled a drop and turned. Francesco held his breath.

'Relax. Don't tell me you're so European that you don't believe Muslims can be doctors.'

He inserted the needle. Francesco watched the brown hand slowly injecting the liquid from the syringe into his body. The doctor withdrew the needle, wiped some fluid over the wound, pressed a ball of cotton wool on it and taped it down. Then he went over to a washbasin and dismantled the syringe. Francesco pulled up his trousers and seated himself on the bench.

'Here.'

The doctor held out a glass of something for him. Francesco took it and sniffed at it. He looked up in surprise.

The doctor chuckled, 'A man shouldn't be too Muslim.'

Francesco downed the contents and made a face. The doctor chuckled again.

'I thought alcohol and sedatives shouldn't be combined?' He handed the glass back.

'Lots of people say that. But not all. Alcohol and sedatives can have a mutually enhancing effect. And that's what you need right now. Try and rest for a while.'

Francesco lay down on the bench with one arm over his eyes.

'What about Maheeba? Is she asleep?'

'On her mother's lap. She had the same dose as you, but not the slug of spirit. Obviously.'

The doctor drew a stool up to the bench and took his pulse.

'Relax now. The army's here, and they've found the bodies; they're searching for tracks. The bodies have been washed and laid out and – shall we use the word restored?'

Francesco gasped.

'How is it possible? How can such brutality be possible?' The doctor didn't answer.

'Is it true they were members of your family?'

'Yes. The daughter of one of my wife's relatives. And her fiancé.'

Francesco lowered his arm.

The doctor was looking down at him. 'I think this island has much sorrow yet to come. We've only seen the beginning.'

He stood up and left the room.

————————

Francesco was lying on his side with his hands between his knees when he woke. He didn't want to wake up, he wanted to return to the darkness, but the cries from the yard outside prevented him. He rose and went over to the window, straightening his clothes and looking out. In the centre of the yard were two biers with bodies on them, wailing women round the end of each. Some were beating their brows, some imploring the heavens, some pressing handkerchiefs to their eyes. The corpses were shrouded in white from top to toe, and it was impossible to tell which was the man and which the woman. The mourners were wafting palm fronds to and fro to keep the flies away.

He moved across to the door. Maheeba was in another doorway, with her arms round an elderly weeping woman. He looked across at her and she shook her head. He closed the door behind him, went to one side of it and leant against the wall of the house. At a little distance from the bodies, sitting under a tree, was a group of men dressed in white. They were talking animatedly, chopping the air with their hands, slamming their fists into their palms. Maheeba's father was among them.

Francesco shut his eyes and rested his head against the wall. He took a deep breath, inhaling everything: the smell of a fire, the smell of flowers, the smell of death; the sounds of mourning, the sounds of anger, the sounds of life. Maheeba came over to him, and he opened his eyes when she spoke and turned his face towards her without raising his head from the wall.

'Slept?'

He nodded, giving her an enquiring look.

'You?'

She nodded. Francesco pointed at the biers and at her. She lowered her eyes, then turned and called in a low voice to the woman she had been embracing. The woman came over to them, dragging one leg a little but obviously accustomed to it. Francesco proffered his hand in greeting. Maheeba quickly stopped him.

'No.'

The woman regarded him for a moment. Maheeba said something to her, the woman answered.

'Mother.'

Maheeba indicated with her hand.

'My. Mother.'

Francesco nodded. Her mother opened the door and the two women beckoned him inside. Glancing over his shoulder as he went in, Francesco saw her father watching them from over by the tree. He went in and closed the door behind him, following the women into a passageway, past the doctor's surgery, into a dining-room and out to a patio, a little garden enclosed by walls on all sides, with a stone table and two benches. The garden must have been about five metres square, half of it paved around the table and benches, the rest thick green grass. There were big pots of flowers along the walls, and on one wall a basin of water had been built in with a tap above. The mother said something to her daughter, sent her to fetch something. Francesco examined the patio, wall by wall, each flower tub in turn. Maheeba came back with a jug and a glass, set them on the table in front of him and poured out a drink for him. Francesco tried it, and then gestured at them both, 'Aren't you two having any?'

Maheeba shook her head. Her mother looked at her. Maheeba went off and returned with a dictionary, found a word and pointed to it, 'Wake.'

Then she pointed towards the yard on the other side of the house. Francesco averted his gaze. She frowned in concentration, consulted the book again and pointed, 'Bodies. Wake.'

She raised her eyes to the sky. 'Spirits. Watch. Evil spirits.'

Then she pointed at him, 'Muslim. No.'

Francesco nodded, understood. Her mother moved the jug nearer his glass and gave him an enquiring look. He declined. Then the mother turned to her daughter and took her by the arm, led her out of the patio and into the house, but first with a rapid movement taking the hand that held the dictionary and scanning the cover. Maheeba drew her hand back equally quickly.

'How do you make this?'

Francesco was holding the glass out in front of him. The wake was over; the two men were sitting alone in the patio garden.

'The same way you make grappa. We distil it from the grape skins after the juice has been pressed.'

'And the juice?'

'Wine.'

'Not bad.'

'As you say.'

They were on their fifth not-very-Muslim round, their conversation came and went. The charcoal grill and the torch had both gone out, the moon had climbed higher in the sky and was right above them now, and the doctor had brought out two blankets to put over them. Francesco had spoken of his Italian childhood and his Portuguese adulthood, the doctor of his South African student years and his time as a hospital doctor in the capital.

'And then?'

'A man always comes back to his roots.'

Both men raised their glasses with a smile. Death was dancing between them in the darkness; it came in the sound of a dirge from the other side of the house, a low monotone, now almost inaudible, gliding up and over the roof and down into the patio, feeling its way along the walls past the flower-pots, touching the door handles, brushing across the benches where they sat, capering on the table between them, lying down and looking at them, biding its time.

'You asked me if this was the first instance. It isn't. But with each one there's something new, something worse.'

The doctor pulled the blanket closer round him. Francesco leant back and listened.

'It began with us burning one another's crops.'

'Us?'

'Would you rather I said "Muslims" and "Christians"? We're us, all together.'

'Go on.'

'Did you see the fields on your way here?'

'Yes.'

'Then you know that we can't afford to burn each other's crops. You come from a country with olive trees, you know how upsetting the pictures are of Israeli soldiers tearing up Palestinian olive trees by the roots. It takes fifty years to grow an olive tree: what sort of monster is it that can rip out people's trees? It's the same here: it takes a whole family a whole year's work to get a crop. What sort of monster is it that burns people's crops just when they're ready to harvest?'

They sat there quietly for a while. The doctor took a sip from his glass before going on, 'Then it escalated to house-burning. You can see it every morning if you look up at the hills from the hotel: smoke in one place or another, much bigger than a bonfire. If you see an army helicopter fly in over the fire, you can be sure it's a house. Families managed to save themselves at first, because the arsonists were always careful to wake them before it was too late. But we all knew it was only a matter of time before even that would change, and change it did.'

The doctor closed his eyes.

'When a house burns down in Europe, the main cause of death is smoke inhalation, isn't it?'

Francesco nodded.

'That's not the case here. Eighty per cent of houses in the countryside are built of a mixture of bamboo, branches and masonry – they burn down instantly. Someone who dies in their sleep of smoke inhalation is more often than not lucky enough to be unaware of anything; sleep will just merge into deeper sleep. But a person who is suddenly engulfed in flames will almost always be woken up, if by nothing else then by the noise, and then has to face the most gruesome final minutes of life it's possible to imagine.'

The doctor opened his eyes.

'You see how important a wake is for us. Between ourselves, we can ignore all that stuff about evil spirits, but see how therapeutic a wake is for the bereaved. They can sit for a whole day and a whole night with the deceased, the corpse has been washed and laid out and dressed in its best clothes; they can weep and kiss and stroke the deceased, they can get used to the fact that he or she is dead, they can say a provisional farewell; they can spend twenty-four hours going over to the bier, touching their loved one's face, sitting down for a while and weeping, viewing and touching the body as much as they like, and the process helps them over their grief. But people who die as a result of arson can't be laid out on an open bier. They are so disfigured that no one would be able to bear the sight. We tried it once, and many of those who took part in the wake needed psychiatric care afterwards. The recognition factor had gone, and with it the human dimension.

'After the first arson attacks we also knew it was only a matter of time before the conflict escalated, and that is in fact what happened. First slit throats, then severed heads. So even now the bodies can't be put on open display: a father's hands will always run over a dead son's wound from ear to ear; a mother's lips will always find the axe blows on her daughter's neck.'

Francesco gave a shudder. He too wrapped himself more tightly in his blanket.

'So that's where we are now. We're waiting for the next

development, and find it hard to imagine what it will be. We only know that it will come.'

The doctor gave the earthenware jug a little shake and divided what was left between them, two glasses filled to the brim. Francesco had to use both hands to steady his as he raised it to his lips.

'We know the others are organising themselves. There are rumours of a shipload of reinforcements on their way to us.'

The words 'the others' and 'us' hung in the darkness between them for a moment before dissolving and disappearing, giving off a faint glow. Both men looked at the words with a mixture of surprise and alarm.

———————

In a village further east on the island a young European woman was writing a letter. She was sitting with her back against a stone wall and a glass of tea at her side. The village was Christian: a woman could sit outside on her own. She had short brown hair and a dark tan, as if from months of sun and sea.

'Hello, little Fresco-Pesco,' she wrote, 'are you OK?' She smiled and took a sip of tea. 'Is it spring at home? Are the apple trees in bloom?' Her face showed her longing, she was day-dreaming. Then she went on, 'In this part of the world people say that travelling is like rinsing your eyes. It's a good expression, that's just how it feels.'

She came to an abrupt halt, as though a thought had struck her, then drew a little sun at the top of the paper, with a smiling mouth and eyes and the words 'I'm fine' beneath it. 'Are you?'

'Rinsing your eyes and seeing something you've never seen before, something that also makes you see what you have seen before in a new way.' She threw back her head and laughed, then she read the sentence over again and underlined two words to show how it should be read to make its meaning clear. Then she drew a male figure, and wrote a name by the side of it: 'Meseo = friend, Christian, some Portuguese blood in his veins, just a little.' She sketched a droplet, then carried on writing.

'Meseo has described what it was like growing up as a Christian in a country where Muslims decide everything: suddenly one day the nursery place withdrawn, suddenly one day Christianity taken off the timetable at school; he has talked of permits that never came, of student places cancelled, always without explanation, but everyone knew: you are Christians, you have to be kept down; he has recounted the difficulties of getting work, of finding somewhere to live — sorry, the position has been filled, sorry, the apartment has been taken — and though it was never said openly, he knew it, you are Christian, you have to be kept out.'

She broke off to have another sip of tea. The main street of the village ran for fifty metres in both directions from where she sat; the view of a house was obscured by the wall behind her. There were not many people about, just a few cars and a flock of goats. She continued writing.

'It's true that on this island the Christians enjoyed privileges in colonial times, but that was a generation ago; how long should they go on being punished for it? Meseo and his companions hadn't been born in colonial times, they were born long after independence. Should they inherit the sins of their fathers?'

She paused again and pensively drew a heart, a heart of intimacy, and wrote, 'On the other hand, Fresco-Pesco, on the other hand persecution obviously gives them a sense of identity, resistance to growing Muslim oppression brings them together.'

A young Asian man came and squatted beside her, stroked her arm and whispered something to her. She smiled and nodded, held up her writing pad and said, 'Coming, just coming.' He stroked her arm again and left her. She wrote, 'But it's something else, something completely different, that gives young people here their identity.' She furrowed her brow a little now, trying to find the right words.

'Meseo has described his youth, when life was church on Sundays and school on weekdays and all they saw of naked flesh was their little sisters. When the priest was away visiting other parishes, they used to go down to the beach to make offerings to the spirits of their forefathers, as if at a given signal, never talking about it. The moment he had gone, people would just start gathering on the beach. In church they used to pass horoscopes to one another, tucked in the hymn books. This is my son's horoscope, how does it fit with your daughter's? A sidelong glance, an inclination of the head, the European missionary priest never knew what was going on, though their own priest may have done, but never said anything. If the horoscopes tallied, there might be a note in the hymn book when it came back, with a suggested sum and a question mark, and so negotiations had begun, and they looked at the chosen one with the long slender arms and the long bony legs and thought, how shall I cope? But they married because their fathers said so, and they coped because their fathers expected it, and they began the training their fathers had selected for them, and they entered the profession their fathers had decided for them.'

The young woman checked her watch and started writing faster.

'Can you understand why Christian youths here are rising in rebellion? Everything is decided for them, absolutely everything has to be in accordance with God's scheme, with that of the clan, and of their forefathers; they have two words for "we" ' – and now she drew again – 'Little We = we who are living now, Great We = we who lived before, we who live now and we who will live hereafter; can you understand why the young here are trying to find out who they are, trying to find their own identity?'

She turned the page over and wrote in smaller writing: 'On the other hand, when everything is part of a grander scheme, you don't need to explain so much, whereas we, we have to explain everything: how can evil exist when man is created in God's image?'

She wrote her father's name and address on an envelope, read quickly through the letter, didn't seem entirely satisfied, but let it go. She drew a smile at the bottom of the last page and wrote two more words: 'Love Anya.' Then she stood up and ran along the street. She licked the envelope and stuck it down as she ran, whispering, 'I hate losing you, but I must.' Then she seemed to become aware of what she had said under her breath, stood still for a moment and said it aloud.

Then she ran on.

If she had had more time, she would doubtless have added another reason why the young people on the island were experimenting with violence – they wanted excitement. For them as for many others the modern world had only one day, and that came every day. But on top of that, the content of that one day was decided for them by others.

7

PARABLES

'It's unbelievable.'

Helen crumpled up an empty cigarette packet and threw it on the table.

'It's fucking unbelievable. You both go out and get a girl, one Christian and one Muslim, and then you end up taking sides in the conflict. That's all we need.'

Francesco replied angrily, 'Neither of us has got a girl, as you put it.'

'But that's what's bloody happened.'

'Could you possibly refine your language? Be more ladylike?'

'That's how Danish ladies speak.'

The three of them were sitting on their own as usual in the breakfast room. Helen had finished eating and had lit a cigarette. Kurt was reading an old English newspaper and didn't bother looking up.

Francesco turned to him and said, 'Why don't you say something? Or do you agree with her?'

'I've heard it all before,' Kurt replied, still without raising his eyes from the newspaper. Helen blew a smoke ring over the top of the paper, and he wafted it away.

Francesco said: 'What about being a bit more aware of the Muslims' viewpoint? They're poor, they're starving, they're desperate.'

'Does that give them the right to resort to violence?'

'Not the right. No one has the right to use violence. But it's understandable. More . . . understandable.'

Francesco checked himself. He had almost used the word 'natural' – that frightened him: all his adult life he had insisted that violence was not part of human nature.

Kurt folded the newspaper and laid it on the table. He looked at them in turn and ventured a cautious smile.

'Shall we try and be friends? Two of us have made contact with the locals, one of us hasn't. That can easily give rise to envy.'

'Kurt!' Helen exclaimed, and they glared at each other across the table.

Francesco was about to intervene when suddenly there came an enormous explosion from the street. The curtains at the open window blew inwards. They all three hurled themselves to the floor and crawled over to the window wall as fast as they could. There was the sound of shouts from the street; in the distance blasts from a police whistle. Helen tucked herself in between the two men, linking arms with both of them.

'Help! I'm not up to this,' she said with an intake of breath that was almost a sob. Francesco put his arm round her shoulders. Kurt hesitated a moment and then took her hand in his. They lay huddled together, expecting another explosion, heard running footsteps on the pavement outside and were about to stand up to take a look when they heard a voice from the hall doorway:

'No. Not look. Dangerous now.'

They turned and saw the young girl from reception gesturing a warning from floor level. They dropped down again. There was the sound of breaking glass and angry voices outside. Then more running feet, but this time getting fainter. The girl crouching in the doorway stood up and brushed herself down, the three Europeans exchanged glances, rose to their feet and took a cautious peek out of the window. The street outside was strewn with shards of glass and bits of metal. The windows of a shop opposite were shattered, the display cabinets empty. The policeman in the track suit was standing beside the shop with a pistol in his hand.

Francesco pointed at him discreetly and said, 'He can't possibly have been standing there when it went off?'

The girl from the desk came over and looked out of the window with them. She shook her head dolefully.

'Gangs. Steal,' she said.

Francesco asked, 'What sort of gangs?'

She indicated herself: 'Young people.'

The three Europeans stood looking at the broken shop windows and the policeman until a police car and a fire engine arrived and blocked their view. One of them was still scared to death and wishing herself somewhere else, far from the island, away from all this; another was wondering why the policeman hadn't been on duty when the attackers or robbers came, and didn't much like the obvious answer; the third was thinking about the natural violence that arises when authority structures collapse, like adults no longer having control over the young, and for the second time in a matter of minutes he noticed that he was putting the words 'violence' and 'natural' into the same context.

Suddenly they were all three roused from their reflections. Out at sea a huge white wave came surging in at a tremendous pace, seeming to extend from harbour to horizon, before collapsing on a totally calm sea as abruptly as it had arisen. Their eyes met and they edged even closer together.

———————

The police captain was examining a fax from the capital. It bore the national coat of arms at the head, was signed by three officials, stamped with the ministry's official stamp and authenticated by a numerical code. He checked the signatures and the code against a secret manual. They were all correct.

'All correct, yet the content is just as absurd.'

He tightened the belt of his uniform as he spoke, took his cap with the shiny peak down off the shelf and stood at the little mirror above the basin to put it on.

'My entire adult life I've never been able to discuss politics, not even with my own reflection, or I'd have been arrested. Now it's over, the old times have gone and new times have come, now I can discuss politics as much as I like. I can talk about corrupt politicians, I can talk about economic crises, I can talk about incompetent ministries. I can talk and talk and talk, I can stand up in a public square and shout, I can write, on walls or in newspapers – but the result is always the same: the politicians are just as corrupt, the economic crises just as grave, the ministries just as incompetent.'

He looked down at the fax on his desk.

'And their faxes just as absurd.'

He picked up the fax and went out of his office, down the corridor, across the yard and out into the street. The police guard on the gate presented arms. The police captain saluted and beckoned the jeep.

'Army HQ.'

He didn't look at the driver as he said it, and the driver merely nodded. The police captain put on his sunglasses.

'The colonel. I've got an appointment with the colonel.'

One of the two guards at the entrance to Army Headquarters replied, 'Yes, we know. Would you mind raising your arms?'

He spoke in an undertone, as if a little ashamed.

'When did you introduce body searches for the police?' the police captain asked as he complied.

'This morning. Colonel's orders.'

One removed his pistol from its holster and laid it on the desk, the other ran his hands along his arms, armpits, sides, legs, round the ankles and up the inside of his thighs, over his back and stomach, and nodded. The soldiers were young and dark, darker than the police captain.

He went up the stairs, along the corridor with its worn red

carpet, and stopped in front of the solid dark-brown door. He knocked and looked out of the window as he waited yet again; he observed the throngs of white-clad figures in the mosque compound, and the cranes down at the harbour.

'Come in.'

He opened the door and went in. The colonel was sitting at his desk by the window, silhouetted against the light. He stood up and gestured towards the easy chairs. The police captain thanked him.

'How are you, Captain?'

'Fine, thanks. And you, Colonel?'

'Fine, thanks. And your family?'

'Fine, thanks. And yours?'

'Fine, as far as I'm aware.'

The colonel pressed a bell and a soldier entered and took an order for tea.

'Has it been a quiet night for your men, Colonel?'

'Not as bad as some. Five houses burnt down in the early hours, another exchange of fire near the Christian Rehabilitation Centre just after midnight, four small bombs in the Muslim business district. How about your men, Captain?'

'More or less the same.'

The colonel and the police captain took stock of each other as usual, the soldier brought the tea, and they each took a sip.

'There seem to be more and more refugees in the mosque?'

The police captain gave the impression of asking a question, but only just.

'Possibly. Are new refugees still streaming into the church?'

'Maybe. You'll be speaking to the leaders of the mosque at Friday prayers, no doubt?'

'Quite probably. And you're still talking with the church fathers even though you don't attend Mass?'

The two men drank more tea, slight smiles flickering at the corners of their lips.

'You mentioned having received a fax from the capital, Captain?'

The police captain drew a folded sheet of paper from his breast pocket and opened it out.

'A ship with seven hundred seasonal workers is on its way here from the regional capital. The Ministry wants us to try and take them.'

He handed the fax to the colonel, who read it, glanced up at the police captain, re-read it.

'What's the problem? There's still work and accommodation available here?'

'We've heard about ships like this before. One landed at Sumbalawa. Three days later the island exploded.'

'Because of the ship?' The colonel had lowered his voice, and a silence descended on the room. 'You're choosing your words carefully, of course, Captain?'

'Of course. But as head of the civil police force in the town it's my duty to be prepared. If the ship turns out to be full of Muslim men, it might be more appropriate at present to refuse disembarkation.'

'In a Muslim country it's not beyond the bounds of possibility that there will be Muslims among seven hundred seasonal workers.'

'And only men?'

The colonel shrugged his shoulders, 'We're not keen on women travelling. Men are the providers, they have to go where the work is. Like here.'

The police captain emptied his glass of tea and set it down delicately on the table before saying, 'I'm sure you understand, Colonel. The word "insurgents" was used on Sumbalawa. We'd rather not have to use that word here.'

'Words can sometimes do harm, true enough. We came here as reinforcements for you. The army can't afford to keep

us here for long. Let's hope the phrase "excellent cooperation" can apply to the whole of our time on this island.'

The two men rose and shook hands.

———————

'Who is it?'

Helen sat up in bed and looked towards the door. Her face
was indistinct behind the white mosquito net.

'Who is it?'

She began to feel apprehensive, leant over on her elbow
and wriggled one hand under the edge of the net to find her
watch on the bedside cabinet. She held it up to the grey light
from the window and then looked at the door again. She
waited a moment, put the watch back on the cabinet and lay
down with her eyes wide open. After a while she closed them
and breathed more calmly. But then something made her
jump.

'Who's there?'

She sat up and threw back the sheet. She was naked, with
red lines on her body from the wrinkles in the sheets. She
climbed out gingerly from under the mosquito net, covered
herself with her arms and crept over to the door.

'Who is it?' she said softly, with her mouth close to the door
frame. 'Is that you, Francesco?'

Silence.

'Kurt?'

She waited. Then went back to the bed, lifted the net and
was about to crawl in when she gave another start and looked
at the door again. She felt vulnerable and gripped the
mosquito net with both hands and draped it round her. It
came off the hook in the ceiling and fell on top of her, like a
gossamer coverlet over a white flesh statue. She returned to
the door, hesitant, listening, put her mouth to the frame and
whispered, 'Who are you? What do you want?'

The door handle moved against her bare stomach. She put her hand round it and it stopped. She tried to push it down, but it resisted. She tried a second time, but the handle wouldn't budge, and then it started rising slowly upwards. Helen used the full force of both hands, with her face pressed to the door, then let go suddenly and shut her eyes, as if to listen. The light from the window was brighter now, and showed up her body more clearly under the net.

———

Was she in a queue? Bodies were pressing against her on all sides. Helen opened her eyes and looked up. It was an entrance hall, five or six metres long, with a massive stone wall at the end. She felt disorientated, tried to turn round, a woman behind her smiled and pointed at the left-hand wall of the room, where a little staircase with narrow steps led downwards, so narrow that the women were having to descend in single file. Above the stairs hung a small metal mask, brass or copper, the mouth frozen in a shriek, as if at birth or death. Helen stretched up and tried to touch it when it came to her turn to go down the stairs, but the woman behind made her desist. This will be about a child, she thought, whispering the words as she walked down, this will be about a child, a child either being born or dying. It was getting darker and darker with every step, as if the faint dawn preferred to stay up above, didn't dare venture down the stairs; this will be about a child, my child, she whispered the words again, and there were tears in her eyes now, the light from a paraffin lamp revealed them, made them sparkle. The lamp was hanging from the ceiling of a little room at the foot of the stairs, which was full of women, tightly packed, saying something, or sighing something, the sound filled the room, accumulated beneath the ceiling. The women were still making their way to something, pushing forward towards something. Helen was pushed along with them, squashed against them, drawn into the sighs from them, breathed out and sighed, closed her eyes, breathed in and sighed. A voice sighed in her ear, the woman behind her, dressed in a simple white blouse and full-length silk skirt, dark-skinned, perhaps in her late twenties, with painted fingernails and broad rings on each thumb. Helen reached down and found the hands with the silver rings, took them in hers and turned to ask, 'Do you speak English?'

Her stomach and breasts were pressing against the woman, and she slid her arms around her, as if to make more space. The woman put her forearms on Helen's shoulders and clasped her hands behind Helen's neck, leant forward and blew gently in her left ear, drew back again and looked at her, leant forward and blew in her right ear.

'Do you speak English?'

The woman smiled and turned her round, pushed away the bodies on both sides and turned her round. Now Helen was facing a hole in the wall, a narrow passageway; the woman in the queue in front of her was on her way in, twisting sideways to ease herself through. Helen hesitated, it was her turn, she hesitated. The woman behind her said something in a low voice. Helen tried to turn her head while keeping her eyes on the passage, *do you speak English*, she put her hands on the walls of the passage, which must have been less than half a metre wide, *do you speak English*, she pulled herself in and entered sideways, *don't tell me you don't speak English*, the woman was following close behind, *how shall I find my way out of this if you don't speak English*, the light faded completely, only the sound and the smell of them were in the dark passage now, the sound of breath, fearful breath, steady breath, the sound of sighs from ahead and behind, the smell of warm bodies, of cotton and silk. The passage must have had a bend in it, for suddenly a square of light became visible up ahead, growing slowly into an aperture. Helen went through and out into the light – warm golden light from many paraffin lamps – and she was naked now, with her trousers and jumper rolled up in her hand. The woman behind her was also naked, she had rolled up her silk skirt and hung it across her neck like a towel and tied her blouse round her head. Helen paused momentarily and looked about her: the room consisted of a pool surrounded by lamps, and was full of bathing women. From the far end a channel continued onwards, that too illuminated by lamps. She turned to the woman with the silver rings, *do you speak English*, the woman smiled and took her by the hand, led her the few steps into the water, took her clothes from her and laid them by the pool, put her own silk skirt with them, tightened the blouse she had knotted round her head, and drew her down with her into the water. Helen gasped, then laughed; the water was less cold than she had expected. They swam a few strokes side by side, over to the channel, floated in the water and watched as the other women swam into the channel in twos and threes and disappeared behind a projection. Helen looked at the woman with the silver rings, nodded enquiringly at the channel; the woman shook her head, put out her hands instead and laid them on her shoulders, turned her over and swam on her back with her. Helen let herself float along, her legs extended and her head tipped back. They reached the side of the pool, the woman sat herself on an underwater ledge, put an arm round Helen and pulled her downwards. Helen brought her hands under the woman's legs, pulled herself down, let herself float up, pulled herself down, let herself float up. Then she submerged herself completely, and when she came up again the woman wiped the water out of her face and hair. Helen leant back and laid her cheek against the woman's cheek, put a hand behind her head and brought her closer. Then she shut her eyes. The woman sang something in her ear while gently stroking her. Helen seemed to be asleep, breathing slowly, her body relaxed. The pool was gradually emptying of bathers, the last ones were coming down the steps from the passageway, swimming for a while and then vanishing into the channel beyond the projection.

Helen sat up with a jerk, looked about her in fright, looked at the woman behind her. She pushed her away and swam a few strokes out into the pool, saw their clothes on the side and swam over to them. The woman reached them before she did, tied them in the blouse she had knotted round her head and swam towards the channel. It was almost wide enough for them to swim into it together. Helen held back a little, her eyes level with the woman's waist, cast a swift sidelong glance at the body next to her, looked up to see whether the woman had noticed, turned her head and looked a little more.

The channel came to an end, and steps led to a doorway from which light and laughter emanated. Helen went up the steps first, the woman following her. The door led into something resembling a cloakroom, with hooks on all four walls and a stand in the centre of the room with eight washbasins. The room was full of women; some were drying themselves, some were standing at the basins combing their hair, some were dressing, others were going out through a door behind a curtain. Helen looked uncertain, and a woman in a white uniform came over to her and gave her a large blue towel. Helen thanked her, and saw the woman with the silver rings being given one too. The woman unfolded the towel and wrapped it round Helen. She tried to pull away, but the woman held on to her, patted and rubbed her dry, her back, shoulders, arms. Helen unfolded her towel and put it over the woman, rubbed her back, shoulders and arms dry, accepted the intimacy. The woman shut her eyes and said something. Helen drew nearer, as if to listen, went right up to her, let her towel slide off her shoulders towards her waist and legs, the woman smiled, responded by letting go of the towel she was holding, as if in a game. Helen watched the towel falling from her own body, watched the towel falling from the woman's body. For a moment they stood there as both towels fell to the floor, and held out their hands as if to touch each other; for a moment gentle fingers stroked white and brown skin, an instant only, and then it was over. Helen gasped and turned away, looked for her clothes, suddenly remembered that they were wrapped in the blouse which the woman had tied round her head, reached out to take them, seemed embarrassed at stretching out naked. The woman loosened the blouse to let the clothes spill out, and they dressed in silence, side by side, facing away from each other; then they stood up and their eyes met.

'Do you speak English?'

Helen pointed at the curtain as she asked. The woman smiled, went over to the curtain, held it aside for her.

'Do you speak English?'

Helen ducked under the curtain, the woman following her at a short distance, and behind it was a hall with pillars and benches, on which sat the women who had just been in the cloakroom, seemingly reluctant to leave the bathhouse. There was noise coming from a door at the end of the hall, bright white light and traffic. She walked towards it, with a brief glance over her shoulder to see whether the woman with the rings was still following. They reached the door simultaneously, stopped and looked at one another again.

'It's a pity you don't speak English.'

Helen had to shout now to make herself heard above the cacophony from the street. She bent forward quickly to give the woman a brief kiss on the lips, and left. The sun was up now, it had dispersed the mist from the ridge, and sunshine filled the street with contrasts and shadows. She walked fast, without a backward glance; the woman with the silver rings stood at the door gazing after her. Helen knew she was, and increased her speed, as if to escape. She came out into a main road with a wider pavement and more space, walked even faster, with a hectic flush on her cheeks.

'Could this be about a child?'

Helen spoke to herself in a tone of surprise and wonderment. Could this be about a child? She put a hand on her bare stomach to cover it, or feel it; could this be about a child? She tried to work out where she was, shaded her eyes and squinted towards the mountain, looked up and down the street and at the houses on both sides. From a stall came a harsh cry; two hands appeared through the counter hatch, two hands and a harsh voice. She jumped back in shock, then walked on; the voice in the stall shouted louder, the hands clutched at the air. She went to cross the street and a voice and two dark eyes shouted at her from a doorway on the other side. She stopped in the middle of the street and turned; a rickshaw driver yelled at her and she only just managed to jump aside. The noises in the street were getting louder and louder, and seemed to be aimed specifically at her. She stood under a tree, covering her ears. Two shoe-shine boys immediately pounced on her, their hands on her shoes; she kicked them away, took a few more steps, began to run. Three street-vendors chased after her, thrusting their wares into her face, postcards, wrist-watches, jewellery; she knocked them away, running for all she was worth. There were shouts coming from every direction now, from the stalls on both sides, from the street-vendors, from shop doorways and entrances. She was weeping as she ran, coughing and wiping away the tears as she sobbed, *I thought it was about a child, I thought it was about a child*. Then suddenly the tumult subsided. She came to a halt in amazement, looking at the cars and people and vendors. Not one of them was shouting, at least not at her. Suddenly a shadow was gliding alongside her, a rickshaw driver, and she had a feeling she had seen him somewhere before.

'Kurt, have you got to the sports pages yet?'
    'Mmm.'
    The receptionist had brought them another British

newspaper, two months old, and they were taking turns to read it.

'How many are there?'

'How many what?' said Kurt, looking at her blankly.

'Sports pages.'

Helen leant across the table, took the paper out of his hands, counted them and gave it back.

'Eight. So I've got time to tell you a dream. Do you want to hear it?'

'Mmm.'

They were sitting at the breakfast table with a water jug, a coffee pot and two empty cups, their plates empty except for breadcrumbs and the remains of some red jam. It was obvious they had plenty of time.

'Do you think dreams are influenced by the places we're in? Do you think we absorb our surroundings for our subconscious to work on and then release again in dreams, so that our dreams are an image of the encounter between our emotions and our environment, an encounter of the possible with the actual?'

'Mmm. Absolutely.'

'I dreamt that I was woken up early one morning by a knock on the door. At first I didn't believe it, I dreamt that I was dreaming, but eventually I went over and opened it. It was here in the hotel. I dreamt that I climbed out from under the mosquito net and there was a woman outside in the corridor, probably in her late twenties, wearing broad silver rings on each thumb. She didn't say anything, just made a sign for me to go with her. I asked whether she spoke English and she shook her head and made a sign again. I remember hesitating, the dream faltered for a moment, as if I didn't want to go. But then I got dressed as fast as I could while she waited. I think she must have been Malay: she had dark skin and hair and was wearing a simple white blouse and full-length silk skirt. She explained something to me about a child,

126

pretended to be holding a baby in her arms, then held her hand half a metre above the floor as if to indicate the height of a child.'

Helen picked up her cigarettes and went over to the window, leant her elbows on the sill and lit up.

'Kurt, have you ever had the feeling of watching yourself in a film? That's exactly the feeling I have right now: I'm sitting telling you about a dream, pick up my cigarettes and go over to the window before continuing. That's exactly what they do in films. I'm talking about something unreal, in an unreal fashion.'

'Mmm.'

'We came down to reception, I woke the night porter and asked him to get us a rickshaw. Somehow I must have known where we were going, because the rickshaw driver started cycling in one direction and I got angry and ordered him to cycle in the other. He obeyed, and it was quite a good feeling, in control, I was fully in control. It was cold, the rickshaw driver had a woollen rug lying on the footboard, but I didn't want to ask for it, didn't want to humble myself, would rather freeze.'

She came back to the table and sat down.

'For some reason the woman wasn't in the rickshaw with me, nor was she running alongside; the streets were empty, just a few people lying around fast asleep. The strange thing was that as we passed a side-street it would suddenly be full of light and life, then all went dead again until we came to another side-street, also full of people, and there she stood.'

'Mmm.'

'We went down the side-street, she in front and me behind; she turned from time to time to make sure I was still there. It was really crowded, but everyone gave way for us, as if there were something radiating from us. We came to a place where a lot of women were standing in a queue, and they too moved aside to let us in first. We went into a hall, down a staircase, into a room and then a tiny passageway. Just before entering the passageway, which was so narrow that we had to turn sideways, one after the other, I noticed something: all the women in the queue were carrying a bundle. It was completely dark, completely silent; the only sound was that of my own breathing. I can't remember how long I dreamt I was in the passageway, but when I eventually emerged I had the feeling that something had happened to me. I found myself in a room with a large pool, which was full of women with children, babies, which must have been the bundles they were carrying. The women were washing the babies, tending them, stroking their hair, cleaning their ears, rocking them to and fro in the water. I wonder if the narrow passage could have symbolised a birth.'

'Mmm.'

'Or can there be such a thing as a reverse birth, where we leave reality and go back to the foetal stage?'

'Mmm.'

'I suddenly had the feeling of being a baby, of floating, of being cared for. Almost the way it must feel to be a foetus: soft, calm, warm.'

Helen paused, propped her chin in her hands.

'There was a channel flowing out from the pool leading to a cloakroom. We got dressed and went on, and beyond it was a peristyle where the women from the pool were sitting, and then I saw something I hadn't been aware of before in the dream: all the babies were dead. The women were sitting with dead babies on their laps.'

Helen closed her eyes.

'All the babies were dead. And the women just sat there, as if they couldn't bring themselves to leave them. I wonder whether the passageway to the pool actually symbolised death, whether the women were tending their dead babies in the pool and then sending them out on their journey to the grave, the channel, but then couldn't bring themselves to abandon them. The woman who had fetched me tried to tell me something as I left, tried to explain something, but I couldn't understand. It was the same out on the street, people tried to tell me something, but I couldn't make out what they were saying. I remember dreaming that I was in despair.'

Helen stopped talking, tilted her cup a little. A soldier came into the room and greeted them, pointing to the door. Kurt folded the paper, laid it on the table, stood up and said, 'Nice dream. Are you certain it was a dream? I saw you in a rickshaw at dawn this morning when I was coming back to the hotel.'

———

The colonel read the report by the light from the window. Only once did he look up at the soldier who had brought it.

'At ease.'

The soldier set his feet apart and clasped his hands behind his back. The colonel finished reading.

'Who was the woman in the pool?'

'One of ours.'

'And who overheard the conversation in the breakfast room?'

'The receptionist.'

The colonel laid the report on his lap and swung round in his chair towards the window. He closed his eyes and breathed in the smell of cotton, different from in the passageway to the pool; this was the smell of white cotton, freshly ironed, under a higher sky, where bodies are cooler, silk smoother.

'She could have made her escape there.'

'Pardon?'

The soldier looked unsure of himself. He was young and slight, with a hint of black down on his upper lip.

'The European woman. She could have saved herself. In the pool. But Europeans are so wrapped up in their own ideas. Are you from these parts?'

'No, Colonel. Further south. Irian.'

'Then you won't know that this island lies in the strait between east and west, the thousand-year-old trade route where Hinduism from the west met Buddhism from the east?'

The soldier shook his head.

'The trade route where Taoism from the north met Islam from the south?'

'No, Colonel.'

'Buddha's parable about the burning house, d'you know that?'

The colonel waited for his reply. The soldier shook his head again in mortification. The colonel turned back to the window.

'It was afternoon. The Master sat under the tree with his disciples in a circle round him. Life went on in the village behind them: three women were fetching water from a well, a potter was throwing a pot, a group of men carried a shrouded corpse above their heads. The birds were singing in the endless sky. It was a hot day, but cool in the shade beneath the tree, the leaves like an immense canopy over them.'

The soldier kept his eyes cautiously on the colonel.

'The Master told them to give themselves up into The One, their minds empty of desires.'

The colonel swung round to the soldier. 'Soldier, why do you think he said The One? Wouldn't Nothingness have been more correct?'

'Hard to say, Colonel.'

The colonel nodded and turned back to the window.

'Hard to say, hard to say, just so. In Buddhism all words are wrong in any case. Liberation is a process, and you can't put words to a process without fossilising it. The One is better than Nothingness for anybody who is afraid of emptiness. Some people can meditate on emptiness, some can't. In Europe in the Middle Ages they had a theory that in nature there was a fear of emptiness, *horror vacui*, that made water follow when a piston was drawn up. Europeans have always been a bit odd. But in this respect they're like many of us: seeking wholeness, completeness, fearing emptiness.'

The soldier shifted position.

The colonel continued, 'A disciple wanted to know more about The One, and the Master replied, "Imagine you're lying on the deck of a ship on a fine day, the sun warming your face and feet, you're almost asleep, but only almost; there's nothing you have to achieve and nothing you haven't achieved, all is well; there's nothing troubling you and nothing you wish for, all is well; you lie there feeling the boat swaying up and down in the swell, up and down, up and down, oh so tranquil, oh so tranquil, you hear the gentle slap of the waves, oh so tranquil, oh so tranquil, and all at once you feel you're rising, you float slowly off the deck and rise upwards, upwards, you look down, see the boat far below, and yourself lying on the deck, you continue rising, upwards and upwards, towards the sun, towards the skies. You turn, lie on your stomach and look down, stretch out your arms like wings and fly, you lean into a dive, first to one side and then the other, dive and loop the loop."'

The colonel paused.

'The Buddha wouldn't exactly have used the word "loop".'

'Certainly not, Colonel.'

'But a loop is what you do, in any case, with your hair flying out behind you, if you have any.'

Another pause.

'He probably didn't say that either.'

'Probably not, Colonel.'

'But anyway, loop or no loop, hair or no hair, "you'll be dancing up there, *with the birds in the endless sky above you, and the leaves of the tree like an immense canopy, and one day you will go up into The One*". Not Nothingness. The One.'

'If you say so, Colonel.'

'Then one day a disciple asked, "What is The One, Master? Tell us whether this One that we shall give ourselves up into – is it like being at one with all creation, like lying in water in the middle of the day feeling a lightness of body, your head empty of thoughts, dozing in the water or falling asleep – whether this One is goodness and happiness, or simply Nothingness, empty and meaningless?" '

The soldier cleared his throat.

The colonel went on. 'Buddha was silent for a long time, then he said indifferently, "There's no answer to your question." But in the evening, when the disciples had gone, the Buddha remained sitting under the bread tree and told the others, those who had not asked, this parable: "I saw a house recently, a house on fire, the flames licking around the roof. I went closer and saw there were people in the house; I called through the door that the roof was on fire and that they should get out quickly, but they didn't seem in any hurry. One of them asked me, his eyebrows on fire, how it was out there, whether they spoke English out there, whether it was raining, whether it was windy, whether they spoke English out there." '

The colonel picked up the report and ran his finger along the edge.

' "Truly, my friends, to those who don't feel the ground burning so hot beneath their feet that they move anywhere rather than staying where they are, to those I have nothing to say." '

The colonel turned to the soldier, 'The European woman could have saved herself in the baths. She could have got out of the burning house. But she wasn't courageous enough. Even with her eyebrows on fire.'

He thought for a moment.

'Do you think I'm being too hard on her?'

'Not at all, Colonel.'

'Hasn't she the right to change?'

The colonel turned back towards the window.

'To change is not a right. And for some people life is simply not long enough. Like the police captain, for example. Why doesn't he leave the burning house?'

8

RETURN

Kurt shivered slightly. It was early morning, not yet daylight, with glimpses of fires here and there. The mountains loomed in the background, black, massive, discernible only in outline, the night still concealing their features. Above them the sky was taking on colour, first deep-red, then gently lightening. The red was reflected in the water between the camera and the mountains, extending its long crimson fingers towards the beach and the people sitting on it, as if trying to grasp them. They were sitting in small groups round their fires, most of them wrapped in rugs draped over their heads, giving them the appearance of monks, with their faces in the shadow of the cowl. Only intermittently would a face be illumined as a fire flared up, and then it was always just lips moving, as if in prayer, with the eyes fixed on the water.

Kurt had been up all night. He had walked with the villagers up the steep mountainside, had asked if he could precede them to the reservoir and film them as they arrived. The tribal elders had agreed. Kurt had set off, but then changed his mind; something made him decide to return to his previous place, roughly in the middle of the procession. He had filmed them instead as they made camp, lit fires, ate their meals. They had invited him to their fires; at every single fire he had filmed they had invited him to sit down, wanting to give him food and drink and show him family photographs. Tattered blurry photographs in garish colours of severe elderly people in rigid poses. He had studied each picture carefully and got an interpreter to ask which were their parents, which were their spouses, which were their children, what had happened to them? The people had answered eagerly, almost shouting, gesticulating towards the water of the reservoir.

Kurt had turned to look at the reservoir with firelight reflected in his eyes; he looked very relaxed. He had gone from fire to fire with his camera, and had finally filmed the empty pipes from the upper reservoir and walked out on the dam and filmed the water flowing out from the lower one. He had continued further out along the dam, which was three to four metres wide, and found a spot where he could get the morning light coming from the right and the people directly opposite. He had approached the tribal elders and asked permission, and they had smiled and nodded and gestured: you film there, we stay here, you go down there, we go down here, we all meet in the middle. He had sat with them and shared his brandy flask with them, a careful unstable capful each; they had talked to him and he had listened, without an interpreter, without comprehending anything, but he had listened anyway, with no sign of impatience, and when he got up to go it was reluctantly, as if he would rather have sat there longer but there was work to do.

He sat now on the side of the dam with a cigarette, studying the reservoir and the people on the other side. When he took a puff he blew the smoke down over himself, as if to avoid disturbing or annoying anyone.

The people opposite also looked across at him from time to time. He became increasingly distinct as the light grew stronger and the darkness around their fires dissolved. A woman was the first to see him stand up from the dam, extinguish his cigarette with his foot and go over to his camera. She pulled her woollen blanket off her head and called out, pointed, and several of the others sat up and stared, their blankets sliding off them as the darkness slid off the surrounding landscape.

Kurt leant over and looked through the viewfinder, saw what it was that had prompted him to stand up: the outline of a roof. He moved the camera slowly along it, could just make out another one beyond it, still under water, but visible nevertheless. On the other bank people were crowding on to what was becoming a shore, an open grassy slope, apparently unable to see anything yet. They were watching the man with the camera, watching his camera. Could it see something they couldn't? Kurt took his eye from the viewfinder and waved to them: patience, patience, it's coming. Then turned back to the viewfinder.

Suddenly the sun rose over the mountain and bathed the reservoir in light, and someone on the shore yelled out, lots of them yelled, all of them yelled, and all were pointing: a roof was rising slowly up out of the water near where the man with the camera was standing, then another emerged, and another. They clapped their hands, shrieked, sobbed. Kurt tilted the camera down towards the roofs, filmed them in sequence, then levelled the camera to take in the whole reservoir, with the people on the other bank. He took his eye away from the viewfinder again to survey the scene he had filmed: the outlines of a village rising infinitely slowly from the water while a hundred or so villagers stood weeping and praying on the opposite bank. The water was subsiding, millimetre by millimetre, centimetre by centimetre, house roofs were continuing to emerge, one here, one there, another at the upper end of the reservoir, then another at the lower end. The people on the shore had stopped crying now and were laughing instead, clutching one another and pointing, there's my house, there's yours; someone had brought out a drum and started beating it, others were ringing small brass bells. The sounds of laughter and drums and bells rolled out across the water and rooftops. The village was rising and shaking itself in confusion, as if it had been asleep for a whole year and was still not quite awake, did not yet quite understand where it was. It regarded the people and then the man with the camera and shook more water off itself, stretched itself drowsily. The movement made more water flow off to reveal doors and windows; soon the first street appeared, the first steps.

Kurt filmed with a steady hand, the village rising from the water, the people on the shore. As he was turning the camera back towards the village he checked himself, looked up from the viewfinder at the villagers, was amazed, and shifted the camera back towards them. Now he filmed the shore, which was getting broader and broader as the water withdrew, but the people were no longer moving forward. They stood where they had been standing when the village first became visible, as if they wanted to wait until all the water was gone, as if the water were a curse that had to run right out before the village could reawaken to life.

All the houses were overgrown with algae, the steps and alleys covered in mud, but they were there, all the houses and steps and alleys were there, and suddenly the laughter and the drums and the bells on the shore ceased, suddenly everything went quiet. Again Kurt took his eye from the viewfinder and looked at the people opposite. They waved at him: get ready. Kurt coiled the microphone lead round his shoulder, stuck the microphone in his headband and raised the camera on to his shoulder and waved back: ready. They lined up three or four across, with the village elders in long white robes going first. Several drummers stepped forward, finding each other in a slow solemn rhythm, boom, pause, boom, pause; a chorus of male voices resonated below the drum beats, gave them bass and depth, drone, pause, drone, pause, then a choir of women's voices filled in the pauses, a high, graceful carolling, drone, screech, drone, tra-la, and the procession moved off down towards the village. Kurt ran towards them over the dam, dropped to his knees to film from the flank a hundred singing villagers approaching their own past in slow rhythmic motion, drone, tra-la, drone, tra-la. The sunlight played on the white robes of the elders, drone, tra-la, drone, tra-la, the overgrown doors and windows and walls of the village silently watched the approaching procession, as though the houses were holding their breath – only the mist rising from them in the sun's warmth gave sign of life; drone, tra-la, drone, tra-la, and an extra long, drawn-out tra-laaaa when two of the elders at the head of the procession slipped on the mud of the steep slope down to the first houses, an extra beat of the drums as their legs shot into the air and two white robes landed on their backs in the mud and floundered and slithered on downwards. The procession stopped, the drums stopped, the men's chorus stopped, the women's chorus stopped. They all stood still and watched the two figures slowly hauling themselves to their feet, now in mud robes rather than white robes, their eyes glaring furiously out of mud masks. A hundred hands went up to a hundred mouths to stifle grins of amusement, or at least to conceal them, but too late. The elders roared, the people jerked back in fright and took up position to resume: no one returns to his own past with a smirk on his face. Kurt had to bite his lip as he filmed, tightening his facial muscles to control his expression. The villagers regrouped: three by three, four by four, and the drummers had signalled to one another and were about to begin again when a sudden bickering broke out among the elders at the front. Those still in white robes were pointing at the two with muddy robes and shaking their heads; the two were protesting but were outnumbered by the many and eventually gave in, taking off their robes to stand naked. Their white-attired brethren shook their heads even more emphatically and pointed to the procession behind. Kurt went on filming the two old naked backs making their way into the centre of the procession, among women and children and younger men; the drums started up, the men's chorus came in, the women's chorus came in, drone, tra-la, drone, tra-la, and then there was an additional chorus of amusement from the women around the naked men, like a half-beat, drone, tra-la, oops, drone, tra-la, oops, and the women round the two men looked at one another and giggled and bent down, and in their mud masks two pairs of eyes tried to pretend that everything was normal, and so the procession approached the village again, drone, tra-la, oops, drone, tra-la, oops, in a hobbling, almost dancing rhythm.

Kurt ran behind them, filming, filling the picture with the village that had risen from the water and the procession of people on their way down into it, the mountains beyond that had regained their features and the high, still sky above. He was about to walk back out on to the dam to carry on filming from the flank when the rear half of the procession drew to a halt again; this time it was the women round the two naked men shouting something, obviously wanting something. The elders at the front stopped in annoyance and looked behind them, called out. The women pointed down at the two men and made a sign in the air with thumb and index finger of something long, a stick, or a rod, or a prayer flag. It turned out to be a prayer flag: the elders patted their white robes and brought out red and white prayer flags covered in painted signs which were sent back through the crowd, and for a few seconds the top halves of the naked men were visible with stooping women all around them, the movement of the women's shoulders indicating that they were tying the prayer ribbons on to them, and the eyes in the mud masks pretending disinterest. The elders gave the signal to set off yet again, and once more the crowd reversed and took up position, three by three, four by four, the drummers sighed and started up, the men's chorus sighed and joined in, the women's chorus sighed and followed on, drone, tra-la, drone, tra-la, and the two naked men sighed as strong female hands lifted them up and bore them above their heads, as if carrying the dead, except for the two short masts sticking straight up into the sky with their red and white prayer flags fluttering in the breeze.

So the old approached the old, that which was and that which once had been, with the exception of the symbols of new life, a new time, blessed with prayer flags. Kurt ran further along the dam and headed towards the village from the opposite side of the procession. He stopped at the first house and waited for the procession to arrive before he went down one of the narrow alleys. He kept on filming while it was out of sight until it reappeared at the end of the alley. The drums were silent now, the men's chorus was silent, the women's chorus was silent: the procession entered the village as in a silent film, down alley after alley, across a little market-place, over to a brick well with winch and bucket. Kurt followed them, filming all the time. When they halted at the well he kept in the background, as if uncertain whether he was now filming a religious ceremony and not wanting to disturb or offend. One of the elders climbed up on the well and spoke in a loud voice, his audience attentive. He pointed at the houses around them, and all heads turned in that direction. Kurt took his eye from the viewfinder to listen and his expression changed to incredulity, fear almost. There were voices coming from the empty houses: a woman laughing, children singing, men talking. The villagers exchanged glances, and it was clear that they had experienced this before and had been hoping for it now, but had not been sure of it. Kurt looked as if he didn't know what to think. He took the microphone from his headband and went over to the nearest house, pushed it through an open window and watched his control panel. The needle didn't move. He stood listening to the voices from inside the house for a while longer, tried again at another window with the same result: the machine recorded nothing. The people round the well were beginning to disperse now, obviously to their own former houses. Some were already scrubbing the algae off the walls, others sweeping the mud off the floors. Kurt beckoned to one of them, a young girl, took her over to another house, listened, looked at her, as if to ask if she could hear anything. The girl nodded and smiled, made a scissors movement with the thumb and fingers of her right hand to indicate talking. Kurt tried to ask, who, who are they? The girl smiled again and made a big arc with her arms, an arc that took in the well and the people moving away from it and the overgrown village and the mountains beyond and the sky above: Us – We who are now, We who were before, We who will come later. Kurt pointed the camera at her, pointed at the house; could he film her while she talked to the voices inside? The girl agreed with a smile, squatted in the doorway and called something into the house, received an answer, laughed, said something in response. The voice asked something, the girl answered, struck her open palm with her other hand, as if to emphasise something. A young girl sitting in a village just arisen from the water talking to those who had lived there before her.

Helen shivered slightly. It was early morning, not yet daylight, with glimpses of fires here and there. The mountains loomed in the background, black, massive, discernible only in outline, the night still concealing their features. Above them the sky was taking on colour, first deep-red, then gently lightening. The red was reflected in the water between the camera and the mountains, extending its long crimson fingers towards the beach and the people sitting on it, as if trying to grasp them. They were sitting in small groups round their fires, most of them wrapped in rugs draped over their heads, giving them the appearance of monks, with their faces in the shadow of the cowl. Only intermittently would a face be illumined as a fire flared up, and then it was always just lips moving, as if in prayer, with the eyes fixed on the water.

Helen had been up at the reservoir the day before and decided where she wanted to be filmed. The guide who had led her there had shown her the grassy slope where the tribe usually gathered to watch the village reveal itself. She had a small viewfinder with her, through which she examined the bank and the water, took a few steps forward, turned and pretended she was holding a microphone and looking into a camera, introducing the view behind her with gestures: here is the tribe, here comes the village.

She had suggested they hire porters to carry a little inflatable boat up to the reservoir; after filming her with the tribe and the emerging village as background they could cut and hurry over to the dam, get the boat that on her instructions the porters would have carefully camouflaged in leaves, put it in the water and film the tribe from the village, film their faces as they saw their houses seeming to rise from the water, film her as she sat in the prow of the boat and described the mood in a low, intense voice.

Kurt had not been entirely convinced.

'Kurt, don't you see what we'll get? The water will be subsiding while we're sitting in the boat, we'll subside with it, the camera angle will be dropping, we will *be* the water subsiding. When all the water has gone and the boat is grounded we will be there to receive them, we will *be* the village; *they* will be coming to *us*, it won't be *us* following *them*.'

'But this is holy for them. This is their ancestors, this is their history. Have we the right to paddle a rubber dinghy over something holy?'

This conversation had taken place in the breakfast room, where they had been alone. Helen had stared at him open-mouthed.

'When did you start bothering about things like that?'

'Now.'

'Is it that dusky little piece of skirt that's turned your head? Firm flesh, exotic aroma, and no doubt some new positions. Is that all it takes?'

'Mind your own business.'

Kurt had glowered, and Helen had held her tongue, even though she wanted to say more. They had sat in silence for a while, then she had asked, 'Have you any suggestions as to how we should go about it?'

Kurt hadn't replied.

Later that day she had written *poor man* in her diary. Poor man, he knows my proposal is a scoop, and he's a photographer, above all else, but he's approaching the age when a hand on a young female breast is increasingly important.

Now they were both sitting in their folding chairs, both with cigarettes. Their porters had lain down a few metres away, behind them. They each had a hip flask and were taking an occasional swig. The tribe was sitting on a grassy bank thirty metres from them, right down by the water's edge. Kurt had measured the distance and calculated the camera angle, explained to her that from here he could get her, the tribe and the village all in clear focus, and then he could zoom in, first on the tribe, then the village as it became increasingly exposed.

'I think I'll try and doze for a bit. Can you wake me when it's light?'

He nodded, and she unrolled a sleeping bag and lay down on the ground. Kurt gazed at the fires by the water, saw the dark figures round them, the dark water beyond. Then he looked down at the face with closed eyes in the sleeping bag at his side, the short blond hair, the laughter lines radiating from the eyes, the tiny creases in the upper lip. He smiled, a little sadly, and took another swig from his flask. Helen opened her eyes a chink and glanced up at him, but he seemed not to notice.

An hour later he bent over and shook her. 'It's getting light.'

She got up, ran a brush through her hair, opened a silver powder compact, checked herself in the mirror, powdered both cheeks and round her eyes. Then she took the caps off eye-liner and lip gloss, held the mirror away from herself and applied her make-up carefully, with precise, deliberate movements. Kurt watched in fascination.

'Kurt, look the other way.'

He turned aside until he heard the powder compact snap shut. Helen came over to him, notebook in hand, reading something under her breath. She reached the end, flicked the pages back, started again and gave him a quick glance.

'Can we do a test?'

He walked towards her with the camera, looking in the viewfinder, seemed satisfied.

'We can start as soon as the light is a bit better. Ready for testing?'

'Ready.'

She picked up the microphone, undid the top two buttons of her blouse, straightened her safari jacket and spoke to camera.

'Have we humans lost the ability to wait? Erasmus says that the ability to wait is what distinguishes us from animals. If we lose that, we lose our humanity and become animals ourselves. Is this what has happened to us? Is this the era of instant gratification? Have we lost the ability to wait, particularly for others? If so, then others no longer have any place, constructive waiting no longer has any place. We have travelled thousands of miles to an Asiatic spice island to visit a tribe that knows all about waiting. They are sitting right behind me now.'

She half-turned and pointed without taking her eyes off the camera. Kurt raised his head from the viewfinder and said, 'Good.'

They stood in silence and gazed at the mountain ridge behind the reservoir, watched the first rays of the sun appear, turned back to camera and microphone. Helen opened her blouse a little more at the neck; Kurt bent forward and squinted through the viewfinder, gave a signal. Helen put on her serious expression for the lens and started again:

'Have we humans lost the ability to wait? Do we live in times of instant gratification so that we no longer have the time to wait, particularly for other people? Damn.'

She stamped her foot. Kurt looked up.

'I had "times" and "time" in the same sentence.'

'And Erasmus got left out.'

'And Erasmus. Damn, damn, damn. It's too early in the morning for me.'

They did two more takes before she was satisfied. Then they moved on to the next shot, where the camera followed her walking down to the tribe by the water's edge.

'Have we in our modern society also lost our rituals? There was a clear trend away from ritual in Western Europe in the Seventies. Everything had to be individual to be genuine. But what are rituals? Rituals are society's way of regulating emotion. Rituals are community, rituals are formalised emotions. Can there be a connection between the two things – between our lack of ability to wait, to wait for others, and the absence of ritual, the absence of an emotional solidarity with others? We think part of the answer is to be found on this island, with this tribe, and in the history of this tribe.'

They had reached the shoreline now. Helen squatted down by a group of people round a fire and lowered her voice. 'This tribe is descended from the original inhabitants of the island. Their religion is animist, which means they believe in the spirits of their ancestors – in trees, in water, in stones – and they believe there is a god who is both the great creator and the great destroyer. They are also determinists. For instance, a baby born with a strawberry mark on its face is sure to be eaten by a crocodile. They tell a tale about a family who moved with their baby to a village where there weren't any crocodiles, in the hope of saving the infant. But it was eaten by a paper crocodile that someone in the playschool had drawn and cut out.'

Kurt swung the camera away from her and round the fire, dwelling on each face in turn; a little child, an old woman, a youth, a man. Helen beckoned to one of the porters, who came running over. Kurt switched off the equipment temporarily.

Helen gave the porter her instructions; 'Tell them I'll ask them two things: what is God? – that's the first, and what is the past? – that's the second. When I speak to them the first time, it will be the first question; when I turn to them the second time, it will be the second question. OK?'

The porter nodded and translated for the people round the fire. They listened in wonder, but gave their agreement. Helen crouched down again and watched for the red light on the camera.

'I asked these simple but happy people the most basic question there is: what is God? This is the answer I got:'

She held the microphone towards the old woman, who said a few words into it. Then she directed it to the young man, who spoke into it a little longer than the old woman. Helen turned the microphone back to herself.

'Then I put another question to these people who live in such harmony with nature: what is the past? A hugely relevant question for people who live a cyclical life. These were their answers.'

She held out the microphone to the little child, who drew back in fear. His father said something to him with a smile and the child spoke into the microphone, just one word. Helen directed the microphone at the father, and he said somewhat more.

'That'll do,' she said to Kurt as she stood up, and he switched off the camera.

Helen turned to the porter. 'What did they reply?'

'That a god is someone who always waits. And that the past is the Great We.'

Helen thanked him, thanked the people round the fire and set off for the dam. Kurt followed.

'When did you stop using an interpreter during takes?'

'It's better without.'

'So it looks as if you understand what they're saying?'

They walked on to the dam. Kurt raised his hand in response when some of the people waved to them.

'God is someone who always waits, and the past is the Great We. Now we're getting somewhere, Kurt. Shall we carry on? You know this documentary might be something no one else gets. I can tell you're annoyed, and we can talk about it, but later, OK?'

'I just have my doubts.'

'We've always worked like this. What's made you start having doubts?'

Kurt didn't reply. He put the camera on his shoulder again and let it roll. Helen picked up the microphone.

'We are the first white people in the world to have been able to share this ritual of a tribe which returns every year to its own past. Our journey has not been without its difficulties and dangers.'

She turned and indicated the tribe behind her.

'For eleven months of the year this tribe lives in the present, an ordinary Asian present of hunting and fishing and birth and death; in the twelfth month they stop time and wind it back. That's when their village rises from the water, like a hand from the realm of the dead, beckoning them. They begin the ritual by gathering for a wake on the shores of the submerged village, behind me here. Every family slaughters a cockerel and smears its blood on their eyelids to protect themselves against evil spirits.'

Down at the shore someone had switched on a transistor radio. Helen gesticulated frantically at the porters and pointed towards the noise, no, no. The porters understood and went over to one of the fires to have a word, and the radio was silenced.

She continued: 'The ritual requires that all the water should have run off the village before the people go back in, otherwise they risk the water spirit getting angry and punishing their houses.'

They switched off microphone and camera and settled down to wait for the water spirit to leave. After almost an hour's silence Kurt turned on the camera and focused on the people at the shore. They had taken up position now, in rows of three and four, with the elders out in front. Some were beating drums, some singing, as the whole group slowly moved off. Helen stepped into the picture with her microphone.

'Now the big moment has arrived.'

She was almost whispering, standing in profile to the camera, her eyes on the scene before her.

'At the head of the procession are the village elders, all men, the bearers of wisdom. Behind them the women, in order of purity, the ones who are menstruating or have been with a man in the last twenty-four hours at the rear, as unclean, while the clean take up a forward position, directly after the male elders.'

She fell silent as the two men at the head of the procession disappeared into the mud on the floor of the reservoir, then went back to the procession and had to take their robes off.

'This ritual is unique to this tribe. Two of the village elders are bathing in the mud that covers everything in their village, and will go back to the others and remove their clothes. This is a symbolic purification; in this way they take upon themselves the time that has elapsed since the previous visit, the time represented by the mud, and return to the tribe and cast it off; in this way they bring past and present together.'

Kurt pulled a face. Helen remained silent while the two naked men made their way back through the procession, which then set off again.

'Once more the tribe approaches its own past. We can just

make out the two naked men, who in a symbolic gesture have not removed the mud from their faces, to show that time is something that exists on the surface of mankind, not inside.'

The procession stopped yet again, and retraced its steps to its starting point. Something was handed back, there was movement in the women's group, then the two naked men were lifted up and borne aloft, with prayer flags fluttering from them in the wind, and they all set off once more.

Helen caught her breath. 'This is the part of the ritual which is hard for us modern people to grasp. The tribe approaches the village time after time; apparently some years it has taken eighteen attempts to go in. The explanation is that the elders listen to the spirits in the buildings and don't enter until the spirits grant permission. And the tribe brings an offering: the women in the procession arouse the naked men sexually, and then they tie the prayer flags round their erections and carry the men aloft into the village, as a fertility prayer for everyone in the houses.'

The procession advanced towards them down an alley, across a little market-place, over to a well. One of the elders climbed up on to the well, and it was clear he was about to address the tribe. Helen ran forward with the microphone. 'Now comes the moment when the leader of the elders will bless the houses. Until then no one may go in. He entreats all who can to have intercourse as soon as they are in their house, to restore life to it. In the course of the next few minutes this tribe will cast off all its sexual inhibitions, just to embrace its own past, but only for this one brief instant.'

The man on the well began to speak; Helen pushed the microphone under his nose and he made a little grimace. She climbed up next to him, nodding her head as he spoke. Kurt stepped nearer and filmed them both in close-up, then he went round the well and filmed them from behind, with the tribe and the village in the background. The man on the well went on speaking at great length and increasing volume.

Helen lost interest and switched off the microphone. Kurt turned off the camera.

'We've got enough of this bit.'

She took out her powder compact and examined her face in the little mirror.

'Kurt, shall we try to film a family going into their house? Give the film a human touch?'

'And film them while they have sex? Uninhibitedly? Mother and father, brother and sister?'

Helen looked a little shamefaced.

'Some exaggeration must be permitted. And it's not un-thinkable . . . They might eat first. Don't you think? What about ourselves? What do we do first when we get to our holiday homes?'

'Have a drink.'

'And then?'

'Have another drink.'

Helen smiled and shook her head. The man on the well came to the end of his speech and she hurried over and took him by the arm.

'May we follow a family into their house?'

He gave her an uncomprehending look. The people round the well began to show signs of moving. Helen called out to them, making signs for them to stay. Then she summoned one of the porters still standing on what had been the shoreline. 'Could you ask this village elder whether we could go with a family into their house?'

The porter translated, got an answer, translated in return.

'Of course. Just choose a family.'

Helen thanked him and went slowly through the crowd, looking at clothes and appearances; she selected one young and one middle-aged woman, the young one dressed in red, with gold embroidery, the older one in black and wearing pearls.

Kurt whispered to the porter, 'Could you hear the speech from where you stood?'

'Most of it.'

'What was it about?'

'Don't slip over on the mud. Remember your children have grown since last year, so mind they don't hit their heads on anything. And distribution of communal tasks.'

Kurt thanked him. Helen motioned him across to the two women, and he took the porter with him.

'Which part of the village has the best light?'

Kurt surveyed the scene. 'Right at this minute, down there.'

He pointed to a house at the end of an alley.

Helen asked through the porter if they could film the two women going into that house.

The porter translated and they looked at him in surprise before replying. Then they went on to say more while he listened and nodded.

'They say they're not from the same family, don't come from the same house.'

'That doesn't matter. They could be.'

Helen started walking towards the house. The porter stopped her to add, 'There's another thing – the older woman says the young one has taken her husband.'

Helen came to an abrupt standstill.

'Fantastic. It couldn't be better.'

She took them with her to the house at the end of the alley as she practised her commentary. 'When this tribe returns every year to its former village, time is rolled back: in the outside world this young woman has become the mistress of this woman's husband, but here they are no longer rivals, here they are like mother and daughter; back here in the village the outside world has not happened.' She directed them when they got to the house; you come in here with the camera and film them as they come, from inside; you two open the door when we call, and they can hold each other and look excited. She made sure the porter had translated: you look excited,

OK? Kurt went into the house ahead of her, measured the light with the door half-open, seemed satisfied, ran his finger over the green algae on the walls and shook his head. Helen came in and glanced about her, went a little way through the hallway and peeked into the rooms. Then she shut the door. In the sudden darkness they could hardly see one another. Kurt went up to her and put his arms round her.

'Is this when we should restore life to the house?' he said.

Helen didn't answer, just looked at him.

He pulled her closer. 'Is this when we should follow the village elder's advice?'

'Kurt.'

It came out as a whisper, midway between a gasp and a sob. He put his hands around her waist, up her back and down again, under her blouse. She closed her eyes. He put one hand on her lower back and one on her stomach, let them glide downwards and meet. She leant towards him, put her arms round his shoulders. He held her for a moment, then took her head in both hands and kissed her.

'Kurt.'

She was crying now. He stroked her hair, adjusted her blouse, smiled.

'Shall we open the door?'

She nodded in the semi-darkness, nodded without taking her eyes off him.

'Or shall we say that we've got enough, and go and film their daily life instead? As a documentary?'

She bit her lip and lowered her eyes.

———

Some hours later Kurt lay with his hands behind his head, gazing at the bamboo ceiling. He was on a wooden bed between a washstand and a bathtub. Rosalind was sitting at the foot of the bed, facing away from him. In front of her on the floor was a half-metre-long bamboo pipe with bowl and mouthpiece of polished ivory. She rolled a little ball against the inside of the bowl, lit a paraffin lamp and held the ball over the flame in a pair of tweezers, turning it carefully. Kurt gently caressed her back. She continued with her task. After a few minutes she put the hot ball in the bowl of the pipe, pricked holes in it with a needle and handed him the pipe. Kurt turned on his side and took a deep drag. Rosalind bent over him and stroked him on the cheek.

'Are you sure your parents aren't coming?'

He lay on the bed and closed his eyes. He was actually no longer bothered about her parents. They were only the uppermost layer of something, something that was on the point of vanishing. Rosalind stroked his neck, his lips; he raised himself a little to take another drag and sank down again. Her hands found his, linked fingers, she kissed him. She picked up the pipe and put the mouthpiece between his lips and he inhaled deeply. She had told him that a skilled opium smoker could empty a pipe in one drag, but he didn't want that, didn't want to be skilled. He reached out a hand and undid her blouse, let his fingers run over her breasts, closed his eyes, slid into the first ten minutes of the endless sleep that opium gives, as clear as crystal.

'Why are you copying my videotapes?'

He took another puff. 'Why are you copying my video-tapes?' Another puff. How many hours between each? Or days? Rosalind bent over him again and put her lips to his cheek. She drew her fingers through his hair and massaged his scalp.

Try not to get worried, try not to turn on to
Problems that upset you (oh)

Kurt gave a sigh of relief, as if a further layer of what was on the point of vanishing had gone.

Don't you know everything's alright
Yes, everything's fine

Was that two more hands stroking him now? Was that her sister? Rosanna? Did it matter? No matter. No matter. Hands were stroking him.

Close your eyes, close your eyes
And think of nothing tonight

Two hands, three hands, four hands, five hands?

Close your eyes, close your eyes
And relax, think of nothing tonight

He reached out in the light darkness or dark light and found a hand, another layer in what was on the point of vanishing.

'Was that how we filmed the village?'

'That was how we did it,' a voice whispered in his ear.

'That was how we did it,' a second voice whispered in his other ear.

'Another pipe?' Both voices? He nodded.

Close your eyes, close your eyes
And relax, think of nothing tonight

He felt around until he found cotton with warm skin beneath, ruffled the material gently, played with it. *Was that how we filmed the village?*

That was how you did it. That was how you did it!

Gentle breath in his ear. *That was how you did it.* Faint peppermint. Very faint.

'Why are you copying my videotapes?'

Someone put the pipe between his lips, she, or she, her, her, he took a long, deep drag, *why are you copying my videotapes*, another drag, and in the crystal-clear peace of the opium intoxication he suddenly saw the answer: he suddenly saw Christian congregations sitting watching copies of his videotapes; he was gliding over the water from island to island and saw them cross themselves at the sight of blood, saw them put their hands to their mouths at the sight of fire – look, look at that throat – and the women in the congregation pressed handkerchiefs to their eyes; a voice whispered *try not to get worried, try not to turn on to problems that upset you (oh),* and a woman in one of the congregations whispered what was that lace design she had on her blouse, right under the wound, was it Melanesian, *everything's alright, yes, everything's fine,* and hands lifted his legs up and his arms away from his body, *close your eyes, close your eyes and relax, think of nothing tonight.* He woke up, midway between one sleep and the next, midway between two sisters, and said it would be a weird reality if my videotapes were used to stir up Christians elsewhere, and he felt for the pipe and took another drag, when they were intended to bring reinforcements to calm thing down, calm things down, and two voices were whispering, like an echo of each other, wouldn't it be, wouldn't it be, a weird reality, that's how it is with the reality we have inside us, it is weird, like an Asian woman, or two, still crouching and making opium pipes for a European man, well into the twenty-first century, or two Asian women singing to him as he vanishes, or you filming the village the way you wanted to film it, not the way she wanted to; we are the reality we have inside us, aren't we, weird reality, *close your eyes, close your eyes and relax, think of nothing tonight.*

Rosalind closed his eyes with her thumb and forefinger and gently stroked his cheek. 'We shall subjugate you,' she whispered, and held his hand. 'We shall subjugate you; you can't just come here, and from the wrong Flemish region to boot.' Another pair of hands stroked his hair and whispered, 'We shall master you, we shall master you, we are two sides of the same thing, two *modi*, we shall enter into you from two directions; you have already been seduced by one of us, the other is waiting, is ready, we shall each make love to you and say you have to choose, the very compulsion neurosis of European culture, choice, we shall make love to you together and say that you can have us both, have us both, but only with opium, only in opium.' Kurt opened his eyes and nodded, in agreement, in the crystal-clear peace of opium intoxication; he mumbled, choose the one, you'll regret it, choose the other, you'll regret it, choose the one or the other, you'll regret both, whether you choose the one or the other you will regret both; laugh at the folly of the world, you will regret it, cry at the folly of the world, you will regret it, laugh at the folly of the world or cry over it, you will regret both, whether you laugh at the folly of the world or cry over it you will regret both, and naked flesh caressed his lips, first from one side, then the other.

Poor Kurt. Everything would be forgotten the next morning, but in one place or another, deep inside his mind, a seed would have been sown.

9

STORM

The drums started up early in the morning. Single beats and then silence, more single beats followed by more silence. Faces appeared at doors and windows, faces gazing out at forest and mountain, uncertain faces. Until the drums started beating the morning had been like any other: pale, quiet, slow. Here and there a cockerel, here and there a dog, here and there an outboard motor, and then, suddenly, drums. Now it sounded like a dialogue: one drum would beat two long, two short, two long; some while later a distant drum answered with two long, two short, two long. Half an hour would pass, and then the same rhythm would sound from yet another location. People began to come out of their houses now, conversing in low voices, looking up at the mountains. A man yelled out as he stared at a point on a mountain from which drumbeats emanated; he shook with fear and said he could see the shadows of the drumbeats. Shadows of drumbeats? Everyone laughed, his family felt ashamed. Shadows of drumbeats? The man dropped to his knees in prayer. Shadows of drumbeats, dark, deep shadows of drumbeats, and a movement in the shadows?

The drumbeats multiplied as the morning advanced to noon and the sun climbed in the sky. It was easier now not to hear them, it was easier now to hide behind the barrier of daily life, the noise of scooters and motorcycles, building work and cranes and people. From time to time someone would stop and listen, others would exchange nervous glances, but for most of them the drums registered as a mere flicker of expression. Apart from one place, one street: the street with the house where the twin sisters lived. In that street the drums brought all activity to a halt, as if the whole street were holding its breath while it waited for the next beats, knowing they were coming nearer all the time, nearer and nearer, with relentless inevitability.

The young European woman looked at the young European man with the TV camera. He was facing her and their eyes met. She went over to him to say hello. Her name was drowned out by the drums.

'Hi. I'm Kurt.'

They shook hands.

Pointing at him and then at herself, she said, 'People here are a bit chary of the natural kinship that Europeans feel for other Europeans, but they can't have everything their own way. What tribe do you belong to?'

'Danish. Danish-Danish. Plus a bit further south. D–Danish.'

He stammered and shook his head ruefully. The woman laughed.

'Do I get the slight impression that you're a TV cameraman?'

Kurt smiled. 'Documentaries. Scandinavian. And you?'

'Portuguese.'

'Amazing. We were shipwrecked with a Portuguese.'

'Shipwrecked?'

'The ferry sank on the way here. We got ashore on a life-raft with a Portuguese guy.'

The woman looked momentarily disconcerted, but brushed it aside, 'Well, Portugal made quite deep inroads into these islands some centuries ago.'

Why did neither of them see the connection? For Kurt it wasn't unusual to meet young Europeans travelling, he hadn't caught the girl's name, and he couldn't know that there was only one other European on the island when they arrived. It was different for Anya: she had never thought of her father as anything but Italian, so she wasn't alarmed to hear of a Portuguese on a life-raft. And naturally enough she was more interested in the shipwreck itself than who the others on the life-raft were. But even if they had both realised the connection it would not have changed the course of events. The Asians in the vicinity did not appear to be taking any notice of them, and they went and sat down on a bench against the wall of a nearby house. Kurt proffered a pack of cigarettes. Anya checked the brand, thanked him and took one. He lit it for her and lit one for himself. A young man in a red headband and warpaint gave them a quick glance from the washstand.

'What are you doing here?' asked Kurt without looking at her.

'Travelling,' she replied, without looking at him. 'I had almost got all the way round the world when I fetched up with the chap over there.' She nodded towards the washstand. 'What about you? I got the impression there might be something between you and one of the twin sisters?'

'Yes. I think we're a couple.'

They went on smoking in silence. More young people had arrived, the yard in front of the house was almost full now. They were wandering in and out of the house, and it was obvious that the parents must be at work. Anya stubbed out her cigarette.

'Does that worry you?'

'Getting together with someone from here?'

'Yes.'

'I have trouble envisaging any future in it. But I'm enjoying it while it lasts.'

Anya leant back and closed her eyes.

'Same here.'

Rosanna climbed up on a wall with a megaphone, tested it, adjusted the volume. She shouted out a slogan and got an answering cry: young people shouted the slogan back at her amidst smiles and laughter. From further down the street another loudspeaker voice could be heard, and another one from higher up.

Anya spoke without moving, without opening her eyes. 'I don't like the look of this. They say it's only meant to intimidate, but I'm worried that things could get out of hand. How much do you know about it?'

'Only that there's going to be a demonstration. Rosalind has asked me to film it. Tell me what you know.'

'Have you seen the commercial centre down by the harbour, the brown brick building? It's enormous, it extends two hundred metres in both directions, and it's entirely Muslim. All the shops fronting the street are Muslim, and all the ones inside are Muslim, all the stalls in the covered market inside the buildings are Muslim. I'm no good with figures, but I reckon there must be several hundred shops and stalls in that building. Meseo says the idea of the demo is a show of power, to prove that the Christians can be united if they want to. He says it's important to get that message over to Muslim traders in particular, because they have both influence and power. If anyone can control the masses, it's them. But I'm afraid – the atmosphere is so electric, I don't think it would take much to spark off a riot.'

She paused before continuing, still with her eyes closed. 'Gandhi had a very apt comment on the law of an eye for an eye, a tooth for a tooth – if you adhere to that, you end up with a world which is blind.'

Kurt looked at her in astonishment. In that instant he realised who she was; he had heard her father say exactly the same thing on the hotel balcony only a few nights before. He started to speak, but was interrupted by the young man at the washstand. Anya stood up and went over to him. Kurt tried to follow, but Rosalind put her hand on his shoulder and stopped him. She whispered in his ear, 'Be careful not to film people without kerchiefs covering their nose and mouth and their clothing inside out. Otherwise you'll make yourself very unpopular.'

'How on earth will I be able to manage that?' said Kurt, his eyes still fixed on Anya.

'Keep well to the front. They'll all be masked. Further back there'll be the supporters. Like the girl you were just talking to.'

Rosalind turned his head to face her and held him at arm's length as she spoke. Rosanna was on the wall again with the megaphone, shouting out a slogan, the crowd responding. They were raising clenched fists in the air now as they shouted, their responses whipped up like a storm raging across the skies. Kurt put the camera on his shoulder and began filming. Anya returned and stood by his side.

'Can you understand what she's saying?' he asked, having to raise his voice.

Anya came closer, and he breathed in her cool skin and brown hair. Rosanna was shouting again, the crowd responded, she shouted something back.

'St Luke's Gospel. In Gethsemane. Jesus knows the soldiers are on their way to arrest him, and asks his disciples *how many swords do we have?* They answer *two*, and he replies *it is enough.*'

Rosanna was chanting repeatedly *how many swords do we have?* The crowd roared *two*, and she responded *it is enough*, raising and lowering her arms as she danced in time to the rhythmic chant, *two swords are enough.*

'Why is that so significant?'

Anya yelled into his ear, 'Because Jesus was on the point of wrecking the whole Christian message of love. When he was preparing his disciples for his arrest, he said that those who had no swords should sell their garments and buy one. You don't say that to people when you want them to turn the other cheek. That's when they say, "Lord, behold, here are two swords," and he answers, "It is enough".'

She gave his shoulder a squeeze and ran off into the crowd. Kurt yelled after her, *wait, I've got something to tell you*. Rosanna was dancing, the crowd was dancing, their voices rising to the heavens. *Wait, I've got something to tell you*. Bright flashes now in the hubbub. *Those who have no swords should sell their garments and buy one. Lord, behold, here are two swords. It is enough, it is enough, it is enough*. Rosanna loosened her cloak and swirled it around her, the crown roared, she swayed her hips and danced, raised her arms, small pearls of sweat in her armpits, small pearls of sweat on her upper arms. Rosalind jumped up on the wall and danced with her, she too with her cloak open, and the shouts from the crowd became ever more frequent; people were loosening their clothes and dancing with each other.

The two sisters turned to Kurt. 'Come on, come and see what's the other side of the wall.'

Kurt kept the camera running as he followed them, pushing the thought of Anya out of his mind; there's a time to film and a time to talk, and now is the time to film. The sound of singing was coming from further down the street, from many voices, a steady rhythmic clapping, with the drums like a deep, threatening pulse. He hurried into the street to look: a hundred metres away was a great throng of people with banners and red headbands, marching towards him shouting and singing. He filmed as they approached. All those at the front and as far back as he could see had kerchiefs over their noses and mouths and clothes inside out. He stood among them and went on filming, the demonstrators flowing round him on both sides. He filmed until he caught sight of a face without a kerchief, switched off the camera, waved at the face and the face smiled.

Rosanna was declaiming into the megaphone as the procession went by. The young people in the yard thundered a response, raised white banners bearing a text in red and leapt over the wall to join the demonstrators in the street. Kurt filmed them from behind as they raised clenched fists and added their voices to the singing and chanting of the marchers ahead of them. Anya was there, towards the rear. She covered her face as she passed the camera.

It was a beautiful day, with clear skies, which made the procession look harmless, almost unreal, made it impossible to imagine that force could encounter force on such a beautiful day. The crowd continued up the street, and from one courtyard after another a new procession emerged to swell the numbers, and around them all the noise of the drums grew louder and louder, faster and more aggressive. Kurt ran on in front, filming. There must have been over a thousand now, and it showed in their demeanour: they were marching with the confidence of demonstrators who know they are a force to be reckoned with.

———————

The colonel received his first telephone call only minutes after the march had set off. He listened, took out a map, marked a point just outside the town, wrote '1000+' by it and put down the receiver. Ten minutes later he had another call. He listened, took out the map, marked a new place, closer in, wrote '2000+' by it and hung up.

'If people keep joining at this rate, there'll be five thousand by the time they get here. And they'll be here in half an hour.'

He pressed a button. An officer appeared at the door.

'Give orders for all our machine-gun posts around the commercial centre to be pulled back. The same goes for roadblocks and checkpoints. Don't let there be a military uniform in sight. Tell the troops they've got twenty minutes. And put them all on full alert. Twenty minutes.'

The officer nodded and left. Nothing in his face gave any indication of whether he understood or approved of the order. The colonel's reasoning was clear: the sight of military positions might provoke the demonstrators and cause unnecessary violence. He picked up the telephone and dialled a number.

'How are you, Captain?'

'Fine, thanks. And you, Colonel?'

'Fine, thanks. And your family, Captain?'

'Fine, thanks, And yours?'

'Fine, as far as I'm aware. You know, of course, Captain, that there's a Christian demonstration on its way to the commercial centre?'

'Of course. You'll have calculated, Colonel, that they'll be there in about half an hour?'

'Something like that. And how many do you reckon there'll be, Captain?'

'Probably the same as you, Colonel. Five thousand?'

'Something like that. It's a huge crowd. How are the police intending to deal with it?'

'We'll play a waiting game. Our task is to ensure law and order. The marchers have assured us they'll behave peacefully. We trust them. So we have to hope no one provokes them.'

'How, for example?'

'By threatening them, for example. Or humiliating them. Or, in the worst case scenario, attacking them.'

'What will the police do then?'

'Defend them. It's our duty. And we've got enough fronts on this island, haven't we?'

The colonel smiled at the covert threat, then concluded the deal: 'We're pulling back so as not to be provocative. But we're on full alert. In case the situation should get out of police control.'

On the other end of the line the police captain smiled at the counter-threat. They bade one another a good day and rang off.

The colonel went over and sat at the window and gazed at the sky. 'From up there you get an overview of history. From up there it's clear whether a tactical withdrawal is a good move or madness. Down here we can't see that, not yet. Down here we see only the honour of the armed forces.'

———————

Did the demonstration stop and hesitate for a moment when it swung into the main street and saw the commercial centre two hundred metres ahead of it? Did the drums let up momentarily?

There was talk afterwards of people hearing the sounds of teams of oxen, of weapons, of swords being drawn, of bugles and heavy drums. None of that is correct – but it could have been the expression of the demonstrators' sense of participation in a historic event.

It was true that the procession came to a temporary halt, or at least slowed down, when the foremost marchers first caught sight of the commercial centre. All those in the front line were wearing long dark cloaks; as if on command they linked arms to hold the procession back, exchanging glances, twelve across, long cloaks and red headbands; as if on command they loosened their cloaks and brought out spears, black, shiny metal spears. Rosalind and her sister were in the middle of this first line, long cloaks, red headbands and black spears; if the colonel had seen them then, he would have realised that it had been a mistake to pull back his troops, but he didn't see them – his face was no more than a vague shadow at a window many blocks away, one of many, many faces at many, many windows, and the young people in the front line called out an order and headed for the commercial centre; if it had been uncertainty that had made them hesitate, or the wish to savour the feeling of having five thousand supporters behind them, it was over now. Twelve young people in long cloaks and red headbands brandished their black spears and cried *the power of the cross*, the marchers behind them responded with *the power of the cross*, and suddenly the drums were back, the roar of the crowd and the beat of the drums rolled down the street and reached the commercial centre, where shutters were hastily closed and steel grilles slammed shut, *the power of the cross*, and now the procession had reached the centre, the silent, sealed centre where not a shop was open and not a face to be seen, but the demonstrators knew that it was full of Muslims inside, behind the façade. The leaders in their black cloaks marched more slowly now, linking arms again and walking in step; behind them ten thousand feet found the rhythm, the drums found the rhythm and intensified it, and that would be the noise the Muslims inside came to associate with the attack, more strongly than the sounds which followed. In a café behind the shops a council of elders held a meeting, proud, smart businessmen, who needed only a few minutes to agree that orders must still remain the same: no provocations, no attacks. They looked up when they heard the noise, ten thousand feet marching in step to the accompaniment of strident, ominous drums, no provocations, no attacks, for a moment they seemed to waver, then they found support in one another and went back to their respective parts of the centre, no provocations, no attacks; the noise of the demonstrators thundered down one side of the centre and along the next, no provocations, no attacks, inside the centre everyone held their breath, standing still and listening to the drums and the slow rhythmic tramp of ten thousand feet, up two blocks, along two; now the demonstration had circled the whole centre, they could let it go at that, no one was in any doubt about their message, and the Muslims inside had listened, but the five thousand Christian demonstrators were too fired up now, they were carried away on a tide of adrenalin; the twelve leaders in their long cloaks set off on a new circuit without stopping, turned and signalled a new slogan: *God is ours, we are His*, the marchers behind them responded with *God is ours, we are His*, the roar rolled along the little alleys into the centre and the market, *God is ours, we are His*, and now the countenances of the Muslims took on a dangerous expression, no provocations, no attacks, whatever happens, whatever happens?

It only took one, a single one who couldn't contain himself, or perhaps it was a Christian demonstrator who was sent down an alleyway as an agent provocateur, but either way the cry was exquisitely timed; if the demonstrators had not been marching in step it would have been inaudible, but it came exactly between two beats, and since it was bellowed through a megaphone, everyone could hear it, *Mary was a whore*, and the procession of five thousand people erupted.

There was also some dispute afterwards about what happened next. The marchers streamed in two directions, howling with fury, along both sides of the commercial centre. They thronged into the alleys that led into the centre, four on each side, eight in all, and paused and waited – for a signal? Was it carefully planned or spontaneous? There were roughly equal numbers of demonstrators pushing into each alley. Was that coincidence? And what about the eight entrances to the centre on the sides where there were no demonstrators, why weren't they included?

There was also much dispute about the subsequent sequence of events – the church bells started ringing, first from a church nearby, then from one further away, then another, then another. Was that also a coincidence? Would they normally have rung just then? Or was it a signal, and in which case, for what? An attempt to calm the demonstrators, to call for peace? Or a signal to storm the centre?

It was the latter. Rosalind pulled out a mobile phone and tapped a number. She was standing at the entrance to one of the alleys with her arm propped against the wall as a barrier. The crowd behind her were chanting and yelling, but stayed back. She got an answer, but couldn't hear it over the uproar. She tried to quieten them a little, listened to her mobile again and looked up over the rooftops on the other side of the street towards the sound of the bells – she then lowered her arm and let the avalanche roll.

It might have seemed a small episode in the context, but for one person it was big, ultimately almost too big. Kurt was filming the demonstrators surging into the alley, but he filmed these few seconds without looking through the viewfinder; his face turned away from the camera towards the young woman in the long cloak and red headband with the black spear at the head of her troops, the woman he had spent long, soft hours exploring the taste and smell of, but never this, never this.

The shouts of the demonstrators echoed off the walls of the alley. The noise was heard and understood by the demonstrators waiting in the other seven alleyways and they stormed the centre instantly, simultaneously. Running feet, running feet, the sound of thousands of running feet, and over it the sound of breath, gasping breath, and over that the sound of cries, the cries of the species, which distinguish humankind from all other species when they attack, human cries of joy, of excitement, of ecstasy, the sound poured into the centre and met other sounds, voices praying, voices imploring, voices weeping in fear, the screams of attack flooded forward, overwhelmed the voices, brought in their wake the sound of blows, the sound of steel, of pain, the sound of breaking, splintering, tearing, the sound of feet kicking and stamping on shops and stalls, and the wave of sound swept through the centre and out the other side, a wave that contained all the sounds of primeval man: the sound of anger and the sound of fear, the sound of victory and the sound of defeat, the sound of violence, which goes on and on and on.

———————

In the window a few blocks away the colonel pressed the bell. The officer came in before it stopped ringing. He must have been standing at the window right outside the door. The colonel gave him a brief order, emphasising the key points on his fingers, one by one; the officer nodded and left. Then the colonel picked up the telephone and dialled a number.

'Shall we assume that both we, ourselves and our families are still well?'

'Certainly. If you're pushed for time, Colonel.'

'More so than when we last spoke. My men have now been given orders to move back in towards the commercial centre. Their instructions are to advance slowly and rev the engines of their tanks. They'll be there in ten minutes. The helicopter will come in and hover overhead at the same time. That should provide plenty of noise. And I'm sure you don't think, Captain, that empty vessels make the most noise?'

'Of course not. Perhaps the demonstrators would withdraw from the centre if they knew.'

'Or could be persuaded to?'

'Exactly.'

'Do you know of anyone they might listen to, Captain?'

'It would have to be someone representing law and order.'

'They would have our full support. We're here to keep the factions apart. We haven't succeeded this time, which is why we're moving in now. But we have no wish to engage in battle with anyone, not with anyone at all.'

The colonel uttered these last words emphatically.

'Understood. Ten minutes.'

'Nine. And remember – my men are coming from the south and the west.'

He put down the phone and turned back to the window again, muttering slowly to himself, 'It is said dictatorships breed nihilism. All values disintegrate and disappear, leaving only religion, the last chance to save yourself as a human being. We've had a dictatorship in this country for thirty years now, and a huge increase in religiosity. What irony. Dictatorship prolonged by believers.'

He looked towards the commercial centre. All the demonstrators had vanished inside. He could just make out the female European reporter at one of the entrances. She was sitting on the pavement with her back to the wall in the empty street. It almost looked as if she were crying.

The colonel waited. No sign of any armed police in the streets on the two sides he could see.

'They must be going in from the north and east. Can they be intending to drive the demonstrators out on this side, right into the arms of my men? Are they deliberately trying to provoke battle?'

He was about to pick up the phone when the scene changed. In the main street behind the centre young people with white placards were appearing, a few to start with, then hordes of them. They were running, away from the commercial centre, away from the city centre.

'So the police must have brought them out. And if they managed, was it the police who sent them in in the first place?'

The first question was easy to answer. The demonstrators scattered when the police arrived with piercing whistles in all the alleys on the north and east sides. The second was more of a rhetorical question. But it didn't go unnoticed among Muslims that the demonstrators ran towards the alleys where the police were.

The sound of sirens filled the air as the fire engines approached. Thick black smoke rose from the commercial centre.

————————

In the next few days large numbers of people in the city abandoned their homes and took flight. Many headed for the mosque compound and the feeling of security afforded by holy ground; others made their way to the harbour and the hope of escaping on a ship. Most fled the way people usually flee in a war zone, on impulse, terrified by rumours. And the fear was contagious: with every family that left, those who remained felt even more vulnerable. Most belonged to clans, and any rumour that the leaders or families from the upper echelons of the clan had left made hundreds of the rank and file rush to do likewise. Few made it very far.

10

NIGHTLIGHTS

D uring the night the jetty filled with people. The night-watch woke the first mate, who went up on to the bridge to check and then told the watch to wake the captain. The first mate was peering through his night glasses when the captain arrived. He handed them over and the captain put them to his eyes and scanned the jetty.

'How many do you think there are?'

'I've done a rough count of the fires, and make it just over a hundred, and it looks like about ten people round each, so there could be more than a thousand.'

They were speaking English to each other, but English obviously wasn't their mother tongue. The first mate sounded Flemish – Dutch or Belgian – and the captain could have been Scandinavian.

'There are army guard-posts over there. Haven't they tried to stop them?' the captain asked.

'Not as far as I could see.'

'And the police?'

'No sign of them.'

The captain took out a packet of cigarettes, offered them to the first mate and the watch, and lit one himself. He leant his elbows on the rail of the bridge and blew smoke towards the jetty, a hundred fires with a thousand people round them wrapped in blankets and veils, cardboard boxes tied with string, bundles on sticks, sleeping children nestled in their parents' arms, babies crying in baskets. Food was being cooked on the fires, and tea being brewed. The captain breathed in the smell and stared at the town beyond the jetty. All was quiet there.

'I don't like it. I have a feeling they'll try to board the ship. A thousand refugees. There's no way we're going to leave with them on board. We'd never get rid of them. There isn't a country on the globe that would let us into port.'

The captain seemed to be talking mainly to himself. The first mate didn't comment.

'Captain?' called the watch from the other side of the bridge. They went over to him. He pointed. Alongside the rusty cargo ship at the other jetty, fifty metres away, the sea was full of small boats: flat-bottomed long narrow boats with outboard motors. All were packed solid with people, just like the jetty. The captain swore and turned to the first mate: 'Wake as many of the crew as we need to prepare to sail, but no noise. Cover portholes and windows with black plastic before any lights go on. Don't use torches on deck – the moon should be enough to work by. Tell the crew to keep below the tops of the rails. Have we finished taking on water and fuel?'

The first mate nodded.

'Is everyone on board?'

'Some of the men are ashore getting a taste of local life, but only a few.'

'That's just too bad. They may as well stay in the beds they're in and carry on tasting. We'll sail at first light, without warning.'

The first mate and night-watch divided up the cabins between them, going from door to door, knocking, opening, whispering. In the course of the next half-hour the crew assembled in the galley, which was windowless. The first mate fetched the captain, who addressed them in muted tones. They nodded, murmured, understood; the majority of them were East Europeans, used to taking orders without asking questions.

They spread through the ship, silently and stealthily. Jobs

were allocated, windows blacked out, hawsers loosened, engines checked; the instrument panel was read by torchlight. From the jetty the ship still appeared to be asleep, as if it had all the time in the world to wake up and stretch in the new dawn. Nevertheless something must have transmitted itself to the people round the fires and in the boats; several kept glancing up at the ship as if alerted by a sound or a movement. Four men carrying a large bundle between them made their way slowly along the jetty towards the ship, passing from fire to fire, edging a metre closer, then sitting down, advancing a metre at a time. At the far jetty one of the motor boats started up, then a second; the engines roared, the drivers called to each other, and under cover of the noise three men paddled towards the opposite side of the cruise ship, with a dark heap in the bottom of their boat.

On the island a cock crowed, then another, the starry sky lightened, the mountains revealed themselves in outline. The captain went up on the bridge, feeling his way over to the loudspeaker apparatus and fumbling for the microphone button. Two pairs of sailors crawled across to the forward and aft hawsers, with instructions to abandon the hawsers if they couldn't pull them in.

A third cock crowed, the sun began to rise over the mountain, the captain switched on the loudspeaker and gave the order to cast off, the engines started with a jolt, lights came on over the entire ship, the sailors stood up normally above the rails and got the hawsers off at the second attempt. As they were hauling them in they heard three sharp thuds against the side of the ship: four men had attached battery-driven electro-magnets to the side of the ship and were rolling out a climbing net to the jetty, thirty metres long. The people round the fires were on their feet, picking up their belongings, taking their children in their arms, and some were already running towards the ship. From the other side there came two similar thuds and the captain leant over to look down: three men in a decrepit boat had fixed a climbing net there too, and a fleet of small boats with sputtering outboard motors was already on its way across from the far jetty.

The captain yelled out, in anger, in distress. As he watched, the net from the quayside was filling with clambering refugees; he tried to count them, got to a hundred, rushed to the other side, where at least twenty boats had already arrived, and refugees with bundles and boxes and children were climbing the net; he ran back to check the refugees swarming up from the quay, and back again to the opposite side where in those few moments the number of boats had already doubled.

The mate came up on to the bridge to report that the nets were attached too low down for the refugees to reach the rail; a rough count suggested there were a couple of hundred on each side. The captain thanked him and told him to wake the orchestra. The mate obeyed, without asking questions. The captain explained to the helmsman how he wanted the ship manoeuvred: full ahead, hard over, full astern, hard over to the other side. The helmsman nodded, understood, the captain wanted the ship turned round in the harbour between the two jetties, ready to sail straight out. Full ahead, hard over, full astern, hard over to the other side, full ahead, hard over, full astern, hard over to the other side: the refugees on the jetty dropped the net amidst screams, the refugees already on the net smashed against the side of the ship. On the opposite side the small boats screeched away in a maelstrom of froth, full ahead, hard over, full astern, hard over to the other side, and the mate reported over the walkie-talkie that the orchestra was ready on the aft deck.

'Ravel's *Bolero*,' the captain ordered. The mate passed on the instruction to the orchestra, who looked at him in disbelief.

'Ravel? *Bolero*?' With a piano and two strings?'

The first mate nodded, 'At five o'clock in the morning.'

The captain was standing with the helmsman on the bridge, full ahead, hard over, full astern, hard over to the other side;

the ship was turned more than halfway now, its bows facing the other jetty, pointing just past the rusting hulk; another two or three manoeuvres and they'd be able to sail straight out. The captain took the helmsman by the shoulder and pulled him away from the wheel, taking over himself.

'You're excused this manoeuvre.'

Then he steered the ship forward in a broad arc towards the cargo ship at the far jetty. From the aft deck came the sound of the orchestra, increasing in volume, a crescendo to accompany engine roar and refugee screams, and he steered towards the cargo ship, hard over, first one side, then the other. The refugees clinging to the net on the starboard side shrieked in terror when they saw the rusty cargo ship suddenly looming up ahead of them. The captain put the wheel hard over again and ran the ship along the cargo boat with only centimetres' clearance. The refugees on the net wept, prayed, yelled; some vomited, others tried vainly to turn away from the side of the cargo ship that was scraping them off, scraping the magnets and the nets off the whole length of the ship with the refugees, their bundles, their boxes and their children too. Ravel's *Bolero* was so loud now that it could be heard above the screams and the desperate tumult in the water.

The captain shouted at the helmsman, 'Check whether they're all off!'

The helmsman reported back, 'All clear.'

He had turned pale. The music from the aft deck was becoming more insistent with every note, the pianist was pounding the keys, lights were coming on in cabin after cabin, frightened faces peeking out to see what was happening. Those on the starboard side saw only the end of the other jetty and open blue sea; those on the port side could not see the refugees on the net below them, they saw only a jetty full of people and a chaos of small boats around the cruise ship. But they could all hear the music.

The captain had turned the ship and was steering straight

towards the end of the first jetty, which ended in a fifteen-metre-high lighthouse rising from the water on an extension of the jetty. He was muttering as he steered and the helmsman stood beside him, mesmerised. There were shrieks from the refugees on the net on the port side; they couldn't have seen what had happened to those on the starboard side, but they must have heard the screams and the crunch of ship against ship, bodies against metal. And now they could see the net full of the dead and dying astern, and flailing figures in the water gasping for air. They stared in silence and wide-eyed horror at their ineluctable convergence with the lighthouse. The ship was gaining speed, and above and behind them an orchestra was playing, the same music over and over again, louder and louder each time.

'Go down and tell them we're sending a peacekeeping force,' said the captain, still looking straight ahead, his eyes not wavering from the lighthouse. The helmsman saluted as he went: a military element had entered the scene.

The first refugees started jumping when the ship was more than ten metres away from the lighthouse. They looked at the helmsman shouting, *we'll be sending a peacekeeping force*, they looked at the massive concrete lighthouse hurtling towards them, they looked at one another and they jumped. First they threw their bundles and boxes tied with string, then they threw themselves, some with children in their arms, some holding each other's hands. Those nearest the bows jumped first, those who would have been the first to be crushed, to be scraped off the ship's side, followed by those next in line, as if the reaction were contagious, or as if the first ones had taken a decision on behalf of all of them. They dropped down the side of the ship, down into the seething, foaming water between ship and jetty and lighthouse, and were immediately sucked in by the maelstrom and disappeared. Those watching on the jetty wailed, ran to the quayside to look over, saw people being spun round and sucked under in the swirl of the multiton steel propeller. It might have been their parents they saw, or their sons, daughters, relatives; an unnatural silence descended on the jetty, people were on their knees staring into the water, the noise of the ship's engines receding further and further into the distance. Only the music from the aft deck still hung in the air, like a climax slowly diminishing.

The helmsman reappeared on the bridge.

'Did they all jump?'

'Yes, every single one.'

'That's what I was counting on.'

The captain handed the wheel back, indicated the course and switched on the public address system.

'This is your captain speaking. We apologise for waking you so suddenly and so early, but a little crisis arose that we had to manoeuvre ourselves out of. Everything is under control again now; I repeat, everything is under control. The ship was attacked by terrorists, but we have managed to evade them, thanks to the heroic efforts of the crew. Not a single terrorist succeeded in getting aboard, so I repeat, everything is under control, there is no danger; you can come out of your cabins whenever you like. Breakfast will be served as usual in the dining room from nine o'clock; for those of you who require something before then, there will be coffee, tea and rolls available. And I would like to take the opportunity to thank the ship's musicians, who kept up the morale of the crew in our hour of need.'

Applause could be heard rising from inside the ship as the cruise passengers opened their cabin doors, and the captain straightened his uniform and smiled. For the passengers, seeing one another in dressing gowns and slippers in the corridors for the first time broke the ice, as did the fact that they had all been in mortal danger and been saved. It brought them together, and they stood talking as they applauded: what a fantastic captain, what a fantastic crew, what a fantastic shipping line! A man in a burgundy silk dressing-gown was the first to get his video camera; two more followed his example, then more, and soon there was a trail of men in flapping dressing-gowns with video cameras making their way up on deck, all intent on filming the attack while it was still fresh, while it was still dangerous. They filmed the climbing net that the crew had pulled up with boat-hooks – this was the net the terrorists used for boarding us, it must have been planned long ago, one of the crew says the net is Iraqi. They filmed the two jetties and the island receding – look carefully and you can just make out some of the terrorists swimming there, defeated – and they persuaded the orchestra to carry on playing while they filmed the ship and the horizon – here you see the orchestra, a trio of brave men who kept everyone calm during the attack and did their bit for humanity, three brave men who proved that in the midst of chaos we represent civilisation, and won't let ourselves be oppressed by evil. And the men in dressing-gowns clambered laboriously up the steps to the bridge and took turns filming one another with the captain, their arms round his shoulders and an uninterrupted, unfathomable sea behind them; an uninterrupted, unfathomable sea that suddenly struck and so quickly that many didn't even realise: it lifted the ship up for an instant and swung it through forty-five degrees before setting it down again. On the bridge the helmsman went white, and the captain's smile froze on his face for the video cameras.

———

The same high room, the same silhouette of the colonel, the same leather chairs, the same glass table, the same portrait of the President on the wall.

'How are you, Captain?'

'Fine, thanks. And you, Colonel?'

'Fine, thanks. And your family?'

'Fine, thanks. And your family, Colonel?'

'Fine, as far as I'm aware.'

They smiled quietly at the ritual, as if it gratified them. The colonel rang the bell, the same soldier appeared, took the same order. Neither of them said anything else until their tea was on the table and the soldier had gone.

'You sent for me, Colonel?'

'Yes,' the colonel replied. 'My men have arrested a European. An Italian. He was in an area where he shouldn't have been. Since the army doesn't have police powers on the island, we'll have to hand him over to you.'

'The book restorer? How long have you been holding him?'

'One night. Well within the limits.'

'The police can start again on the forty-eight hours the law allows, but we can't detain him longer than that.'

'But if you charge him?'

'For what? We'd never get a judge to put a European in custody for having been in an unauthorised area. Everyone knows that Europeans have no sense of direction, they wander all over the place.'

'But if you charge him with sedition?'

The police captain fell silent, stared at the colonel, took a sip of tea, put the glass down slowly, as if playing for time.

'Can you be more precise?'

'The man has a daughter, a backpacker.' The colonel pronounced the English word as if it left a nasty taste in his mouth. 'She's in a relationship with one of the leaders of the Christian militia. We thought her father might be a good card to play. And we thought you, Captain, would have no objection to having this European in custody.'

'None at all.'

The two men exchanged glances.

'It goes without saying that we need this European? That it's important nothing happens to him?'

'Certainly. You said yourself, Colonel, that you hoped the

words "excellent cooperation" could apply to the whole of your time on this island.'

The colonel grinned at the police captain's wiles. He stood up, put his hands behind his back and went over to the window. 'Attitudes are hardening out there. If it flares up any more, we'll need reinforcements.'

The police captain smiled, as if to show that he understood what the colonel was implying. He answered in a steady voice, 'In the spirit of cooperation we could say that we'll make sure we keep the groups in check as they are now, or at least after we've arrested someone the Christian militia are likely to listen to. It would be a shame if the balance were suddenly disturbed, for instance, by a shipload of Muslim men.'

Now it was the colonel's turn to smile. He walked across the floor and held out his hand. 'It's a pleasure to work with you, Captain. It had occurred to me that the ship's papers might turn out to be defective.'

The police captain was on the point of leaving, but seemed suddenly to think of something else and came back. The colonel hardly had time to cover his mouth with his hand.

'There was one other thing. You ought to know, Colonel, that six American rock musicians were left ashore when the cruise ship sailed. Four with ponytails. About our age. They've been given permission to perform a peace concert in the village that's normally under water.'

'Was that a difficult permission to grant, Captain?'

'Not really. They made a generous donation.'

'To what?'

'The police-force Sunday school.'

The colonel put his hand over his mouth again.

Francesco was afraid. He was being led down the narrow corridor with the dark-brown doors, one policeman in front of him, another close at his heels. The corridor was empty and quiet now, no weeping women, no screams. Ceiling fans at ten-metre intervals, and still none of them functioning. The policeman in front of him stopped at a door, knocked and waited. After a while he knocked again, and this time a voice responded. He opened the door and spoke, turned and nodded curtly. Francesco entered with a sense of doors slamming behind him.

The police captain was sitting at his desk, the same dark circles under his eyes and a cigarette burning in the ashtray. Francesco attempted a greeting. The police captain made no reply. The policemen took up position by the wall.

'Could you please tell me why you've arrested me? First the army, and now the police?'

He could hear the tremor in his own voice. It had been building up over several hours, from the moment when one soldier had searched him while another held a gun to his neck, the hours alone in a dark, damp bunker listening to voices outside, the hours in the back seat of a car with a blindfold over his eyes, a car that seemed to keep stopping all the time. They had been waiting for him at a checkpoint on the return journey to town. Maheeba and the bodyguard had been taken aside. She had tried to remonstrate with the soldiers, but an officer had brusquely told her to hold her tongue, though at the same time lent her a phone to ring her father.

The police captain touched a sheet of paper on the desk in front of him. 'Because we're bringing a charge against you.'

'A charge?' Francesco exclaimed, staring in disbelief at the police captain. 'For what?'

'Sedition.'

'Sedition?' Francesco almost shouted. 'Is it sedition to visit a Muslim family? Is it sedition to talk to a Muslim waitress?'

The police captain held up a hand to stop him. 'You said you had come here to search for your daughter. We have found her.'

Francesco caught his breath. The police captain continued without giving him the chance to ask anything.

'She's perfectly all right. Nothing has happened to her. She's with the leader of one of the youth militias on the island. The charge is that your real reason for being on this island was not to find your daughter, you knew she was here, but to give money and instructions to the militia. You're a courier for a fundamentalist Christian group that wants to destabilise the island – this island and others.'

Francesco's eyes filled with tears. He felt unsteady on his legs, looked round for a chair and sat down, tried to speak, but nothing came out. The police captain held up the charge sheet, and Francesco eventually managed to stammer weakly, 'Rubbish. It's absolute rubbish.'

The police captain stopped him again, 'Choose your words carefully. Anything you say from now on may be used against you.'

'But this is pure fabrication. You can't have a shred of evidence.'

The police captain smiled, almost as if he had been waiting for this moment. 'Lex Americana, Gringo.'

Francesco stared at him uncomprehendingly.

'Inverse burden of proof. It's not us who have to prove you guilty – you have to prove that you're not. Saddam didn't succeed.'

The police captain rang a brass bell and waited. A few minutes later a policewoman entered, with a black truncheon at her belt, and saluted. He spoke to her with a nod at Francesco, who could see they were discussing him and watched her expectantly. She met his eye and beckoned him to follow her. He tried to ask the police captain something but got no response. At the door the policewoman gave him a brusque order. He sighed and followed her, out of the room, along a corridor, up some stairs. They came out on to a roof terrace, crossed it and paused at another staircase, iron this time, leading steeply up a concrete wall. She must have been in her early thirties, with two gold stripes on her epaulettes. She gestured to him to turn round, then she drew out her truncheon, leant backwards and a bit to one side as if wielding a baseball bat and thwacked him across the back of the knees. He screamed and fell forward, put his hands behind his knees to rub them. She prodded him in the ribs with the truncheon and pointed wordlessly at the iron staircase. He got to his feet with difficulty and hobbled to the stairs on bent legs, his hands still clutching the backs of his knees; he used them to lift his legs up one step at a time. The policewoman followed three steps behind, with an expression of indifference on her face, as if she had all the time in the world.

Francesco was brought to a halt at the top of the stairs by a steel door. The policewoman came up beside him, took a key-ring from her belt and selected a key. Her hands were brown and strong, with an engraved silver ring on her left thumb and red nail polish. She opened the door and nodded at him to enter. Francesco staggered inside, out of breath; she poked him in the spine with her truncheon to get him to move further in. The room was an empty rectangular guard-room containing two cells, which were built as cages along one wall with vertical steel bars and flat crosspieces. On the opposite wall facing the cells was a small window, high up, also with a metal grille. Near the door stood a little table and a chair. On the table was a portable radio.

The policewoman pointed with her truncheon to one of the cells, the door of which was open. Francesco hesitated, unable to believe what was happening to him. She stuck the truncheon between the bars and rattled it impatiently. He went in quickly and she slammed the door behind him and turned the key. The cell measured two metres by three, with a bed along the dividing wall to the adjoining cell, where the bed was similarly positioned, only bars separating the two. There was a blanket on the other bed with something under it, apparently lifeless. He tried to make out whether it was a person, looked over at the policewoman but she did not react. She sat down at the table, switched on the radio and filled the room and the two cells with tinny pop music. He tried the bed in his own cell, leant back against the bars and then, remembering the bundle on the adjacent bed, jerked upright again.

Sunlight was streaming in the high window, sunlight with a smell of heat and the sound of traffic. He got up and went along the wall facing the window, trying to find the place that afforded the best view. He stopped near the cell door, put his face between the bars and hoisted himself up by holding on to the crosspiece. He could see a street with houses on both sides. Stretching up on tiptoe gave him a longer view, like a film camera moving into a picture. There were street lamps hanging from cables above the road, and further up a crossroads with traffic lights, at a busier road than the one he was on.

Later in the afternoon the policewoman was relieved by a colleague, a slightly older woman who came in, exchanged greetings and sent the younger woman off. The new police-woman laid her truncheon on the table, switched off the radio and began reading a battered paperback. Francesco didn't try to communicate with her.

The light from the window changed slowly as evening approached; first it turned softer and warmer as the shadows lengthened, then gradually faded. A woman in a blue apron came padding in with food, setting a metal soup bowl and a plastic jug of water by the door of each cell. Francesco got down on his knees and pulled the food carefully in, emptied the jug in one gulp, raised the soup bowl in trembling hands and tasted it. The woman in the blue apron rattled the door of the next cell and spoke in Malay to the bundle on the bed. It didn't move. She rattled the door again and said something else, almost chanting, like a dirge. The guard rose from her chair and came over to the door, peered at the bundle on the bed and shouted something, not loud or hostile in manner. The bundle didn't move. Francesco put his hand through the bars to touch it, shake it, but a sharp admonition from the guard made him withdraw. He went back to his bowl of soup and sipped at it, keeping his head down. The woman in blue left, and the guard returned to her book. Francesco pushed his empty water jug and soup bowl out through the cell door and cast a glance at the untouched meal in front of the adjacent door.

Then the door to the room opened and the younger policewoman reappeared, letting her replacement go with a brief exchange of words. She sniffed the air and furrowed her brow. Francesco knew what she meant and indicated the enamel chamber-pot under his bunk with an apologetic grin. She unlocked the door of his cell and nodded at him and the pot. She ushered him out ahead of her and down the steps, holding the end of her truncheon against the nape of his neck in silent warning.

He emptied the pot in a toilet without door or window and rinsed it under a tap on the wall. The policewoman looked at him and pointed at the lavatory pan. Reluctantly he guessed her meaning and unbuckled his belt, took down his trousers and sat. She watched his every move. He kept his eyes down and shaded them with one hand.

At the foot of the iron staircase she struck him across the back of the knees again. He swore, in Italian, and irately. She just stood there impassively, with her truncheon at the ready. He had to exert considerable self-control not to retaliate but to continue up the steps. She locked him in his cell, pointed at her wrist-watch and held up five fingers, then pointed at the bulb on the ceiling and made a cutting motion with the flat of her hand: dark. Francesco nodded and sat on the side of the bed while he massaged the backs of his knees. After five minutes the policewoman switched off the light and left.

Francesco lay down on his bunk with one arm over his eyes, turning from side to side. The bundle next to him remained motionless. It wasn't entirely dark; there was a faint gleam from the window. He got up quietly and crept over to the place where he could see the street best, held on to the crossbar and raised himself on his toes. The street was faintly lit by two lamps a hundred metres apart illuminating the areas directly beneath them. In between all was in darkness; when someone entered the pool of light they appeared to step out of nowhere, walk a few paces and disappear again into nothingness. Then there would be a long gap before they suddenly stepped into the next field of light, out of nowhere. Francesco watched them, his lips moving soundlessly. He was about to get down and go back to his bed when something out there riveted his attention. He quickly stood up on tiptoe and craned his neck for a better view.

The furthest pool of light was filled by a group of young people, eight or ten of them, walking fast, in long flowing cloaks and red headbands; the one in front looked like a young woman, with the springy gait of a trained athlete. Just as she left the circle of light she opened her cloak and pulled out a spear. All the others following her were opening their cloaks too as they moved out of sight. Francesco waited expectantly, trying to stretch higher and staring at the next pool of light. But the group didn't reappear. They must have taken a side-street between the two lamps. He lay down on his bed again, loosening his clothes and trying to sleep. Then he stiffened. A thin hand emerged from the bundle in the adjoining cell, felt its way to his eyes and closed them with two fingers, then found his ears and covered them for a moment, one at a time, after which it slid over his cheek and pressed his lips gently but firmly together before vanishing back between the bars and in under the blanket.

11

AN AGREEMENT

The police captain came to see him after four days. Francesco had used his belt buckle to carve a notch in the cell wall for each day that passed. He was sleeping so little and so restlessly that he would probably have lost count otherwise. His predecessors had made their marks on the wall before him. It was not encouraging.

'How's life here?' the police captain asked in a not un-friendly voice.

'May I please talk to my daughter?'

'In a day or two. If you cooperate. Strictly speaking we could forbid you visits.'

'How is she?'

'Still fine. We don't think she knows you're here.'

For a moment the police captain was also a father. Then he gave the guard a nod, she switched off the radio, handed him the keys of the cell and left the room, without a word. Francesco watched her go.

'Why is she on duty all the time?'

'It's the rota. Two weeks on, one week off. Do you like her?' He had a twinkle in his eye.

'I would like her better if she stopped hitting me behind the knees every time we go up the staircase,' Francesco replied, rubbing the backs of his knees to illustrate his point.

The police captain grinned, 'It's her way of showing that she likes you.'

He unlocked the cell door. Francesco gave him a questioning look and he indicated the guard's table and chair.

'Come and sit down.'

Francesco left his cell with some reluctance, and tested the chair before sitting down.

'How long can you hold me here?'

'As long as we want.'

'Without charge, without formal indictment?'

'You have been charged. With sedition. We'll draw up the formal indictment when we've completed our investigations.'

'And when will that be?'

'When the investigations are finished.'

'Are the investigations going on now?'

'We must assume so.'

Francesco fell silent. Imprisonment had in many ways made his stay on the island simpler, especially now that he'd heard that his daughter was all right.

'And the Embassy?'

'We're still trying to phone. The exchange is noting it every time we ask for the number. They haven't managed to get through yet.'

'And we're supposed to believe that?'

'Are you suggesting we're lying?'

There was a hard edge to the police captain's voice. Francesco didn't reply. He felt exhausted. The police captain leant against the desk.

'How are conditions in custody?' he asked, reverting to his old self again, without a hint of friendliness or humour. Francesco still made no reply.

The police captain looked round and went on, 'They could be better, but they could also be worse.' He was watching Francesco's face as he said it. 'It wouldn't take much to make it worse,' he added, leaning forward as if to check that the threat had struck home. 'On the other hand, what would it take to make things better?' He appeared to be enjoying his role.

'Going to the toilet on your own? Not having to use a chamber-pot? No more truncheons across the backs of the knees when you climb the stairs?'

Francesco raised his head and waited for him to continue.

'We had you under surveillance before we arrested you. We know a bit about you. Can you get to sleep without alcohol?'

Francesco averted his gaze.

'Can you?'

Francesco closed his eyes.

'Here's a proposal,' said the police captain in a neutral tone, neither friendly nor unfriendly. 'I need you for something specific. You'll get payment in alcohol if you help me. Wine doesn't keep well in this heat, and beer is probably too weak, so it will have to be spirits. We know you like brandy. How much do you need to relax in the evenings and be sure of sleeping?'

Francesco opened his eyes and said, 'What do you want from me? Information?'

'No.'

The police captain pulled the door ajar and called to someone. A policeman climbed the staircase and brought in a covered basket, set it down on the table and left. The police captain removed the cloth and displayed the contents: two cans of beer glistening with condensation and a package in waxed paper tied with brown string. Francesco drew a line in the condensation on the beer cans with his finger. The police captain undid the package and flicked through a bundle of papers with his thumb as if he were going to shuffle them. Francesco lunged forward to stop him.

'What are you doing, man? You'll tear them!' he shouted, trying to push the police captain's hand away.

The police captain smiled, 'That was the reaction I was hoping for. Would you like a beer? It's just gone twelve, so I should think it's permitted.'

He opened a can of beer without waiting for an answer and handed it to him. Francesco took it cautiously and put it down on the table.

'You're a book restorer. All I'm asking is that you restore these documents. In exchange you'll get two cans of beer every day at twelve and a half-bottle of brandy and a bottle of mineral water every evening at nine. We'll collect the bottle and whatever's left in it every morning, just to keep things orderly. What do you say?'

Francesco bent over and carefully extracted the documents from the waxed paper, freeing the top sheet with his fingertip and lifting it up to see it better.

'What are these?'

'Sheets of paper.'

'From a book?'

'No.'

'How old are they?'

'Exactly thirty-eight years.'

Francesco looked up; the police captain had paused slightly before answering and his voice sounded a little odd. Francesco did a swift calculation back through the history of the country and turned pale. 'The coup?'

'The rumour of a coup,' the police captain replied, emphasising the word *rumour* with a hand gesture. 'A rumour that the army used as a pretext for a counter-coup. And then the executions began.'

Francesco sifted through his memory for a quotation; 'One of the most savage acts of mass murder in modern political history?'

'Correct. *New York Times.*'

'Over half a million executed?'

'Or over a million. The count of mass executions is always dependent on who's doing the counting.'

Francesco lowered his eyes. Silent seconds ticked away.

'I'll need a few things.'

'Just make a list.'

Francesco took a swig from the can of beer, the first long swig of a man who is thirsty. The police captain watched him.

'I'll send in a bottle of brandy tonight. Then you'll be well rested before you start work tomorrow.'

He got up and went to the door, called in Malay and stood there till the policewoman arrived. Then he left, without another word.

The first bottle of evening brandy was delivered to the door just as the sun went down. The policewoman took it in and spoke to someone on the steps, closed the door, came across the room, set a glass and two bottles on the floor in front of the cell door and nodded. Francesco waited until she had turned away, then got down on his knees and slid the glass and bottles inside. He inspected the half-bottle of brandy, read the label, shook his head, then unscrewed the top, sniffed and smiled. He picked up the bottle of mineral water and tried to read the label on that too, opened it, took a sip and smiled again. Then he blew hard into the glass to clean the dust off, wiped it on his shirt, and halfway filled it with brandy. He tasted it, a tentative sip, closed his eyes and swallowed, and then sighed, a long sigh of well-being, or perhaps relief. He topped up the glass with mineral water and watched the little bubbles of carbon dioxide rising to the surface, then put the glass to his lips and drank.

'God bless king and country.'

At that very instant there was an explosion in the street near the crossroads. He went to the bars and watched the aftermath of the wave of destruction, which had travelled down the street in the unnatural silence that always follows a bomb, just before the policewoman leapt across to reprimand him and hoist herself up to have a look out of the window. Francesco pretended not to understand, stayed where he was, standing on tiptoe to see; he watched the people come running panic-stricken down the street, heard cars hooting beyond the crossroads. The policewoman noticed he was still there and seemed about to knock him away with her truncheon, but then something out in the street distracted her. Francesco could see what it was: the same young people in cloaks, with the same graceful young woman at their head, but this time there were more of them, at least twenty, and now they had their weapons at the ready: spears, clubs, bows and arrows, even a few with home-made guns. Then came another sudden explosion, smaller than the first, from an alley behind the house on the right-hand side of the street. It was succeeded by a shot, and then two more. The young people turned round, their leader held up her hand and shouted an order and they rushed off down the alley.

Then more figures appeared from the crossroads, ten to fifteen youths in white headbands. Behind them a silent wall of men in white tunics. Francesco could see the youths starting to run towards the alley into which the young people in red headbands had disappeared, but the policewoman turned and he took his hands off the crossbar just before she brought her truncheon down between two upright bars and pointed to his bed. He snatched his glass from the crossbar, moved away and sat down. She stood and watched him for a moment, as a threat, then went back to the window and hoisted herself up for another look before returning to her table.

Francesco refilled his glass, held the bottle up to the light to see how far down it had gone, leant back with the glass in his hands and sipped at it slowly while humming a mournful song. The wail of sirens and the blue flash of police-car lights came through the window; he looked up to see but didn't stand. The policewoman went over to the window and hoisted herself up again to look out for a while. Francesco raised his glass to her with a quizzical smile to ask whether she would like to join him for a drink. She shook her head, an ambiguous movement that could have meant no or that he shouldn't have suggested it. She indicated her watch, held up five fingers and glanced at the light-bulb. Francesco nodded. He filled his glass with brandy and mineral water, put it under the bed, straightened out his blanket and lay down. The policewoman looked at him with her hand on the light-pull, made the shape of a pistol with her other hand and pretended to fire at him, a little smile playing at the corner of her eyes and lips. Then she put out the light and left. From the bundle in the next cell came a quiet chuckle.

Francesco lay there listening to the noises from the street: sirens, cars, shouting, and suddenly cries of lamentation in the distance. He raised himself on one elbow and looked towards the window as if to locate their source. They were coming from the sea, and he saw before him the eyes that had stared at him in the moonlight, heard the lamentations getting louder, long-drawn-out and sorrowful.

Francesco emptied the bag of items he had ordered and spread them over his bed: two flat-bottomed plastic dishes slightly larger than the sheets of paper, four bottles of liquid, one brown, one black and two clear, two brushes with grey bristles, two pairs of tweezers, a ball of string and a bag of clothes-pegs. He opened the bottles and smelt them, tried the brushes against the palm of his hand, took a pair of tweezers in each hand and brought the two pairs together, almost like a surgeon. The policewoman seemed uninterested; it was impossible to tell whether she was watching or not. A plaintive voice was coming from the radio.

Francesco sat down with the pack of documents and carefully unfolded and smoothed out the waxed paper. The sheets appeared virtually square, about fifteen by fifteen centimetres, and a bit thicker than the pages of a book. They were completely blank. He ran the tweezers along the edge as he counted, mumbled *fifty* under his breath, then *a hundred*, carried on counting and muttered *near enough two hundred*. Then he picked up the top sheet with the two pairs of tweezers and held it up to the light from the window, turning it slowly. He lifted another to inspect, and another.

'If anything has been printed on these sheets, it's gone for ever. But something has been typed on them, and that can be restored.'

He took the ball of string and tied the end at head height to one of the bars between the cells, pulled it across and fastened it to the bars on the guardroom side. The policewoman didn't look up, the voice on the radio droned on and on. He set one of the plastic dishes upside down on the bed and laid the top sheet of paper on it, opened the black bottle and dipped the brush.

'Do you know anything about ink?' he said, bending over the paper. The policewoman still didn't look up. He stroked the brush carefully over the first sheet for a minute or so, then stood back and inspected it. Some typewritten letters had become visible. The whining voice on the radio had been replaced by music.

'One per cent of everything that's printed in the world is good, professional work, the rest is rubbish. One per cent is printed by skilled printers with insoluble ink on permanent paper. And it will last for ever. The rest is printed by unskilled people, with soluble ink on poor quality paper. Which means that sooner or later it will disappear, first the ink, then the paper. Sooner or later ninety-nine per cent of everything we print will disappear. And then we'll disappear ourselves.'

He gave a slight smile, bent over the paper again and went on brushing. The music on the radio was interrupted by a news broadcast, an animated voice reporting riots in the capital. The reporter was evidently alongside the demonstrators, and their rhythmic chants could be heard in the background. Then the broadcast returned to the studio, where a general gave assurance that the authorities had everything under control. The policewoman was facing the radio as she listened. Francesco didn't look up from his work, but he could sense that the news was important to her, so he kept quiet while it was on. There followed a series of messages of support: businessmen supported the President and his men, the lawyers' association supported the President and his men, the civil service staff federation supported the President and his men. The policewoman switched it off. Francesco registered the fact with a sideways glance, but said nothing. He picked up the first sheet with the tweezers, carried it to the string and hung it there from a clothes-peg. The policewoman came over to look at it. Francesco went and stood next to her by the cell door, one of them inside and one outside the bars. Letters and numbers were becoming visible on the paper now, a line of each, a name, and a number and date.

'What is it?' he asked aloud without looking at her, as if he thought the fact they were standing gazing at it together represented some kind of complicity. She didn't reply, but stayed a little longer before going back to her seat at the table. Francesco set to work again, took a new sheet and laid it on the inverted plastic dish, worked on it in silence, hung it up to dry, and so on, one after another. In an hour he had filled the drying line, so he rigged up a second below the first and carried on until that too was full. Then he took out the pot from under the bed, ducked beneath the two strings of papers and straightened up on the other side. The policewoman raised her head now and stared at him behind his wall of names until he had finished and turned round towards her.

He ducked back beneath the strings, replaced the pot under the bed, felt the ink on the first sheet with his fingers, rubbed his fingertips together and nodded, 'Dry.'

Turning the plastic dish the right way up, he emptied the

two clear bottles into it, put the second dish next to it and emptied the contents of the brown bottle into that. He tried to see the time on the policewoman's watch. He was going to ask her something, but changed his mind. He laid the first sheet in the dish of clear liquid and began counting aloud while beating the seconds with his foot; on every tenth he held up a finger, and on thirty he lifted the sheet out of the dish with the tweezers and put it in the dish of brown liquid.

'Do you know anything about paper?' he asked.

She shrugged her shoulders, 'Nix English.'

Francesco resumed his work and carried on talking. 'Up until the mid-nineteenth century all printing was on paper made from rags. Then wood-pulp paper arrived, and to write or print on that you have to add starch, otherwise all you get is blotting paper. The usual method was to add a mixture of resin soap and aluminium sulphate. And that's where the problem lies, because when aluminium sulphate gets damp it changes to phosphoric acid, which eats into the cellulose fibres of the paper until it is so weakened that it breaks when you fold it once or twice.'

He took the sheet out of the other dish with the tweezers and hung it up to dry, put the next sheet in the first dish and counted off the seconds again. He continued his disquisition as he transferred this sheet over into the other dish.

'The process can't be reversed, but it can be halted. You put each sheet in liquid freon, which contains alkaline magnesium salts which neutralise the acid in the paper. It takes time, and it costs money, but it can be done. And it's important. Take for example the National Library of France. It has 2.6 million books and periodicals printed between 1875 and 1960. An investigation thirteen years ago estimated 90,000 of them to be beyond repair, 900,000 in imminent danger and 700,000 at risk in the longer term. Which meant that sixty-five per cent of France's printed heritage was in the process of disappearing.'

He went on working in silence until there was a knock on the door and the woman in blue arrived with two cans of beer. She set them down outside his cell door and left without so much as a glance in his direction. He hung up the next sheet, retrieved the cans of beer and sat down on his bed to have a drink.

'The problem with paper being broken down by acid,' he went on, talking to himself, 'is effectively over. Resin soap was replaced by neutral synthetic polymers in paper production in the 1980s, so goodbye acid. At the same time an everlasting paper was developed containing alkaline materials. You can recognise it from the watermark, the mathematical infinity sign inside a circle.'

He finished the first beer and opened the next.

'You won't find any such watermark in me. I'm still being broken down. You have to be gentle with me, and not screw me up.'

He was woken by whispering voices. He rolled over in bed and squinted into the gloom. The bundle the other side of the cell bars was silent.

He lay back down and closed his eyes, certain that he must have been dreaming. A few moments later he opened them again, equally certain that he hadn't. He sat up and looked at the two strings of documents, slowly, almost unwillingly, as if he wished he hadn't seen what he'd seen. The whispering was coming from them.

He pressed his back into the wall of bars behind him and gripped the bars with both hands. One of the documents was slowly revolving, in the draughtless, windless room, and a second, on the lower string, was responding. The two documents seemed to be trying to call to one another, but quietly, for fear of being overheard. They were hanging at opposite ends of the cell, one at the far left on the upper string, the other at the far right on the lower one. And there were sounds coming from the documents between them, but of a different kind: they were also sounds of fear, and desperation, but different. He looked down at the floor of the cell, beneath the documents, from where the sounds of the other documents were emanating; it wasn't the sound of voices, it was the sound of drops, drops falling on to a stone floor.

He raised a hand to his face, as if to wipe away a reality, or a thought. He knew the documents had been dry long before he went to bed.

The bundle by his side suddenly moved and said, 'There, there, there,' rocking back and forth, 'There, there, there.' And the documents burst into a wail, a mournful, beseeching wail. The bundle swayed back and forth, offering solace, 'There, there, there,' a lullaby, 'There, there, there.'

Francesco leant his head against the bars behind him and closed his eyes, almost demonstrating to the documents that he was listening; someone or something wants this for me, so let it come; he listened to the sobs rising and falling, to the swell of prayers beneath the sobs, to the whispering voices seeming to cry out under their breath. The bundle by his side was trying to console them, but it seemed that the solace had the opposite effect, provoking more despair, releasing inhibitions. Finally an engine started up and the sounds of weeping and whispering voices died away. The bundle in the next cell sighed, a long, deep sigh, and fell silent.

Francesco sat for a long time gazing at where the sounds had been, and in his eyes were reflected some of the fragments of the country's history that he knew, flickering slowly by, image after image.

———

When morning arrived, he asked for the police captain to be sent for. The policewoman was loath to do so at first, but he was persistent.

The police captain came right up to the cell door before he spoke. 'There'd better be a good reason why you wanted to see me. In this part of the world prisoners don't send for their jailers. Is there something wrong with the documents? Or the equipment you ordered?'

'What sort of documents are they that you've got me restoring?' Francesco whispered, clutching the bars with both hands.

The police captain put his face close to him and replied in the same tone, 'That needn't concern you. Just restore them.'

'The documents cry and whisper at night.'

The police captain blanched. They stood facing each other in silence for a moment, a European and an Asian, before the police captain responded, 'They're identity papers, of people who were executed. Let's just say there are archives waiting for them.'

He raised his eyes towards the two strings of documents and sighed, 'The shame of it. What cruel, never-ending shame.'

'Theirs or ours?' said Francesco, still whispering.

'Take your choice,' said the police captain, and left.

Francesco stayed where he was, his hands gripping the steel bars. He thought, their shame, because they let themselves be executed; our shame, because we Europeans had nearly three hundred and fifty years of colonial history in this country and should have foreseen the outcome. He tried to regard himself as a prisoner of atonement, a white European called to account for centuries of brutal colonial repression, but he couldn't. He knew there was a flaw in his argument, but he just couldn't see what it was. He realised later what it must be: the European perspective.

Francesco lay with his eyes wide open, staring at the identity papers. He held his hand in front of his face in the semi-darkness and murmured to himself, 'In ancient societies people and things were regarded as holy when they were seen to be connected in some way with a reality beyond themselves. In modern society there are no longer any holy people or holy objects. We have only one reality left, a disconnected reality.'

He turned to look at the bundle. Did it just move? He held out his other hand and continued his murmuring; 'Where ancient man had to make his way through gods, demons and spirits, modern man stands alone, in an empty cathedral, alone with himself and his reason. Some call this loneliness progress.'

The bundle in the next cell said something. Francesco smiled and whispered, 'Exactly.' Shipwreck, despair, fascination, indignation, arrest, and now this. Not bad, not bad.

The bundle spoke again, and Francesco made a dismissive gesture, 'You needn't call me Gringo, that's what the police captain calls me.' The bundle sat up slightly to correct him, 'Gandhiist?'

Francesco smiled apologetically. Gringo and Gandhiist, they almost sounded the same. The bundle went on, 'All living creatures are fundamentally one, right?'

'Right,' Francesco replied warily, seeing what the bundle was driving at and wanting to resist.

'So violence against one is violence against all? Right?'

Francesco just nodded.

'The logical consequence of which is that as long as violence exists, there's only one thing to do?'

Francesco nodded again and continued the dialogue, 'Seek out the violence and oppose it.'

'And if you don't manage to? And if you don't manage to?'

The bundle seemed agitated now.

'And if you don't manage to?'

Francesco didn't respond. His eyes filled with tears as he waited for the answer he knew would come.

'Gandhi also talked about the non-violence of the coward. Of the coward.'

Francesco dried his eyes with the back of his hand.

'Those who don't dare admit that violence sometimes has to be eradicated.'

That night, for the first time, Francesco saw himself in a seemingly endless history of violence; that night, to his own horror, he realised that for people who live with the notion of a Great We there is no difference between violence in the past and violence in the present. As a European he was responsible for the violence on the island in the past (and consequently in the present). Which was the courageous and which was the cowardly option, to try to break the chain of violence or to eradicate it altogether? He simply did not know.

12

FATHER

'Are we Israelis? Are we vandals? Will we be ripping up their olive trees next?'

Anya was weeping with rage. Meseo kept his eyes averted.

'Can't you see what you've got me into? Can't you see what you've got the others into? Are you trying to make them hate us?'

They were sitting on a bench down by the harbour. Neither of them was wearing a headband now, neither of them had warpaint on. Behind them smoke was still rising from the ravaged commercial centre.

'How old was that commercial centre?'

Meseo didn't reply.

'How many times have the shops passed from father to son? How many fathers have taught their sons the handicraft that went with the shop? How many fathers have taught their sons to polish the wood in the shops till it shone like that?'

She hugged her knees and stared at the horizon.

'Do you know how long it takes to grow an olive tree to maturity? Fifty years. The Israelis know that. And they know that the Palestinians know that they know. It's hatred they're trying to generate when they tear up Palestinian olive trees. Because Palestinian hatred gives the Israelis their legitimacy. Is it Muslim hatred we want?'

Her voice was shrill now. On the pavement behind her people were staring in alarm. Meseo tried to pacify her, but to no avail.

'Do you hear what I say? It was the family silver we destroyed back there. Every single shop was a monument, to their fathers, and their fathers before them. We have brought shame on them. And you understand as well as any what that means here.'

Meseo stopped her. 'Oh, you know it all. You know what Israelis think and what Palestinians feel. You know what we want and how those over there see things. How have you suddenly become so omniscient?'

He was talking to her without looking at her, but then he swung round and launched into her: 'I know why you're angry. It's because you enjoyed it. I could see it in you while we were doing it. You were laughing, and dancing, you sang as you kicked their shops to pieces. You were exactly how you are when we make love.'

Anya gave a start.

'And now you're angry because you enjoyed it. That's one thing you Europeans do know all about – guilt.'

He really shouted the last word.

Anya hit out at him as she replied, 'Don't be so ridiculous. Whenever you feel unsure of yourself, you criticise Europeans. You know it was madness to attack the commercial centre, you know it's brought shame on the Muslims, and you know they'll have to retaliate, that they won't be able to live with their shame.'

She got up and strode off furiously along the promenade. Meseo ran after her and grabbed her by the shoulder.

'Don't act like you're in some third-rate American film.'

She shook off his hand and turned to confront him. 'Travelling is like rinsing your eyes. Do you remember that expression? Well, this is one rinse I could have done without.'

She was about to go when two policemen came towards her on the promenade, stopped and touched their caps. She was frightened. One of them was looking at a piece of paper in his hand and asked a question in Malay. The colour drained from Meseo's face.

'What did they say?'

'They said your name, wanted to know if it was you. I think it's a photo of you on that paper.'

One of the policemen interrupted him with a curt order.

'They're telling you to go to the police station with them.'

Anya caught her breath. The policemen marched her off, one each side of her. Meseo tried to follow, but they spoke sharply to him and he stayed where he was, watching the three figures as they disappeared into the centre of town. Anya turned her head once but the policemen jerked her round and made her face the way they were walking.

———

They brought her into the room with the desk and the slow fan on the ceiling. The police captain looked up from what he was writing and pointed to a chair. Anya sat down. He nodded at the two policemen, and they left and closed the door behind them.

'Do you speak English?' Anya asked anxiously.

'Of course I speak English. Otherwise I'd have an interpreter here.'

He inspected her in silence, eyeing her up and down from her sturdy boots to her cropped hair. She shifted uneasily in her seat.

'Is this how my daughter will turn out? She's at a boarding-school in Switzerland. I'm not sure I want her to look like this,' he said, dropping his voice at the end as if speaking to himself.

There was a glint of annoyance in Anya's eyes as she replied, 'I've never been to a Swiss boarding-school. Could you please tell me why I've been brought here?'

'Because you took part in the destruction of the commercial centre. And because we have your father here. In a cell.'

He leant back and waited. At first Anya just sat and stared at him, unsure she had heard aright. Then she began to stammer, as if about to say something, checked herself, started to say something else, stopped herself again, and finally uttered two words, 'My father?'

The police captain simply nodded. Anya looked round the room, as if trying to take in the whole building, the building where her father was.

'My father? Here? How on earth can he have got here? And why?'

'On a life-raft. He says he's searching for you. We don't believe him. We think he was going to deliver money and instructions to the Christian militia you're involved with. We've arrested him.'

Anya was speechless. She could hear the Danish camera-man saying *we were shipwrecked with a Portuguese man* and the pieces fell into place. She could see her father in danger of drowning at sea and felt fear; she saw him in his study bent over mediaeval manuscripts and felt tenderness. She scruti-nised the police captain, aware that she must weigh every word now, and concentrated for the next hour on making sure she did so. She made no comment on the absurdity of the charge; she waited until she had her voice under control and then asked calmly about her father's legal rights, whether the Embassy had been informed, whether he would appear before a magistrate and, if so, when. Just once, when the police captain left the room for a moment, she stood up, lifted the chair she was sitting on and banged it down hard on the floor.

'You'll be able to go to him soon. We'll hang on a while longer,' he said as he came back in. He lit a cigarette and glanced at the clock.

'Why wait?'

'Because he's busy right now. An evening ritual. We don't want to disturb him for a bit.'

Anya wrinkled her brow speculatively. 'Do you let him have wine in jail?'

The police captain gave her a stern look. 'Wine in an Asian jail? What an idea!'

They sat in silence until the sun had gone down and the street lamps came on outside the window. Then he got up and gave her a nod: 'You can talk with your father, but not see him.'

'Why not?'

'Don't be impertinent.'

Without another word he got up and went to the door and she followed him into the corridor, at the end of which he preceded her into a little room with no windows or furniture, except for a stool by one wall with a grille above it at head height, a half-metre square covered with black cloth behind the bars.

'There. And talk English, not Portuguese,' he said, indicating the stool. Anya sat down reluctantly and looked up at the bars and the black curtain.

'Dad?' she said in a low voice, then looked down and listened. Not a sound. The police captain stood in the doorway with his arms folded.

'Dad? Are you there?'

She reached out her hand to touch the curtained bars, but the police captain stopped her immediately. She drew back her hand and changed position on the stool.

'How long have you been holding him?'

The police captain smiled without answering. Anya turned back to the grille.

'Dad, if you're there, say something.'

There was a sudden gasp from behind the curtain, so strong that the fabric moved. Anya jumped.

'Dad, are you all right?'

A voice cleared its throat on the other side, preparing to speak.

'Are you hurt?'

'No, Anya, not hurt, not hurt.'

Her eyes filled with tears and she moved to rise from the stool, but the police captain took a couple of steps forward and restrained her.

'How are you?' asked the voice from the grille, steadier now.

Anya looked up in surprise. 'How am I? Here I am having just found out that you're under arrest in an Asian jail and you ask how I am!'

'Tell him,' the police captain interjected.

'I've had a fantastic six months travelling. Africa was like intense heightened reality. Asia is something else; I feel more in contact with something here, something cyclical. As if Africa is the moment and Asia is eternity.'

She glanced at the police captain and said, 'Don't I sound like the daughter of a book man?'

Then she turned back to the grille. 'What are you doing here?'

'Looking for you.'

She stared in disbelief towards the voice and its answer. Then she stood up slowly and addressed herself directly to the grille: 'Looking for me? You travel halfway round the world looking for me?'

'Your last card was from Sulawesi. Then there was nothing.'

She sat down and closed her eyes. Something akin to anger or rebellion flitted across her face, then she smiled, a little sadly, as if the anger might be love.

'Where have you been?' the voice asked with a slight quaver.

'How's Mum?'

'Much the same. Why didn't you write?'

Anya stood up. There were tears in her eyes again, but her expression was different. She muttered, *much the same, why didn't you write*, and then kicked the wall with a thud. The police captain had his eye on her and made a sign for her to sit down.

'Anya, what's happening?' cried the voice desperately from behind the bars.

Anya seemed not to hear and sat down on the stool and addressed the room in a low, firm voice, either for the police captain or for her father: 'Have you ever thought what it's like to be responsible for an illusion?'

She pushed her hair back before going on: 'The illusion of a harmonious family, for example, with mother and father forever loving each other and the children forever innocent, forever the same age? The day you stop sustaining the illusion, the day you leave, the illusion crumbles and the people left behind fall into a panic.

The police captain came over to her, put a hand under her arm and raised her up. After a while she got up and kicked the wall again. Then she turned to the police captain and nodded. He stood and looked at her for a moment before he led her out.

There came a howl from the grille.

13

A COUP

The same desk, the same window, the same back-light. The colonel stood up and waved his hand towards the armchairs, and the police captain thanked him. The colonel had a portable radio on his desk playing martial music. He turned it down and took it over to join him.

'How are you, Captain?'

'Fine, thanks. And you, Colonel?'

'Fine, thanks. And your family?'

'Fine, thanks. And yours?'

'Fine, as far as I'm aware.'

The colonel rang the bell, the soldier came in and took the order for tea.

'Has it been a quiet night for your men, Colonel?'

'Not as bad as some. What about yours, Captain?'

'The same. You sent for me, Colonel?'

The colonel nodded and pointed at the radio. 'There are riots in the capital. Serious this time. It occurred to me you might be interested, Captain. The military radio is broadcasting running news. It's on a frequency that I don't think can be received on normal civilian sets.'

'Not ones made in this country, anyway.'

'And because of that it can be more informative than would be wise on a civilian programme.'

'No doubt.'

The colonel turned up the volume and the military band rose from the table between the two men, passed the portrait of the President and marched out through the open window. A man's voice took over, reading out greetings to the President, from chambers of commerce, societies, foreign ambassadors; the greetings rolled out like a train on rails, rumbling soporifically out of the radio, *dum-de-dum, dum-de-dum*. The colonel sighed.

'Do you play backgammon, Captain?'

The police captain nodded. The colonel went to his desk and brought out a board, sitting down heavily. He opened it, distributed the counters between them, and said, 'The leader of one of the Islamic parties has asserted that he can mobilise a million people to march on the presidential palace and parliament. He's demanding the President's resignation. No such demand has ever been made before. There's every reason to believe that he really can mobilise that many.'

'Unfortunately . . .' said the police captain as he picked up his counters. The colonel gave him a sidelong glance without responding. A new military band replaced the stream of greetings, and for some time the music and counters being laid and moved were the only sounds in the room. Then, still concentrating on the game, the police captain began to speak; 'I was five years old when we won our independence. Can you remember our first leader, Colonel? How proud of him we all were? Can you remember the portrait of him that hung everywhere?'

The colonel nodded tentatively, a little grudgingly, as if sounding a note of caution.

The police captain moved two counters and went on, 'It took me many years to realise why we couldn't keep him. I was only a child then, I only remember the light around him, and laughter, and the happy cries, and then sudden darkness, in the middle of the day. Later on, of course, I both read and realised for myself that it couldn't work, as the world was. But I can't say I ever really understood why, because understanding would be a kind of approval, a sort of silent acceptance.'

The colonel cleared his throat, but the police captain didn't seem to be aware of it, just carried on talking, unperturbed, almost in a monotone: 'The more I read, the more I could see that all the reasons why people were proud of him were the very reasons why we couldn't keep him.' He held up his hand and ticked the points off. 'He thought it was possible to be neutral in the Cold War, thought it was possible to talk to the Americans, the Russians and the Chinese. He expropriated many of the previous colonial rulers' properties and restored them to us. And he refused to bow to demands to clamp down on the Communist Party, a completely lawful party with solid support in the trade union movement and solid success in every election. My father used to listen to his speeches on the radio. He was in a union. Harbour worker and elected official.'

'Stevedore?'

'Crane driver.'

The police captain hardly noticed the brief dialogue. The music on the radio faded out and a voice came in with the news. The two men sat up to listen. Over a hundred thousand demonstrators had congregated in front of the presidential palace and more were constantly arriving; large numbers of police were on standby; the army had so far received no instructions from the President. The colonel and the police captain went on with their game.

The police captain continued, 'My father used to go to a club meeting every Tuesday evening. He would sometimes take my two elder brothers along. I seem to recall my mother being anxious; I think I have a mental image of her standing at the window watching them go. Occasionally when I close my eyes I can hear her sigh as she turns away from the window, presumably because they had gone out of view, and I see her sit down with my little brother, little sister, and me. We were always doing our homework, always, and I can remember my little sister sitting with her tongue poking out of the corner of her mouth when she was doing her sums, like this.'

He stuck the tip of his tongue out of the left corner of his mouth and closed his lips over it.

'Suddenly one day someone said the word *coup*. I had just taught my brother and sister the word *fuck*, and they thought that *coup* was another word for the same thing and started giggling. Our mother shouted at them as she sat with her ear glued to the radio, listening for any sounds suggestive of a coup. My father came home later. We could see him in the distance, talking to someone, then stopping and chatting to several more in the street, and walking on surrounded by others. His eyes were dark when he came in, more serious than usual when he lifted us up and hugged us; his hands were harder. And one thing I remember particularly was that he hugged us longer, held each one of us longer than usual.

'I remember the radio being on for the rest of the evening, even after we'd gone to bed, which was most unusual. I lay there listening for the word *coup*, registered the number of times it was said until I fell asleep, only then to be suddenly jerked awake by the word *counter-coup*, spoken with such excitement, shouted almost, the way some people are said to arouse themselves, almost shouting, when they fuck and counter-fuck.'

The colonel said, 'Can we manage without such references? It is, after all, the turning-point in our country's history you're talking about.'

The police captain nodded, absent-mindedly, as if only partially attending. The music on the radio was interrupted by a short bulletin to say that the army was sending in tanks against the demonstrators. The two men sat for some time in silence without looking at one another. The colonel's knuckles whitened round the counter he was holding. Then they resumed their game.

'I was woken by my mother and father later in the night,' the police captain went on, with his eyes on the board. 'That was nothing new, a family of seven in one room have few if any secrets from one another, but this was different. My mother wasn't making the same noises she usually did. She used to whisper to my father, and sigh, but now she was crying. And my father was talking to her in a different way from usual – he used to call out to her in a low voice, and now it sounded like he was trying to comfort her, to convince her of something.'

The colonel interjected, 'When did the knock on the door come?'

The police captain looked surprised, as if he didn't like the flow of his narrative disturbed, yet at the same time not entirely surprised.

'At dawn. You always come at dawn, don't you?'

'Don't you too?'

'Yes, when the human organism is most defenceless and vulnerable, when the human brain is in greatest need of sleep and rest. There were four of them, an officer and three privates, and they knocked on the door with rifle butts or clubs, in fact there may have been more of them outside doing the knocking, the blows came so fast and furious. My father was already up and dressed; he must have been expecting them or even heard them coming down the street, in the main door, up the stairs. They seized him and tied his hands behind his back, my mother trying to stop them and two of the soldiers beating her off. Then they put a blindfold over his eyes and he turned to look at us children as they did it, one silent glance and then his eyes were covered. They hauled him out on to the landing and my mother tried to cling to him, but they beat her off again. They shoved him down the stairs; he couldn't see the steps and tripped, couldn't save himself, and crashed into the wall of the next landing with the full weight of his body.'

The police captain paused for a moment, seeing the scene before him again and wondering how much to recount.

'We lived on the fifth floor. By the time my father reached

ground level his whole face was bruised and bloodied, he had blood streaming from his nose and he had trouble walking. The remarkable thing was that they let us go with him: my mother, my brothers and me, my little sister, and gradually more and more neighbours. My mother went in front of us with her arms out at the sides as if to protect us or hold us back. When she tried to rush down the stairs to help my father, they pointed their guns at her. It took me many years to understand why we were allowed to go with him, admittedly at a distance, but allowed to go nevertheless.'

The colonel was fiddling silently with a counter, putting it down, picking it up, up, down, up, down.

'They wanted us to see it all, absolutely everything, every tiny little detail. Five other men were dragged out of the block we lived in. They had their hands tied behind their backs and their eyes blindfolded and they stood in the courtyard, all of them bleeding and one with a dark stain on the seat of his trousers. My father was pushed into the row, and there must have been at least thirty soldiers and twice as many spectators. Four more were brought out while we waited there, and then someone yelled an order and the ten prisoners were marched away, out through the entrance and off to the left down the street, the soldiers prodding them along with their guns, steering them, keeping them together. It was a piece of theatre; I can still see it before me now. Every day. The sun was rising and its rays were slanting down on the soldiers and prisoners, as though trying to draw them into itself, and they were walking into the sun, staggering towards the sun, and I later thought: so this is how this country was born.'

'Careful now,' said the colonel quietly. The police captain looked up at him and was about to answer when he was interrupted by a hectic voice on the radio reporting on street-fighting in the capital, and gathering in reports not just from the presidential palace but also from other parts of the centre, from outside ministries and public buildings. They listened until the martial music came on again. The colonel stood up and slowly paced the room.

The police captain spoke to his back, 'I didn't think of making an estimate at the time, but there must have been several hundred of us following the soldiers and prisoners by the time we got to the main square. The soldiers kept us at a distance, but no more than fifteen to twenty metres, and I could see my father's hands, his head and his back. His hands were tied, but his back was straight and his head held high, only now and again drooping forward as it became too heavy to hold up.

'The square was already full of people. There were three army lorries in the middle with prisoners in the rear, mostly men, but also a few women scattered among them, all with their hands bound and eyes blindfolded, most with blood on their faces or clothes. A ring of soldiers kept the onlookers at bay, but now the distance was only about five to ten metres and the crowd was moving all the time. The soldiers were from another part of the country – we could see that from the colour of their skin and hear it from their voices – and they had fixed bayonets on their rifles. My father and the other prisoners we had come with were crammed on to one of the lorries. The soldiers just heaved them up and slung them in with the prisoners who were already there. They got to their feet shakily, hesitantly, tried to make a space for themselves.

'New groups of prisoners kept arriving. The lorry was packed so full that it seemed impossible to squeeze in any more, but they did. Another group, and another, and we could see the prisoners panting for breath. And then nothing.'

The colonel stopped his pacing and turned to ask, 'Nothing?'

'Nothing. The lorries just stood there, the soldiers stood there, we stood there. The sun rose higher in the sky, it got hotter, stiller. The soldiers made the front rows of onlookers sit down and stay seated, and that put a check on the pressure from behind. The prisoners on the lorry looked more and more exhausted, and from time to time one of them would sink to his knees and collapse against the one next to him.'

The news interrupted the music again, only minutes after the previous bulletin, to report half a million people in the square in front of the presidential palace.

The colonel came and sat down. 'There's no way of controlling half a million people.'

The police captain nodded. The colonel looked down at the board; 'Shall we see if we can finish the game?'

They went on playing, and the click of the counters blended with the martial music and the sounds from the open window and combined together into something unreal. This time it was the colonel who reverted to the police captain's story.

'When did he arrive?'

'They. There were two of them. They came in one of our cars, with our crest. It had darkened windows, but not too dark to see that there were two *tuan* inside the car, one in the front and one in the back, two big foreigners with pale white skin and round eyes. Have you heard this story before?'

'Many times, but not from you.'

'The car drove into the square behind us. We saw it first in the eyes of the soldiers who were facing us. Then we heard it, as commotion.'

'You were very aware, for a child.'

'I've had a whole lifetime to analyse my mental images, to listen to the sounds, imbibe the smell. My mother put her arms about us and pulled us to one side as the car approached. The onlookers sitting on the ground in front of us fled in fear. I managed to look in the windows as it passed: one of the foreigners was in uniform, the other in civilian clothes.'

'And there was no doubt about which country they were from?'

'None at all. Americans. Gringos. From the American

Embassy. One of them, the civilian, had some documents in his hand. The car stopped by the lorries and both the men wound down their windows. An officer with a black staff under his arm went over and saluted them, the foreigners leant out of the car windows and shook hands. The officer gave them a clipboard of papers, and we could see their heads bent over it in the car, the one in civilian clothes running his finger slowly down the list and crossing off names on his own documents: one sheet, two sheets, three sheets. Then he looked up and spoke, first to the foreigner in uniform, then to the officer outside the car. And then – then the names of my two elder brothers were called out.'

The radio broke in again with an announcement of the President's resignation. A broadcast speech was expected soon. More music. The two men sat motionless. The colonel folded up the backgammon board.

'Was it the officer who read out your brothers' names?'

'No, he got a junior officer in a steel helmet with a sub-machine-gun to do that: he went along the rows of seated onlookers calling out their names. I can still remember my mother's fingers digging into me as she gathered all five of us in her arms, in a tight grip. It went totally silent all around us. When I think back, I have a feeling of everyone holding their breath, even the prisoners on the lorry, so that the only sound was the voice of the junior officer in the steel helmet with a sub-machine-gun calling out the same names over and over again.'

'But nobody moved, nobody looked at your brothers?'

'Nobody.'

'So in the end one of the foreigners, most likely the civilian, beckoned the officer and pointed at two people at random: two small boys, or a girl with her little sister on her arm?'

'You know that part of the story too, Colonel?'

'It happened everywhere.'

'The foreigner pointed at a brother and sister, ten and

twelve years old, they lived on the staircase next to ours. Two soldiers grabbed them and hauled them towards the lorries, their mother desperately trying to hang on to them. One of the soldiers hit her with his rifle butt. The two children had almost reached the middle lorry when my mother cried out. All movement on the square seemed to freeze, all noise ceased, only my mother's voice arched over the square, my mother's voice shouting out the names of my two elder brothers. It was the last time I heard her speak. She forestalled the shame that would otherwise have come upon us, but she never spoke another word for the rest of her life.'

The two men stood up, and the colonel put the backgammon board away in his desk and came over to the police captain to say, 'Shall we go?' He made a minor adjustment to the police captain's pocket flaps and gestured towards the door. The police captain brushed the colonel's shoulders with his hand. They went outside to the waiting car. They sat in silence for the first part of the drive. The police captain was observing the street life; the colonel stared straight ahead, deep in thought. Then he took out a spectacle case from an inside pocket and polished his glasses thoroughly before putting them on and leaning towards the police captain, as if to see him better.

'You disappoint me, Captain.'

The police captain didn't react.

'Everything you've just told me could have come from absolutely any Western newspaper.'

The police captain didn't appear to be listening.

'Present a handful of individuals, set them in the foreground and let the historical drama be the background, and hey presto, you have your audience. Is it the *tuan* you're living with who's influenced you?'

The police captain didn't reply. The colonel took off his glasses, put them back in the case, opening and closing it as he spoke. 'We don't think like that here. We think the most important thing is to keep our house in order, and we look eight hundred years ahead. A lot of individuals come and go in eight hundred years. If we were to tell the history of each and every one of them, we would lose the overview. But above all, we wouldn't manage to keep our house in order if we let everyone have freedom of choice.'

Still gazing at the street, the police captain replied, 'Could it be that you're judging me too harshly, Colonel? There are many like me on the islands in our country, boys who saw their fathers and brothers executed and gradually realised they had one and only one way of showing their patriotic inclinations: join the police force, join the police and hope that will save the lives of your mother and little brother and sister; join the police and disappear, to some dusty, forgotten outpost. Your mother won't get hospital treatment when she needs it and your little siblings won't get an education, but they'll live, they'll live their whole lives in the shadow of your father's membership of a trade union; for the Americans trade unions are a form of communism, so they have to be eradicated, but your mother and little siblings, not members themselves, they can live. And you'll find a hiding place for yourself, you'll marry a *tuan* who can give your children dual nationality and you'll send them to a boarding-school abroad where the party can't touch them, and you'll live the life you have to in order to get them through. *Tuan* and gin and tonic go together.' A little smile played on his lips. 'But, as you Muslims say, a man will put up with a lot for thirty date palms.'

For a little while they said nothing, until the colonel asked, 'Have you got any more to tell me?'

The police captain responded without taking his eyes off the street outside. 'As the lorries were starting their engines, a man in a white shirt and grey trousers suddenly came running up. He was waving a long strip of paper tickets in the air and shouting a name, over and over again. The soldiers aimed their guns at him, but he took no notice; he pushed forward through the crowd of onlookers, jumped over the seated rows at the front and reached the middle lorry before anyone could manage to stop him. "Mr Suparto!" Mr Suparto!" he yelled, in a shrill, desperate voice. Everyone knew who he was: he ran the tobacco kiosk at the lower end of the square. "Mr Suparto!" A man on the lorry raised his head; it was the one with the dark stain on the seat of his trousers. "Mr Suparto!" The kiosk owner was holding the strip of tickets out to him. "You're a millionaire! I sometimes take a note of who's bought which numbers and when one of mine comes up I often know whose it is. Mr Suparto, you're a millionaire! It can only be you!"

'The man on the lorry seemed dazed, turning his head from side to side, looking as if he was trying to raise the hands that were tied behind his back. The kiosk owner grabbed hold of the tailboard of the lorry and was starting to hoist himself up when the first bayonet slid between his ribs. He turned and stared in utter astonishment at the blade sticking out from his side and at the soldier holding the weapon. Then he turned and watched the other bayonet going in between his ribs on the other side, not in astonishment now but in disbelief; he put the strip of paper tickets to his lips as the soldiers lifted him off the lorry on their bayonets and threw him to the ground, put their boots on his chest and pulled out the bayonets.'

The police captain went quiet.

The colonel took over: 'And then he said, as he lay there, "My father ran this kiosk before me, and his father before him, but never before has anyone become a millionaire from buying a lottery ticket from us, and now when it finally happens, you take him away."'

The police captain nodded. 'Something like that. If he had time to say that much. His internal organs were punctured from two sides and blood was spurting out of his mouth. Pity it wasn't a film, then he'd have had time to say more.'

They had arrived at the police station. The guard presented

arms, another opened the heavy metal door, and the police captain and the army colonel went along the corridor, up the stairs and across the roof. At the foot of the stairs to the cells the police captain paused and asked, 'What about you, Colonel? Is there an American Embassy in your life?'

'Recently, yes. My brother was foreman of several warehouses in the harbour in the capital. He had a wife and two children, a boy and a girl, and lived a good secure life in one of the workers' apartment blocks owned by the port authority. The boy was due to get married with the passing of the monsoon season, to the daughter of an accountant, a step up the ladder. The wedding was arranged, and my brother had paid the first instalment of the dowry. Then suddenly the port was closed, from one day to the next. One day full of normal activity, the next day everything at a standstill. The port authority just kept a small workforce to load the last few containers on ships as they came in. No new containers were unloaded.'

'Why?'

'Because the Americans in what they call the "war on terror" have decided to give priority to so-called secure foreign ports for the shipping of containers to the USA, which means harbours with American inspectors and X-ray equipment that costs fifteen million dollars. My brother's port had neither. There are about twenty such secure ports around the world, and that's where all the containers are now going. People aren't stupid: it costs a thousand dollars a day to have a container lying in port, so they send their containers where they'll be cleared fast, not where they'll be cleared slowly. My brother's port was one where containers were cleared slowly.'

'What happened?'

'Can't you guess?'

'Just himself?'

'And let the others live on with the shame?'

The colonel and the police captain stood for a moment in

silence. Then the colonel said, 'I wonder whether people think about the way they take their own lives, or whether they just choose what's nearest or easiest. Do they know that a bullet through the mouth blows off the back half of their head, and that someone will come and find them? Or is that the idea — are we all being punished?'

They went up the iron staircase to the cells.

14

DEPARTURE

D id Francesco dream that his daughter came to visit him –
in the middle of the day as he was working on the police
captain's papers? Suddenly she was sitting there, her hair tucked
back behind her ears, injecting a fresh breath of life into the cell.

'They can't hold you here for long. As soon as we make
contact with the Embassy, you'll be out.'

Francesco nodded. Anya was sitting on the bed and glanced
across at the bundle in the next cell.

'Revolting.'

Francesco went on with his work. He was immersing sheet
after sheet in the plastic dish of liquid and hanging them up to
dry. Anya sat watching him. She had gone to the police station
firmly determined to try any means to get to visit her father, to
cry or scream, but the police captain had consented to the visit
after only a moment's thought. *Remember that a daughter should
always listen to her father*, he had said, with a glint in his eye.
Now she was sitting on the bed and describing her travels,
from one country to another, meeting a group of young
people with Portuguese blood in their veins, not much, but
enough to distinguish them as a group; she described meeting
one of them in particular. She went quiet when her father
asked her about the rest of her travels.

'Dad, are there circumstances where the use of violence is
permissible?'

She was suddenly twelve years old again, with a tooth brace
and long hair fastened up in a ponytail, sitting in his studio

watching him at work while they talked. They could talk for hours.

'Do you remember the ancient educational ideal? How can you control a city if you can't control your own desires?'

Anya nodded.

'Violence is a form of desire. There are occasions when violence can be understood, but never occasions when it can be condoned. Violence is a lack of identity, lack of empathy with another life.'

'But if you as an individual or as a group have been wronged over a long period of time?' It was obvious who Anya had in mind.

'Do you put that right by putting yourself in the wrong?'

Anya didn't answer. There was silence between them for a while. Then they just chatted until the policewoman rapped on the table with her truncheon and announced that the visit was over.

Anya asked, 'Do you talk to her much?'

Francesco shook his head. 'Not a lot.'

'Is she the only one who keeps an eye on you?'

'By and large.'

Anya gave him a quizzical look and said, 'I like her leather boots.'

Then she left, and Francesco wiped his eyes as she went out of the door.

The visit had not been a dream. He understood only too late why it had seemed unreal to him – instead of intimacy he had used the visit as an attempt to re-establish the relationship between them as it had been, the relationship he had missed and mourned. Only afterwards did he recognise the signs of it having irritated her, only when he sat with a glass in his hand in the evening did he see it and put it into words and wilt a tiny bit, a tiny bit more.

But what was the most striking aspect of the visit? That the daughter had not told her father she was spending a lot of time with the young people of a Christian militia? Or that the father had not told his daughter he had met a young Muslim woman? Neither. Neither of them was aware of motives to be concealed. The most striking aspect of the visit was that Francesco had not mentioned that chance had drawn him emotionally into one side of the conflict on the island, a conflict where violence was not only unavoidable, but perhaps even necessary.

Did Francesco dream that another visitor came to see him in his cell? Maheeba with a basket on her arm? Did she say something to the policewoman by the door?

The policewoman nodded and pointed at her wrist-watch. Maheeba nodded too. Francesco had risen from his bed and was looking at the two women open-mouthed. The policewoman closed the door behind her and left. Maheeba came over to him with a smile, placed her hand on his mouth and stretched up and kissed him on the forehead. She handed him the basket, which he took with cautious wonderment. He put it on the bed, removed the white cloth covering it and pulled out the contents: fruit, bread and cheese, baked sweetcorn in green leaves, a bottle of mineral water and another, smaller, bottle. He held it up, took off the top and sniffed it, glanced at her, had a sip, then another. She sat down on the bed, and he sat beside her. She stroked the back of his hand, smoothed out the wrinkles and spoke to him. He didn't answer, she spoke again, and now he shook his head, but slowly, as if not quite sure.

What he said was clear, the same as he had been saying all the time: it's too late, it's too late. But what was it she said? Did she say something totally new: you'll never be happy anyway, so might I not just as well be with you?

She held his hand up in front of her, took his fingers one by one and stretched them. Then she put her arms round him and spoke again. He looked down at her and laid his hand on her hair and cheek. He smiled now, a little sadly, but he smiled.

Did she say something new to him now after all? Did she

say she would wait for him? Wait for him to come back if he left the island, wait for him to come out of his sorrow if he decided to try and stay with her?

In that case, as was to be hoped, she stood for humanity; she had kept the ability to wait, and thus also the ability to allow room for others.

Maheeba let go of him, straightened up and reached for the basket. Francesco picked up the little bottle, but she took it from him and put it back in the basket, gave him the bottle of mineral water instead, watched him as he drank, took out one of the baked sweetcorn and passed it to him. She talked while he ate, pointing at herself, pointing at him. He listened to her, nodded from time to time, occasionally shook his head. She gave him bread and cheese, he ate it, picked up the little bottle again, looked at her enquiringly, she shook her head, carefully peeled an orange for him and gave it to him segment by segment. Then at last she held out the little bottle and smiled. He took a deep drink, closed his eyes and leant his head against the cell wall. Then he began to talk. She laid a hand on his arm, watching him, attending to his every word.

How much did she understand? Does it matter if it was only a dream? If it was a dream that the police captain suddenly entered the room? Maheeba took the rest of the food out of the basket, wrapped it in the cloth, hung the empty basket on her arm and stood up to go. Francesco stood up with her, held out his hand towards her, heard Anya whisper *has anyone else been to visit you*, changed his mind, took half a step towards her, *has anyone else been to visit you*, changed his mind.

Maheeba went out of the door; the police captain took the top off the little bottle and tipped the contents on the floor, gathered up the bottle of mineral water and the cloth of food and left.

How fortunate that it was only a dream, for in our dreams we can use paintbrushes as much as we like, paint the good in light, bright colours and the bad in dark, threatening hues; in

227

our dreams we can reach out to something and withdraw from it in one and the same movement without experiencing it as strange.

———

Three blocks away round a table in a windowless meeting room sat a group of Chinese businessmen. The table was covered with architectural plans. One of the Chinese was using a white pointer.

'We'll build a hotel here. With a large terrace. The reservoir is here. The village is just visible under the water.'

The others leant forward to have a look.

'One price for the eleven months the village is submerged. We've got diving bells big enough for eight on the drawing board. With five of them we can send forty tourists down in the morning, forty in the afternoon and forty in the evening. We'll give value for money, let them have lots of time.'

A young Chinese woman came and collected up the empty bottles and put out a fresh supply.

In a café down by the harbour the American rock musicians were sitting talking to a group of Malaysian men.

'Music is the only universal language there is, the only universal language. Everybody understands music.'

The musician in the red skullcap was speaking. The one in the colourful waistcoat was waving his cigarette in the air and saying, 'Peace and reconciliation? Bring all races together for a concert of peace and reconciliation? I'm not sure that I like your music, but I'm willing to die for your right to play it? Because that's what freedom's all about?'

The Malaysians sitting with them nodded and exchanged glances.

Two twin sisters sat with a young man in a pavement restaurant near the church.

'Money is one thing. We know what we can use it for, and

we know who to contact. But making our mark is another matter altogether. We'll be revealing who we are. And what we can do.'

Rosalind was emphasising her words by thumping on the table. Meseo was nodding eagerly. Rosanna was tilting her head back and laughing.

'It can't fail. If they attack, we'll be ready – more than ready – to receive them. And if they don't attack, we'll put out a rumour that they were too scared because we were there.'

All three laughed and clapped their hands. Anya arrived and took a seat with them. Meseo greeted her with a broad smile and said, 'Keep this to yourself, but there's a concert being arranged at the village that's emerged from the water, and we've been asked to be stewards.'

Anya looked horrified. Meseo patted her on the knee. 'Status. Christian power.'

In the windowless meeting room the Chinese businessmen were laughing and helping themselves to new bottles.

'And full price for the month when the village is exposed. Full, full price. The tourists will get a package deal: sitting with the tribe and watching the village reappear, joining the villagers' procession, visiting as many houses as they want and listening to the spirits of the ancestors.'

Some of the Chinese were shifting uneasily in their seats and attempting to interject. The speaker continued with a dismissive gesture; 'Already taken into account. We might lose the tribe, but enough of them might stay to make it look genuine to the tourists. It's all a question of price. And if the ancestral spirits fall silent, we've got an alternative.' He smiled. 'Hi-fi technology.'

The others round the table laughed. The laughter swept out of the door as the young woman came in with more bottles; it disappeared out of the house and along a street, found its way to the café down by the harbour where the American rock musicians sat, eavesdropped on the list of equipment they were compiling and swept on further to the pavement restaurant by the church where the Christian group were sitting; the European woman had just got up and left in anger, the young Asian man was laughing and saying how would she react if she knew we were going to use the money for weapons, and the twin sisters were laughing; the laughter from the Chinese businessmen flitted on back to the windowless meeting room where one of the men was explaining that the police would pose no problem, the police captain's wife is a good friend of mine, winking and pressing his finger and thumb together as he said good, and the other men round the table roared with laughter: we've put forward a proposal for an American rock concert in the village and asked the Christian militia to stand by to defend it. Something organised by Westerners on holy ground is guaranteed to provoke the Muslims. We've bribed the leaders of the Muslim militia with money and told them there are rumours circulating that they daren't attack, and that never fails: pussy, honour and money, their three fundamental values.

The men round the table hooted with laughter and slapped one another on the back; the laughter waited until the young woman brought in more bottles, swished out of the door and down to the harbour, gathered up the laughter from the American rock musicians, we are the world, we are the children, passed to café by the church and gathered up the laughter of the young Christians, at last we'll change the rules of the game, at last we'll show the congregations on other islands what's possible; it continued on its return journey to the meeting room, the tribe will leave the village for good after shedding blood over their ancestors' houses, they have a word for it, desecration, desecration, and the man who was speaking shouted the word and the laughter grew, expanding out of the room, twisting itself into a spiral in the air and rising slowly into the sky, Chinese laughter, American laughter, Malaysian laughter; the spiral looked like a flock of birds converging, a flock of pink flamingos rising and rising until they reached an apex, turned and dived down to attack.

Francesco was lying on his side with the plastic glass in one hand and the bottle in the other when his daughter's voice came back to him.

'Dad?'

The light in the guardroom and cells was off, the police-woman was immobile under the blanket on her bed, the bundle on the bed in the adjacent cell was just an outline.

'Anya?'

Francesco looked up at the window. It was open. Low pressure had brought clammy, heavy air. He tried to get out of bed but couldn't manage it. A shadow fell across him.

'Can you stop this?'

Francesco sobbed, 'Anya, Anya, browner, thicker hair than I'd imagined, a stronger physique, no more jeans and T-shirt, or shorts and sun-top, but in a suit, Mediterranean elegance, such a young woman in a suit, and a white blouse.'

He burrowed his face into the pillow as he spoke, but his voice flowed out across the room, headed for the sounds from the window, climbing towards them, his last words emitted like a half-strangled cry.

'Can you stop this?'

Her voice seemed far away now, as if outside the window; he looked up again, *does she want me to stop the sounds?*

'Can you stop this? Huge numbers of people are going to die, many more will have their lives wrecked. The island will never be the same, not in our time.'

Now her voice seemed to be coming from the doorway out to the staircase. He turned in that direction and formed his lips into silent words: 'What is it you want me to stop?'

The voice from the door seemed startled, as if out of a

reverie. It focused on the man with the plastic glass and bottle on the bed and drifted gently towards him.

'What's about to happen.'

There was a knock on the door, short and sharp. Francesco woke up. He had fallen asleep with the glass in his hand, and now set it down carefully. The colonel and the police captain entered. The police captain had brought a bottle, which he placed on the floor by the cell door.

'Your time has come, Gringo.' He spoke the last word with contempt. Francesco didn't know what to think, and looked uncertainly from the police captain to the colonel.

The colonel said, 'The papers hanging up to dry in his cell – has he restored them?'

'Yes,' replied the police captain.

'What are they?'

'Identity cards. Of those who were executed in our block.'

'All of them?'

'No, only those on the American Embassy list.'

The room froze. Whispering voices could be heard from the identity cards on the string.

The police captain said, 'There's been a coup in the capital. The man in your photograph is finished.'

Francesco grew tense. The police captain took his evening bottle away from him and held it up to the light-bulb to gauge how much had gone before he gave it back, and then he tied a blindfold over his eyes. Francesco heard the man in the different uniform, who had been leaning against the wall, say something to the police captain, heard the door creak and someone come into the cell and put a hand on his shoulder. He sniffed, and recognised the policewoman as she pushed him out ahead of her. At the top of the steps she laid her truncheon across the nape of his neck, her other hand still on his shoulder, and gave him a gentle kick on the back of the knee, *go*. He went, feeling for one step at a time; when he got down to the roof and was being led over to the door to the corridor, he heard the man in the unknown uniform stop. The police captain asked him something, the man in uniform answered as they walked past him and the answer disappeared behind them.

The colonel put his foot on the parapet of the roof and looked out over the town. It was dark, here and there an illuminated street, a light in a window, from one direction music, from another weeping, and from the heights above a sound system was being tested.

For many Asians the memory of the Japanese occupying forces during the Second World War is so horrific that no mention of their name is allowed. They are called instead *the long way back* or *the echo from afar*. Their empire has thousands of years of roots, and the roots are twofold: the sword and the chrysanthemum. Their culture is also based on shame. When the echo from afar took American prisoners of war, they didn't understand them. For the echo from afar there was no question of surrendering and being taken prisoner; they could hardly imagine such shame. If the American prisoners were also sick or injured, that increased the shame. The Americans learnt gradually that, among other things, the worst thing to do was to laugh, which indicated that they did not realise their own shame.

In Asia only a European would have shown a picture of himself with the dictator in the capital. It made the police captain lose face in front of the three Europeans and his police colleague. European culture is based on guilt: a European can atone for his guilt, but shame has to be evened up, balanced, avenged. If you react passively to your own shame, it increases – because others can see that you're doing nothing about it.

The sound system up on the mountain ridge was increasing in volume. The colonel glanced towards the door through which the European prisoner had left and heaved a sigh. He took his foot off the parapet, gazed over the town one last time and spoke broodingly into the evening darkness; 'I wonder whether people from shame-based and guilt-based cultures can ever really understand each other. This may be our biggest mistake, believing that others are like us, and think like us. A European has to disassociate himself from himself to atone his guilt. We Asians have to make our mark.'

He turned away and followed the police captain and the policewoman with the European prisoner.

———————

Anya was sweating from running. She stopped and looked towards the village, listened to the village. It was early evening, low sun, warm, a slight breeze, a brief cloudburst, the scent of cloves and nutmeg, white-coloured garments, all the whites of the rainbow; white against the sombre voices, the deeper voices of the Great We, soft, calm, the higher voices of the Little We, sharper, more impatient, and above them, like an echo, other voices, other voices. Anya craned her neck, tried to hear; a face came momentarily into view above the village, looked at her, turned and spoke to someone. Anya felt afraid and tried to shout, and the face above the village disappeared. A saxophone was tentatively warming up, the notes gliding from beat to beat yet suspended in anticipation. She watched them floating up from a stage that had been erected in the square, by the well.

Four loudspeakers had been rigged up in front of the stage, stacked in two pairs; they stood five to six metres high, higher than any of the houses round about. There were two young men on the stage, probably technicians, concentrating their attention on the job in hand, turning knobs, moving leads, tapping microphones on black metal stands. People had started wandering in, some had even been there when the stage was being erected, but it was only when the sound system was turned on and tested that everyone really began streaming in. Some had little stools to sit on, others carried baskets of food on their arms; many were arriving in groups, parents and children, relatives, neighbours, all with their eyes fixed on the stage, as if they weren't entirely convinced it was there, as if they had heard rumours and were coming to check them out for themselves.

An electric guitar was pushed up on to the back of the stage, and a musician came clambering up after it; the audience clapped, laughed, the guitarist smiled and waved, picked up his guitar and hung it round his neck, gripped a fret and strummed a chord, changed his fingering, another chord, then turned a knob, took a plectrum he'd been holding between his teeth and began to play, gently, calmly, simple guitar notes that lifted on the breeze and soared into the sky. The audience stopped chatting, the sound man adjusted the controls on the mixing desk in the centre of the square, the technicians left the stage, the guitarist advanced to centre stage, playing faster now; another musician climbed up and went over to an electric piano, played three chords, leapt into the air, span round in a complete circle and landed on the same spot, played three more chords, to laughter and applause, looked up briefly, grinned at the guitarist. Spotlights were switched on from the surrounding roofs, white, red, blue, and their beams focused on the two musicians, making them stand out clearly in the soft evening light, somehow strangely absorbing the sunlight in the village at the same time as illuminating the stage, absorbing the light in the village and replacing it with shadows, long, dark shadows of walls and buttresses.

Something was moving in the shadows, something darker, a foot in a black boot, a weapon in a black sheath, a blackened face; a white tunic glowed, then another, but no one in the square seemed to notice anything, they had eyes only for the stage. A vocalist had come on now, and the other six musicians were climbing up, eager hands passing their instruments up after them, two trumpets and three saxophones, baritone, tenor and alto; a man sat down at the drums and another lifted a double bass up from a stand while the saxophonists fastened their instruments to the straps around their necks; the vocalist put his lips right up to the microphone and sang, the music built up around him, the bass joined in, as did the drums, the wind section put their instruments to their lips and played a staccato riff, precise, crisp, and the audience in the square jumped in surprise, put their hands to their mouths and exchanged glances, while in the shadows something moved again, but in the opposite direction, a boot, a weapon, a blackened face, and the vocalist sang and the wind section played the same riff and now it seemed that the music and the stage lights were drawing the light from the surroundings and into the square, most strongly on the stage, more weakly on the audience. The sun had sunk below the horizon.

———

After the policewoman had been dismissed, the car carrying Francesco, the police captain and the colonel set off, along a street, across a square, leaving the town centre. The white beams of the headlamps pierced two long tunnels in the darkness, the red rear-lamps closed them off behind. Sleeping vagrants sat up as the car swept by, catching a glimpse first of the white face in the back seat with a blindfold over its eyes and then of the uniforms in the front seat, and quickly lay down again, shutting their eyes as fast as they could. The car sped on, past the harbour, then inland and upward. The houses thinned out and finally ceased altogether, leaving only the moving car.

'Why do you call me Gringo?'

'Because you are one.'

'Gringo? Isn't that a North American? Never.'

'You're all North Americans now.'

Francesco took another swig from the bottle and said, 'How do you work that out?'

'American logic – if you're not with us, you're against us.

Seen from our part of the world it looks like this: if you're not against the Americans, you're with them. We haven't heard any criticism of the Americans from your prime minister, Gringo, rather the opposite.'

Suddenly a tropical cloudburst poured down on the car, the rain hammered against the roof, drowning out the noise of the engine. After a few minutes it subsided into a heavy shower. The police captain switched the windscreen wipers from double to single speed, the colonel wiped the mist off the windows and tried to see out. The car was crawling slowly uphill now, on a narrow track full of deep potholes. The police captain swung off the road and brought the car to a halt under the dark trees overhanging the road. Then he turned in his seat and said, 'In the dark we rely on hearing rather than seeing. Try and find noises that will camouflage you. A waterfall, a generator, a herd of cows.'

Francesco moved his head from side to side, as if listening.

'Are there any of those here?'

'That's your problem. You're the one who's fleeing.'

The police captain untied the blindfold, got out of the car and tilted the seat forward.

'Run.'

Francesco said, 'Why am I fleeing?'

'It's more acceptable to your embassy.'

'Than what?'

The police captain did not answer, merely nodded his head in a direction away from the car.

Francesco sat up. He levered himself unsteadily through the door, put one foot to the ground and was out. The police captain looked him in the eyes, nodded his head and repeated, 'Run.'

Anya was sitting on an empty bench looking at the stage. She was afraid, without knowing why. Fear had made her run. A woman came and sat down beside her, smiled at her. Anya gave her a quick sidelong glance. The woman met her glance and whispered, 'Francesco.'

Anya was completely taken aback.

'Francesco.' The woman repeated Anya's father's name, pointed at her, *your father*, pointed at herself, *him and me.*

Anya was even more startled and said, 'You and him?'

The woman nodded and pointed at her again, then at herself again, and said, 'Francesco and you. Francesco and me.'

She beamed radiantly. Anya's face tightened. Maheeba leant across, put her arms round her, kissed her on the cheek, and said, 'Sister.'

She closed her eyes and swayed to the music. Anya was confused. She didn't know whether to slap the woman or embrace her, break out in laughter or burst into tears. She scanned the square, where the public were still streaming in, and there was Meseo's face, near the well. She got up with a hesitant glance at the Asian woman beside her, then touched her tentatively on the shoulder.

'Bye.'

Maheeba laid her own hand on top of the one on her shoulder and gave it a pat, opened her eyes and smiled again. Anya went towards the well whispering, *aren't you a bit on the young side, aren't you a bit on the young side*, but nevertheless she was grinning inwardly, and shaking her head. Meseo had seen her, he was waiting for her behind the well, and took her hand without a word, dragged her down an alley and out into a large atrium, which was full of young people in warpaint and red headbands, all armed. The twin sisters from the commercial centre attack were there, dancing to the music, happy and excited. Kurt stood against the back wall of the atrium, filming, with a European woman beside him. Anya remembered her from the day of the attack on the commercial centre. The woman wasn't reporting now, she was standing with her microphone lowered and watching the young people as if afraid to put what she saw into words.

————————

Francesco dithered for a moment, then stumbled forward in front of the car and squinted along the beams of its headlamps shining into the trees. He took a few faltering steps, frowned as if he didn't quite understand what was happening to him, and followed the beams into the trees; a confused man fleeing along a corridor of light that gradually grew dimmer and dimmer. He chose what most people would have chosen, to stay in the light as long as possible to see where he was going. It gave a kind of overview, and overview brings a feeling of control, and thus security. Had he run into the pitch-blackness surrounding the car he would have been out of sight in seconds.

He turned after a while to look back at the car, shading his eyes against the bright white lights staring silently after him, abandoned the attempt to see and went on running. The ground was well-trodden and packed hard, which should have made him think, but he wasn't thinking; he tripped instead, gasped for breath, got up and set off again. He was muttering as he ran, incoherent phrases, brief fragments. The lights of the car were getting fainter now, the trees encircling him darker and darker, and suddenly he paused and looked to one side in surprise: something was shining, glittering in the darkness, chain-link fencing? He cast a glance to the other side, more chain-link fencing? He peered down at the ground and could see now that it was a path, and he squinted along it as far as he could see in the darkness and then continued on his way, uncertainly; the path curved, the light disappeared, and on he ran with his arms outstretched in front of him, feeling his way with his feet, until he collided with something cold, chain-link fencing? He slowed down and could distinguish an outline, a gate? He stopped, trying to make out more, a chain-link gate in a tubular metal frame with a handle; he pushed at the handle, opened the gate and still he wasn't thinking, still he didn't ask himself what the point was of three-metre-high chain-link fencing if it had a gate which was unlocked. He went through quickly and shut the gate after him, with a feeling of having escaped from something, unaware that he had in fact shut himself in.

———————

Anya looked about her wildly, tried to count, gave up. The youth militia was in constant motion, dancing in and out of one another's lines, eyes closed as they moved around, playing with their spears, bows and arrows. Many of them were wearing long, dark cloaks, which gave them the appearance of avengers; were they avengers? Anya shouted out the question, are you avengers, what are you avenging? One of the twin sisters came dancing towards her, smiling, dancing in front of her.

'Meseo!' Anya cried, and he came over to her, reluctantly.

'What are you all intending to do?'

She had to yell over the music.

'We've come up to defend the village,' he said, dancing as he shouted in her ear.

'The way we defended the commercial centre? Meseo? Can you hear me? Are you going to defend the village the way we defended the commercial centre?'

She turned to leave.

'Where are you going?' Meseo asked, putting an arm round her neck to hold her back.

'To tell the organisers.'

'You're not going to tell anyone anything.'

He pulled her closer. Anya wrenched herself free and managed to propel herself towards the two Europeans with the TV camera and microphone.

'Please film me leaving this courtyard! Film me so that no one tries to stop me!'

Kurt simply nodded. Helen raised the microphone to her lips and said, *there is a young European woman among the insurgents, and it looks as if she does not agree with their strategy*. Anya walked slowly backwards to the alley leading out of the atrium, her eyes fixed on the camera. The dancing crowd stepped aside and let her through. Meseo stared silently after her.

At the upper reservoir Francesco came to a halt when he caught sight of water. There it was, all of a sudden, still and black. He tried to make out the shoreline to judge its extent, but land and water merged into darkness. The moon had risen, which gave some light, but not enough. He scraped his foot and found a sharp edge, which could have been a wall. Bending down to see better, he lost his balance and toppled into the water with a feeble cry. A brandy a day, at work and at play, but not while you're swimming, he murmured, taking a few strokes. He attempted to find a finger-hold on the wall, but it was too smooth; he attempted to find the top edge, but it was too high. Out of the darkness above and beyond the wall he could hear the sound of metal on metal, like a lock being turned. Much further off he could hear music, and muttered to himself that they may be poor and underdeveloped, but they have damned fine radios. He went on swimming along the wall, trying to get a grip, swimming with his legs and one arm, keeping the other in contact with the wall. A movement in the water made him stop and turn. Fish? The water was eddying, bubbling, gurgling. He murmured again, a brandy a day, at work and at play, but not when the water's gurgling. He turned back to the wall and went swimming on but the water took hold of him and dragged him under. He gasped as he went down, gasped as he came up a moment later; he was very frightened now, and tried desperately to grab at the wall, to save himself.

———————

Anya was out of the alley and running towards the square, towards the stage and the light and the music, her heart pounding, panting for breath, when she saw the steel wire across the narrow street, but too late, too late; she just had time to fling out her hands as she fell forward, grazed her palms on the ground and landed heavily on her knees. She was about to get herself up when strong, brown hands grasped her wrists and ankles and pulled her into a doorway, a voice spat in her face, you're shit, other hands tugged at her clothing, infidel shit; there were white headbands all around her, white headbands and blackened faces, she tried screaming but the music was too loud, tried to defend herself but the hands overcame her, you're shit, the world doesn't need shit like you, infidel shit.

———————

At the upper reservoir the water sucked Francesco under again; he was in no condition to offer resistance. He could hear voices under water, *Great danger, Great We*, was that what they were saying, or was he imagining it? He swam on, gasping for breath, sobbing, still desperately searching for a handhold. Then suddenly he got a grip on the top of the wall, which must have been lower there, or the water higher; it didn't matter, didn't matter. He clutched it with both hands and tried to hoist himself up, fell back into the water, swam to the wall again to make a second attempt. He raised himself a centimetre at a time, got his head and chest over the edge, and found himself staring at a pair of boots. They were welted boots, high and fairly worn.

He took hold of the boots and pulled himself towards them. The boots didn't move. He got a leg over the top of the wall and straightened up, on his knees and elbows with his head hanging down and breathing deeply. Was he crying? The police captain reached down and lifted his face to check. 'Are you crying?'

———————

In the square the audience got their first warning that something was wrong: the smell of blood came wafting down the streets behind them and towards the music, the smell of sweat and tears, hatred and terror, but strongest of all the smell of blood, the sweet, slightly heavy smell of life pumping out, and some of the audience turned their heads and sniffed, whispered to each other; many of the audience turned to look in the direction of the smell, where eight narrow streets led into the square, symmetrically, and the streets each side of the stage were empty; the smell came from the streets behind the audience, and more and more of them twisted round to look in that direction. A group of youths in red headbands passed across the end of one street, and at the end of another a group of youths in white headbands did the same. Could it be some sort of dance routine? Suddenly blending with the smell of blood was the smell of burnt flesh, the nauseating smell of burnt human flesh and singed hair.

———————

By the upper dam the police captain struck Francesco hard across the back of the knees with his baton. Francesco screamed and fell.

'How did you come to meet our President?'
'He had documents in need of restoration.'
Francesco rubbed the backs of his knees. The police captain

unfastened his pistol and gave a sad smile. 'Haven't we all. Haven't we all.'

———————

In the square the wind players in the band took a break while the singer performed a solo, and now there were young people in red and white headbands and men in white tunics in all four streets behind the audience, and it was no longer possible to imagine that they were dancing; the smell was too strong, the smell of anguish and the smell of pain and the smell of a spear driven in with tremendous force and the smell of an arrow finding its target, and all at once the audience was shrieking in panic, because the windows of the houses on the square were filling with white-painted death masks talking and shouting and talking and shouting until it was no longer possible to see in and the houses were quivering and trembling and shaking with voices; the death masks were suddenly everywhere now and shouting at the audience from doors and windows and gateways.

At the upper reservoir the police captain thrust his pistol between the European prisoner's lips, whispered softly, 'Sweet dreams', and squeezed the trigger. Then he pulled the trigger. The back of Francesco's head was blown off and his knowledge of ancient manuscripts scattered among the trees on a tropical spice island, together with his love of a daughter and sadness over a relationship that hadn't lasted.

———————

In a yard in the village a young, bleeding European woman raised her head towards the shot and called *Dad* in a voice stifled by tears; from the sea a roar of movement rose up and in over the island, along the dark mountain tops to the upper reservoir, surged across it underwater and smashed into the sluice of the dam; in the square the wind players lifted up their instruments and prepared for the crescendo leading to the finale, they punctured the universe with unisonous, hard and rhythmic blasts, muffling the shot from the upper reservoir; the vocalist was singing at the top of his voice and did not see the water rushing three metres deep down the four streets behind the stage and thundering into the square, and the audience screamed as the stage splintered and the water carried them off before they even had time to rise from their seats. Some tried to swim with the flow but were sucked under by the whirlpools created by torrents from four streets colliding in the square in a maelstrom that raced on down the four streets on the other side of the square and flushed out all the red and white headbands after felling them with floating benches and bodies and fragments of stage, and the bleeding European woman had just crawled out on to the street on all fours when the water hit her and a few foaming metres further down the street she saw she was being swept past the two TV reporters, lifeless now; she caught a glimpse of her father with the back of his head blown away, she screamed and grabbed at him, let herself be pulled down with him, taking in water; they reached the bottom together, she laid her head on his chest and expelled the last breath she had in her lungs in a final cry; the twin sisters swept past her with eyes that no longer saw and bodies that no longer danced; immediately after them came a young man with hands flailing round his own death mask, hands that had once caressed her.

Standing by the car the colonel sighed and gazed up at the sky. On hearing the shot he had thought, *shot in a prison yard, unacceptable, shot in flight, acceptable.*

He got in the car, ready to go. The police captain joined him a few moments later.

'Will you and your troops be withdrawn now?' he asked as

he reversed the car and turned. In the distance it sounded as if the concert had reached its climax.

The colonel nodded and replied, 'Probably. Following the coup we must await new orders; we no longer have an assignment here.'

The police captain put the car in gear and let out the clutch. The headlights sought their way through the darkness towards the sea and the houses.

'Leave us alone so we can kill one another in peace?'

The colonel looked at the police captain. Then he nodded.

'That's what the world would prefer. To leave people alone so they can kill one another in peace.'

————————

In the village all turbulence in the water came to a standstill; calm, calm, all was calm now, not a ripple to be seen, and so too all noise vanished; silent, silent, all was silent now, not a sound to be heard, only the moon shining down on a dark island and the sea around it, unbroken to the horizon, the sea quietly keeping its eye on the island, watching over it or holding a wake, who knows?

A NOTE ON THE AUTHOR

Gunnar Kopperud was born in Norway in 1946 and studied theatre in Strasbourg and London, later taking a Master's degree in philosophy at the University of Oslo. He has worked as journalist for, among others, Associated Press and the leading Norwegian daily paper, *Dagbladet*. He is the author of *The Time of Light* and *Longing* (both published in English by Bloomsbury). He lives in Norway.

A NOTE ON THE TYPE

The text of this book is set in Bembo, the original types for which were cut by Francesco Griffo for the Venetian printer Aldus Manutius, and were first used in 1495 for Cardinal Bembo's *De Aetna*. Claude Garamond (1480–1561) used Bembo as a model and so it became the forerunner of standard European type for the following two centuries. Its modern form was designed, following the original, for Monotype in 1929 and is widely in use today.